THE
MARBLE COLLECTOR

Cecelia Ahern was born and grew up in Dublin. She is now published in nearly fifty countries, and has sold over twenty-four million copies of her novels worldwide. Two of her books have been adapted as films and she has created several TV series. She and her books have won numerous awards, including the Irish Book Award for Popular Fiction for *The Year I Met You*.

For more information on Cecelia, her writing, books and events, follow her on Twitter @Cecelia_ Ahern, join her on Facebook www.facebook.com/CeceliaAhernofficial and visit her website www.cecelia-ahern.com.

Also by Cecelia Ahern

THE
MARBLE COLLECTOR

cecelia ahern

HARPER

Harper
HarperCollins*Publishers*
1 London Bridge Street
London SE1 9GF

www.harpercollins.co.uk

First published by HarperCollins*Publishers* 2015

This paperback edition published by *Harper* 2016
1

Copyright © Cecelia Ahern 2015

Cecelia Ahern asserts the moral right to
be identified as the author of this work

A catalogue record for this book
is available from the British Library

ISBN: 978-0-00-750185-4

Set in Sabon LT Std by Palimpsest Book Production Limited,
Falkirk, Stirlingshire

Printed and bound in the United States of America
by RR Donnelley

Find out more about HarperCollins and the environment at
www.harpercollins.co.uk/green

For my Sonny Ray

I saw the angel in the marble and I carved
until I set him free.

Michelangelo

PROLOGUE

When it comes to my memory there are three categories: things I want to forget, things I can't forget, and things I forgot I'd forgotten until I remember them.

My earliest memory is of my mum when I was three years old. We are in the kitchen, she picks up the teapot and launches it up at the ceiling. She holds it with two hands, one on the handle, one on the spout, and lobs it as though in a sheaf-toss competition, sending it up in the air where it cracks against the ceiling, and then falls straight back down to the table where it shatters into pieces, murky brown water and burst soggy teabags everywhere. I don't know what preceded this act, or what came after, but I do know it was anger-motivated, and the anger was my-dad-motivated. This memory is not a good representation of my mum's character; it doesn't show her in a good light. To my knowledge she never behaved like that again, which I imagine is precisely the reason that I remember it.

As a six-year-old, I see my Aunt Anna being stopped at the door by Switzer's security as we exit. The hairy-handed security guard goes through her shopping bag and retrieves a scarf with its price tags and a security tag still on it. I can't remember what happened after that; Aunt Anna plied me with ice-cream sundaes in the Ilac Centre and watched with hope that every memory of the incident would die with each mouthful of sugar. The memory is vivid despite even to this day everyone believing I made it up.

I currently go to a dentist who I grew up with. We were never friends but we hung out in the same circles. He's now a very serious man, a sensible man, a stern man. When he hovers above my open mouth, I see him as a fifteen-year-old pissing against the living room walls at a house party, shouting about Jesus being the original anarchist.

When I see my aged primary school teacher who was so softly spoken we almost couldn't hear her, I see her throwing a banana at the class clown and shouting at him to *leave me alone for God's sake, just leave me alone*, before bursting into tears and running from the classroom. I bumped into an old classmate recently and brought the incident up, but she didn't remember.

It seems to me that when summoning up a person in my mind it is not the everyday person I think of, it is the more dramatic moments or the moments they showed a part of themselves that is usually hidden.

My mother says that I have a knack for remembering what others forget. Sometimes it's a curse; nobody likes it when there's somebody to remember what they've tried so hard to bury. I'm like the person who remembers everything after a drunken night out, who everyone wishes would keep their memories to themself.

I can only assume I remember these episodes because I have never behaved this way myself. I can't think of a moment when I have broken form, become another version of myself that I want and need to forget. I am always the same. If you've met me you know me, there's not much more to me. I follow the rules of who I know myself to be and can't seem to be anything else, not even in moments of great stress when surely a meltdown would be acceptable. I think this is why I admire it so much in others and I remember what they choose to forget.

Out of character? No. I fully believe that even a sudden change in a person's behaviour is within the confines of their nature. That part of us is present the whole time, lying dormant, just waiting for its moment to be revealed. Including me.

1

PLAYING WITH MARBLES

Allies

'Fergus Boggs!'

These are the only two words I can understand through Father Murphy's rage-filled rant at me, and that's because those words are my name, the rest of what he says is in Irish. I'm five years old and I've been in the country for one month. I moved from Scotland with Mammy and my brothers, after Daddy died. It all happened so quickly, Daddy dying, us moving, and even though I'd been to Ireland before, on holidays during the summer to see Grandma, Granddad, Uncle, Aunty and all my cousins, it's not the same now. I've never been here when it's not the summer. It feels like a different place. It has rained every day we've been here. The ice-cream shop isn't even open now, all boarded up like it never even existed, like I made it up in my head. The beach that we used to go to most days doesn't look like the same place and the chip van is gone. The people look different too. They're all wrapped up and dark.

Father Murphy stands over my desk and is tall and grey and wide. He spits as he shouts at me; I feel the spit land on my cheek but I'm afraid to wipe it away in case that makes him angrier. I try looking around at the other boys to see their reactions but he lashes out at me. A backhanded slap. It hurts. He is wearing a ring, a big one; I think it has cut my face but I daren't reach up to feel it in case he hits me again. I need to go to the toilet all of a sudden. I have been hit before, but never by a priest.

He is shouting angry Irish words. He is angry that I don't understand. In between the Irish words he says I should understand him by now but I just can't. I don't get to practise at home. Mammy is sad and I don't like to bother her. She likes to sit and cuddle. I like when she does that. I don't want to ruin the cuddles by talking. And anyway I don't think she remembers the Irish words either. She moved away from Ireland a long time ago to be a nanny to a family in Scotland and she met Daddy. They never spoke the Irish words there.

The priest wants me to repeat the words after

him but I can barely breathe. I can barely get the words out of my mouth.

'*Tá mé, tá tú, tá sé, tá sí . . .*'

LOUDER!

'*Tá muid, tá sibh, tá siad.*'

When he's not shouting at me, the room is so quiet it reminds me it's filled with boys my age, all listening. As I stammer through the words he is telling everybody how stupid I am. My whole body is shaking. I feel sick. I need to go to the toilet. I tell him so. His face goes a purple colour and that is when the leather strap comes out. He lashes my hand with leather, which I later learn has pennies sewn into the layers. He tells me he is going to give me 'six of the best' on each hand. I can't take the pain. I need to go to the toilet. I go right there and then. I expect the boys to laugh but nobody does. They keep their heads down. Maybe they'll laugh later, or maybe they'll understand. Maybe they're just happy it's not happening to them. I'm embarrassed, and ashamed, as he tells me I should be. Then he pulls me out of the room, by my ear, and that hurts too, away from everyone, down the corridor, and he pushes me into a dark room. The door bangs closed behind me and he leaves me alone.

I don't like the dark, I have never liked the dark, and I start to cry. My pants are wet, my wee has run down into my socks and shoes but I don't know what to do. Mammy usually changes them for me. What do I do here? There is no window in the room and I can't see anything. I hope he won't keep me in here long. My eyes adjust to the darkness and the light that comes from under the door helps me to see. I'm in a storage room. I see a ladder, and a bucket and a mop with no stick, just the head. It smells rank. An old bicycle is hanging upside down, the chain missing. There's two wellington boots but they don't match and they're both for the same foot. Nothing in here fits together. I don't know why he put me in here and I don't know how long it'll be. Will Mammy be looking for me?

It feels like forever has passed. I close my eyes and sing to myself. The songs that Mammy sings with me. I don't sing them too loud in case he hears me and thinks I'm having fun in here. That would make him angrier. In this place, fun and laughing makes them angry. We are not here to be leaders, we are here to serve. This is not what my daddy taught me, he said that I was a natural leader, that I can be anything I want to be. I used to go hunting with him, he taught me everything, he even let me walk first, he said I was the leader. He sang a song about it. 'Following the leader, the leader, the leader, Fergus is the leader, da da da da da.' I hum it to myself but I don't say the words. The priest won't like me saying I'm the leader. In this place we're not allowed to be anybody we want to be, we have to be who they tell us to be. I sing the songs my daddy used to sing when I was allowed to stay up late and listen to the sing-songs. Daddy had a soft voice for a strong man, and he sometimes cried when he sang. My daddy never said crying was only for babies, not like the priest said, crying is for people who are sad. I sing it to myself now and try not to cry.

Suddenly the door opens and I move away, afraid that it will be him again, with that leather strap. It's not him but it's the younger one, the one who teaches the music class with the kind eyes. He closes the door behind him and crouches down.

'Hi, Fergus.'

I try to say hi but nothing comes out of my mouth.

'I brought you something. A box of bloodies.'

I flinch and he puts a hand out. 'Don't look so scared now, they're marbles. Have you ever played with marbles?'

I shake my head. He opens his hand and I see them shining in his palm like treasures, four red rubies.

'I used to love these as a boy,' he says quietly. 'My granddad gave them to me. "A box of bloodies," he said, "just for you." I don't have the box now. Wish I had, could be worth something. Always remember to keep the packaging, Fergus, that's one bit of advice I'll give you. But I've kept the marbles.'

Somebody walks by the door; we can feel their

boots as the floor shakes and creaks beneath us and he looks at the door. When the footsteps have passed he turns back to me, his voice quieter. 'You have to shoot them. Or fulk them.'

I watch as he puts his knuckle on the ground and balances the marble in his bent forefinger. He puts his thumb behind and then gently pushes the marble; it rolls along the wooden floor at speed. A red bloodie, bold as anything, catching the light, shining and glistening. It stops at my foot. I'm afraid to pick it up. And my raw hands are paining me still, it's hard to close them. He sees this and winces.

'Go on, you try,' he says.

I try it. I'm not very good at first because it's hard to close my hands like he showed me, but I get the hang of it. Then he shows me other ways to shoot them. Another way called 'knuckling down'. I prefer it that way and even though he says that's more advanced I'm best at that one. He tells me so and I have to bite my lip to stop the smile.

'Names given to marbles vary from place to place,' he says, getting down and showing me again. 'Some people call them a taw, or a shooter, or tolley, but me and my brothers called them allies.'

Allies. I like that. Even with me locked in this room on my own, I have allies. It makes me feel like a soldier. A prisoner of war.

He fixes me with a serious look. 'When aiming, remember to look at the target with a steady eye.

The eye directs the brain, the brain directs the hand. Don't forget that. Always keep an eye on the target, Fergus, and your brain will make it happen.'

I nod.

The bell rings, class over.

'Okay.' He stands up, wipes down his dusty robe. 'I've a class now. You sit tight here. It shouldn't be much longer.'

I nod.

He's right. It shouldn't be much longer – but it is. Father Murphy doesn't come to get me soon. He leaves me there all day. I even do another wee in my pants because I'm afraid to knock on the door to get someone, but I don't care. I am a soldier, a prisoner of war, and I have my allies. I practise and practise in the small room, in my own little world, wanting my skill and accuracy to be the best in the school. I'm going to show the other boys and I'm going to be better than them all the time.

The next time Father Murphy puts me in here I have the marbles hidden in my pocket and I spend the day practising again. I also have an archboard in the dark room. I put it there myself between classes, just in case. It's a piece of cardboard with seven arches cut in it. I made it myself from Mrs Lynch's empty cornflakes box that I found in her bin after I saw some other boys with a fancy shop-bought one. The middle arch is number 0, the arches either side are 1, 2, 3. I put the archboard at the far wall and I shoot from a distance, close to the door. I don't really know how to play it properly yet and I can't play it on my own but I can practise my shooting. I will be better than my big brothers at something.

The nice priest doesn't stay in the school long. They say that he kisses women and that he's going to Hell, but I don't care. I like him. He gave me my first marbles, my bloodies. In a dark time in my life, he gave me my allies.

2

POOL RULES

No Running

Breathe.

Sometimes I have to remind myself to breathe. You would think it would be an innate human instinct but no, I inhale and then forget to exhale and so I find my body rigid, all tensed up, heart pounding, chest tight with an anxious head wondering what's wrong.

I understand the theory of breathing. The air you breathe in through your nose should go all the way down to your belly, the diaphragm. Breathe relaxed. Breathe rhythmically. Breathe silently. We do this from the second we are born and yet we are never taught. Though I should have been. Driving, shopping, working, I catch myself holding my breath, nervous, fidgety, waiting for what exactly to happen, I don't know. Whatever it is, it never comes. It is ironic that on dry ground I fail at this simple task when my job requires me to excel at it. I'm a life-guard. Swimming comes easily to me, it feels natural, it doesn't test me, it makes me feel free. With swim-ming, timing is everything. On land you breathe in for one and out for one, beneath the water I can achieve a three to one ratio, breathing every three strokes. Easy. I don't even need to think about it.

I had to learn how to breathe above water when I was pregnant with my first child. It was necessary for labour, they told me, which it turns out it certainly is. Because childbirth is as natural as breathing, they go hand in hand, yet breathing, for me, has been anything but natural. All I ever want to do above water is hold my breath. A baby will not be born through holding your breath. Trust me, I tried. Knowing my aquatic ways, my husband encouraged a water birth. This seemed like a good idea to get me in my natural territory, at home, in water, only there is nothing natural about sitting in an oversized paddling pool in your living room, and it was the baby who got to experience the world from below the water and not me. I would have gladly switched places. The first birth ended in a dash to the hospital and an emergency caesarean and indeed the two subsequent babies came in the same way, though they weren't emergencies. It seemed that the aquatic creature who preferred to stay under the water from the age of five could not embrace another of life's most natural acts.

I'm a lifeguard in a nursing home. It is quite the exclusive nursing home, like a four-star hotel with round-the-clock care. I have worked here for seven years, give or take my maternity leave. I man the lifeguard chair five days a week from nine a.m. to two p.m. and watch as three people each hour take to the water for lengths. It is a steady stream of monotony and stillness. Nothing ever happens. Bodies appear from the changing rooms as walking displays of the reality of time: saggy skin, boobs, bottoms and thighs, some dry and flaking from diabetes, others from kidney or liver disease. Those confined to their beds or chairs for so long wear their painful-looking pressure ulcers and bedsores, others carry their brown patches of age spots as badges of the years they have lived. New skin growths appear and change by the day. I see them all, with the full understanding of what my body after three babies will face in the future. Those with one-on-one physiotherapy work with trainers in the water, I merely oversee; in case the therapist drowns, I suppose.

In the seven years I have rarely had to dive in. It is a quiet, slow swimming pool, certainly nothing like the local pool I bring my boys to on a Saturday where you leave with a headache from the shouts that echo from the filled-to-the-brim group classes.

I stifle a yawn as I watch the first swimmer in the early morning. Mary Kelly, the dredger, is doing her favourite move: the breaststroke. Slow and noisy, at five feet tall and weighing three hundred pounds she pushes out water as if she's trying to empty the pool, and then attempts to glide. She manages this manoeuvre without once putting her face below the water and blowing out constantly as though she's in below-zero conditions. It is always the same people at the same times. I know that Mr Daly will soon arrive, followed by Mr Kennedy aka the Butterfly King who fancies himself as a bit of an expert, then sisters Eliza and Audrey Jones who jog widths of the shallow end for twenty minutes. Non-swimmer Tony Dornan will cling to a float for dear life like he's on the last life raft, and hover in the shallow end, near to the steps, near to the wall. I fiddle with a pair of goggles, unknotting the strap, reminding myself to breathe, pushing away the hard, tight feeling in my chest that only goes away when I remember to exhale.

Mr Daly steps out of the changing room and onto the tiles, 9.15 a.m. on the dot. He wears his budgie smugglers, an unforgiving light blue that reveal the minutiae when wet. His skin hangs loosely around his eyes, cheeks and jowls. His skin is so transparent I see almost every vein in his body and he's covered in bruises from even the slightest bump, I'm sure. His yellow toenails curl painfully into his skin. He gives me a miserable look and adjusts his goggles over his eyes. He shuffles by me without a good morning greeting, ignoring me as he does every day, holding on to the metal railing as if at any moment he'll go sliding on the slippery tiles that Mary Kelly is saturating with each stroke. I imagine him on the tiles, his bones snapping up through his tracing-paper-like skin, skin crackly like a roasted chicken.

I keep one eye on him and the other on Mary, who is letting out a loud grunting sound with each stroke like she is Maria Sharapova. Mr Daly reaches the steps, takes hold of the rail and lowers himself slowly into the water. His nostrils flare as the cold hits him. Once in the water he checks to see if I'm watching. On the days that I am, he floats on his back for long periods of time like he's a dead goldfish. On days like today, when I'm not looking, he lowers his body and head under the water, hands gripping the top of the wall to hold himself down, and stays there. I see him, clear as day, practically on his knees in the shallow end, trying to drown himself. This is a daily occurrence.

'Sabrina,' my supervisor Eric warns from the office behind me.

'I see him.'

I make my way to Mr Daly at the steps. I reach into the water and grab him under his arms and pull him up. He is so light he comes up easily, gasping for air, eyes wild behind his goggles, a big green snot bubble in his right nostril. He lifts his goggles off his head and empties them of water, grunting, grumbling, his body shaking with rage that I have once again foiled his dastardly plan. His face is purple and his chest heaves up and down as he tries to catch his breath. He reminds me of my three-year-old who always hides in the same place and then gets annoyed when I find him. I don't say anything, just make my way back to the stool, my flip-flops splashing my calves with cold water. This happens every day. This is all that happens.

'You took your time there,' Eric says.

Did I? Maybe a second longer than usual. 'Didn't want to spoil his fun.'

Eric smiles against his better judgement and shakes his head to show he disapproves. Before working here with me since the nursing home's birth, Eric had a previous Mitch Buchannon lifeguard experience in Miami. His mother on her deathbed brought him back home to Ireland and then his mother surviving has made him stay. He jokes that she will outlive him, though I can sense a nervousness on his part that this will indeed be the case. I think he's waiting for her to die so that he can begin living, and the fear as he nears fifty is that that will never happen. To cope with his self-imposed pause on his life, I think he pretends he's still in Miami;

though he's delusional, I sometimes envy his ability to pretend he is in a place far more exotic than this. I think he walks to the sound of maracas in his head. He is one of the happiest people I know because of it. His hair is Sun-In orange, and his skin is a similar colour. He doesn't go on any traditional 'dates' from one end of the year to the other, saving himself up for the month in January when he disappears to Thailand. He returns whistling, with the greatest smile on his face. I don't want to know what he does there but I know that his hopes are that when his mother dies, every day will be like Thailand. I like him and I consider him my friend. Five days a week in this place has meant I've told him more than I've even told myself.

'Doesn't it strike you that the one person I save every day is a person who doesn't even want to live? Doesn't it make you feel completely redundant?'

'There are plenty of things that do, but not that.' He bends over to pick up a bunch of wet grey hair clogging the drains, which looks like a drowned rat, and he holds on to it, shaking the water out of it, not appearing to feel the repulsion that I do. 'Is that how you're feeling?'

Yes. Though it shouldn't be. It shouldn't matter if the man I'm saving doesn't want his life to be saved, shouldn't the point be that I'm saving him? But I don't reply. He's my supervisor, not my therapist, I shouldn't question saving people while on duty as a lifeguard. He may live in an alternative world in his head but he's not stupid.

'Why don't you take a coffee break?' he offers, and hands me my coffee mug, the other hand still holding the drowned rat ball of pubic hair.

I like my job very much but lately I've been antsy. I don't know why and I don't know what exactly I'm expecting to happen in my life, or what I'm hoping will happen. I have no particular dreams or goals. I wanted to get married and I did. I wanted to have children and I do. I want to be a lifeguard and I am. Though isn't that the meaning of antsy? Thinking there are ants on you when there aren't.

'Eric, what does antsy mean?'

'Um. Restless, I think, uneasy.'

'Has it anything to do with ants?'

He frowns.

'I thought it was when you think there are ants crawling all over you, so you start to feel like this.' I shudder a bit. 'But there aren't any ants on you at all.'

He taps his lip. 'You know what, I don't know. Is it important?'

I think about it. It would mean that I think there is something wrong with my life because there actually *is* something wrong with my life or that there is something wrong with me. But it's just a feeling, and there actually isn't. There *not* being something wrong would be the preferred solution.

What's wrong, Sabrina? Aidan's been asking a lot lately. In the same way that constantly asking someone if they're angry will eventually make them angry.

Nothing's wrong. But is it nothing, or is it something? Or is it really that it *is* nothing, *everything* is just nothing? Is that the problem? Everything is nothing? I avoid Eric's gaze and concentrate instead on the pool rules, which irritate me so I look away. You see, there it is, that antsy thing.

'I can check it out,' he says, studying me.

To escape his gaze I get a coffee from the machine in the corridor and pour it into my mug. I lean against the wall in the corridor and think about our conversation, think about my life. Coffee finished, no conclusions reached, I return to the pool and I am almost crushed in the corridor by a stretcher being wheeled by at top speed by two paramedics, with a wet Mary Kelly on top of it, her white and blue-veined bumpy legs like Stilton, an oxygen mask over her face.

I hear myself say 'No way!' as they push by me.

When I get into the small lifeguard office I see Eric, sitting down in complete shock, his shell tracksuit dripping wet, his orange Sun-In hair slicked back from the pool water.

'What the hell?'

'I think she had a . . . I mean, I don't know, but, it might have been a heart attack. Jesus.' Water drips from his orange pointy nose.

'But I was only gone five minutes.'

'I know, it happened the second you walked out. I jammed on the emergency cord, pulled her out, did mouth-to-mouth, and they were here before I knew it. They responded fast. I let them in the fire exit.'

I swallow, the jealousy rising. 'You gave her mouth-to-mouth?'

'Yeah. She wasn't breathing. But then she did. Coughed up a load of water.'

I look at the clock. 'It wasn't even five minutes.'

He shrugs, still stunned.

I look at the pool, then at the clock. Mr Daly is sitting on the edge of the pool, looking after the ghost of the stretcher with envy. It was four and a half minutes.

'You had to dive in? Pull her out? Do mouth-to-mouth?'

'Yeah. Yeah. Look, don't beat yourself up about it, Sabrina, you couldn't have got to her any faster than I did.'

'You had to pull the emergency cord?'

He looks at me in confusion over this.

I've never had to pull the cord. Never. Not even in trials. Eric did that. I feel jealousy and anger bubbling to the surface, which is quite an unusual feeling. This happens at home – an angry mother irritated with her boys has lost the plot plenty of times – but never in public. In public I suppress it, especially at work when it is directed at my supervisor. I'm a measured, rational human being; people like me don't lose their temper in public. But I don't suppress the anger now. I let it rise close to the surface. It would feel empowering to let myself go like this if I wasn't so genuinely frustrated, so completely irritated.

To put it into perspective here is how I'm feeling: seven years working here. That's two thousand three hundred and ten days. Eleven thousand five hundred and fifty hours. Minus nine months, six months and three months for maternity leave. In all of that time I've sat on the stool and watched the, often, empty pool. No mouth-to-mouth, no dramatic dives. Not once. Not counting Mr Daly. Not counting the assistance of leg or foot cramps. Nothing. I sit on the stool, sometimes I stand, and I watch the oversized ticking clock and the list of pool rules. No running, no jumping, no diving, no pushing, no shouting, no nothing . . . all the things you're not allowed to do in this room, all negative, almost as though it's mocking me. No life-saving. I'm always on alert, it's what I'm trained to do, but nothing ever happens. And the very second I take an unplanned coffee break I miss a possible heart attack, a definite near-drowning and the emergency cord being pulled.

'It's not fair,' I say.

'Now come on, Sabrina, you were in there like a shot when Eliza stepped on the piece of glass.'

'It wasn't glass. Her varicose vein ruptured.'

'Well. You got there fast.'

It is always above the water that I struggle, that I can't breathe. It is above the water that I feel like I'm drowning.

I throw my coffee mug hard against the wall.

3

PLAYING WITH MARBLES

Conqueror

My neck is being squeezed so tightly I start to see black spots before my eyes. I'd tell him so but I can't speak, his arm is wrapped tight around my throat. I can't breathe. I can't breathe. I'm small for my age and they tease me for it. They call me Tick but Mammy says to use what I have. I'm small but I'm smart. With a burst of energy, I start to shake myself around, and my older brother Angus has to fight hard to hold on.

'Jesus, Tick,' Angus says, and he grips me tighter. Can't breathe, can't breathe.

'Let him go, Angus,' Hamish says. 'Get back to the game.'

'The little fucker's a cheat, I'm not playing with him.'

'I'm not a cheat!' I want to shout, but I can't. I can't breathe.

'He's not a cheat,' Hamish says on my behalf. 'He's just better than you.' Hamish is the eldest, at sixteen. He's watching from the front steps of our house. This statement is a lot, coming from him. He's cool as fuck. He's smoking a cigarette. If Mammy knew this she'd slap the head off him, but she can't see him now, she's inside the house with the midwife, which is why we've all been turfed out here for the day until it's over.

'Say that again,' Angus challenges Hamish.

'Or what?'

Or nothing. Angus wouldn't touch Hamish, older than him by only two years but infinitely cooler. None of us would. He's tough and everyone knows it and he's even started hanging out with Eddie Sullivan, nicknamed The Barber, and his gang at the barbershop. They're the ones giving him the cigarettes. And money too, but I don't know what for. Mammy's worried about him but she needs the money so doesn't ask questions. Hamish likes me the most. Some nights he wakes me up and I've to get dressed and we sneak out to the streets we're not allowed to play on. I'm not allowed to tell Mammy. We play marbles. I'm ten but I look younger; you wouldn't think I play as well as I do, most people don't, so Hamish hustles them. He's winning a packet and he gives me caramels on the way home so I don't tell. He doesn't need to buy me off but I don't tell him that, I like the caramels.

I play marbles in my sleep, I play when I should be doing homework, I play when Father Fuckface puts me in the dark room, I play it in my head when Mammy is giving out to me, so I don't have to listen. My fingers are moving all the time as if I'm shooting and I've built up a good collection. I have to hide them from my brothers though, my best ones anyway. They're nowhere near as good at playing as me, and they'd lose my marbles.

We hear Mammy bellow like an animal upstairs and Angus loosens his grip on me a bit. Enough for wriggle room. Everyone tenses up at the sound of Mammy. It's not new to us but no one likes it. It's not natural to hear anyone sound like that. Mattie opens the door and steps out even whiter than usual.

He looks at Angus. 'Let him go.'

Angus does and I can finally breathe. I start coughing. There's only one other person Angus doesn't mess with and that's our stepdad, Mattie. Mattie Doyle always means business.

Mattie glares at Hamish smoking. I get ready for Mattie to punch him – those two are always at it – but he doesn't.

Instead he says, 'Got one spare?'

Hamish smiles, the one that goes all the way to his green eyes. Daddy's green eyes. But he doesn't answer.

Mattie doesn't like the pause. 'Fuck you.' He slaps him over the head, and Hamish laughs at him, liking that he made him lose his temper. He won. 'I'm going to the pub. One of you come get me when it's out.'

'You'll probably hear it from there,' Duncan says.

Mattie laughs, but looks a bit scared.

'Are none of you keeping an eye on him?' He gestures to the toddler crouched in the dirt. We all look at Bobby. He's the youngest, at two. He's sitting in the muck, covered in it, even his mouth, and he's eating grass.

'He always eats grass,' Tommy says. 'Nothing we can do about it.'

'Are you a cow or wha'?' Mattie asks.

'Quack quack,' Bobby says, and we all laugh.

'Fuck sake, will someone ever teach him his animal sounds?' Mattie says, smiling. 'Right, Da's off to the pub, be good, Bobby.' Mattie rustles Tommy's head. 'Keep an eye on him, son.'

'Bye, Mattie,' Bobby says.

'It's Da, to you,' Mattie says, face going a bit red with anger.

It drives Mattie mad when Bobby calls him Mattie, but it's not Bobby's fault, he's used to us all calling Mattie by his name; he's not our da, but Bobby doesn't understand, he thinks we're all the same. Only Mattie's first boy, Tommy, calls him Da.

There's Doyles and Boggs in this family and we all know the difference.

'Let's get back to the game,' Duncan says as Mammy screams again.

'He's not allowed to play unless he takes his turn again,' Angus says angrily.

'Fine, he will, calm down,' Hamish says.

'Hey!' I protest. 'I didn't cheat.'

Hamish winks at me. 'You can show them.'

I sigh. I'm ten, Duncan is twelve, Angus is fourteen and Hamish is sixteen. The two Doyle boys, Tommy and Bobby, are five and two. With three older brothers I'm always having to prove myself, and even when I'm better than them, which I am at marbles and they can't stand it, then I have to work even harder because they think I'm a cheat. I'm the one who teaches them the new games I've read about in my books. I'm better than them. They all hate it but it drives Angus mental. He hits me whenever he loses. Hamish hates losing too but he's figured out how to use me.

We're playing Conqueror, me, Duncan and Angus. Angus wouldn't let Tommy play because he's the worst, he's so bad he just ruins the game. When my older brothers aren't around I teach Tommy how to play; I like doing that, even though he's diabolical. That's the word Hamish uses for everything. I use my worst marbles, just the clearies for him, because he chips them and everything. Tommy's sitting on the steps away from Hamish. He's afraid of Hamish. Tommy knows that Hamish and his da don't get along so he thinks he has to defend his da when he's not there. He's only five but he's a tough little shit, scrawny and pale like his da too. The lads call him Bottle-washer because he's so skinny and wiry.

What happened to put me in the headlock was that Angus threw the first marble, then Duncan shot his marble at Angus's. It hit and that's why Angus got mad in the first place. Duncan captured Angus's marble then threw another to restart the game. I hit Duncan's, captured his then threw another to restart.

Angus threw his taw and missed mine.

Duncan aimed at Angus's corkscrew, not because it was closer but because I know he could tell Angus was already getting angry and wanted to wind him up. Anyway he missed and it was my turn. I had two targets; I could have chosen Duncan's opaque, which I don't much want because everyone has them – that's marbles that are just one colour – or Angus's Popeye corkscrew, which I've had my eye on for a long time. Angus says he won it in a game but I think he must have stolen it from Francis's corner shop. I've never seen anyone with one like that. I've only ever seen a picture of one in my marble book, so I know that his is a three-colour special called a snake corkscrew. It's a double-twist

and has a green-and-transparent clear with fila-
ments of opaque white. It has tiny clear bubbles
inside. I found it in his drawer a few days ago and
he caught me snooping and kicked me in the balls
to let it go. I didn't drop it though, I know better
than to let it get scratched, but watching him play
with it hurts more than the kick in the goonies did.
He should be keeping it in a box, safe so it doesn't
get ruined.

I decided to do a move I'd been working on and
impress them all by putting a spin on my marble
and hitting both marbles in the one throw. I threw
my taw and it hit Duncan's opaque first like I
planned, then Tommy shouted and they all looked
at Bobby who had a snail in his mouth, shell and all.
Angus rushed over to grab it from him and chucked
it across the road. He opened Bobby's mouth wide.

'The snail is missing from the shell. Did you eat it,
Bobby?'

Bobby didn't answer, just waited for a clatter, his
big blue eyes wide. Bobby's the only blond. He gets
away with murder because of those blue eyes and
blond hair. Even Hamish doesn't hit him half as
much as he wants to. But anyway when they were
all busy wondering about where the slug part of
the snail went, nobody was looking when my taw
hit Angus's marble as well, which meant that I could
capture both marbles in the one throw. They looked
back at me to see me holding two of them in my

31

hand, and that's when Angus accused me of cheating and wrapped me in a headlock.

Free now of the headlock I have to respond to the cheating allegations by trying to repeat the move, which should be fine, I know I can do it, but I can't when they think that I'm a cheat. If I can't do it again it proves to them that I cheated. Hamish winks at me. I know he knows that I can do it, but if I don't win he might not take me out tonight. My hands start to sweat.

Mammy screams again and Tommy's eyes widen.

'Baby?' Bobby asks.

'Nearly there, pal, nearly there,' Hamish says, rolling up another cigarette, cool as fuck. Seriously, when I grow up I want to be just like him.

Mrs Lynch's door opens – she's our next-door neighbour – and she comes out with her daughter, Lucy. Lucy's face is already scarlet when she sees Hamish. Lucy is holding a tray with a mountain of sandwiches all piled up, I can see strawberry jam, and Mrs Lynch has diluted orange in a jug.

We all pile on top of the food.

'Thanks, Mrs Lynch,' we all say, mouths full and devouring the sandwiches. With Mammy in the throes of it we haven't eaten since dinner yesterday.

Hamish winks at Lucy and she kind of giggles and runs inside. I saw them together late one night, Hamish had one hand up her top and the other up her skirt, and she'd one leg wrapped around him like a baby monkey, her thick white thigh practically glowing in the dark.

'That mammy of yours will keep going till she gets that girl of hers, won't she?' Mrs Lynch says, sitting down on the step.

'I've a feeling it's a girl this time,' Hamish says. 'Her bump's different.'

Hamish is serious; for all his trouble he notices things, sees things that none of the rest of us do.

'I think you're right,' Mrs Lynch agrees. 'It's high up all right.'

'It'll be nice to have a girl around,' Hamish says. 'No more of these smelly bastards to annoy me.'

'Ah, she'll be the boss of you all, wait'll you see,' says Mrs Lynch. 'Like my Lucy.'

'She sure is the boss of Hamish,' Angus mutters, and gets a boot in the stomach from Hamish. Chewed-up jam sandwich fires out of his mouth and he's momentarily winded and I'm glad: payback for my headlock.

Hamish's green eyes are glowing, he really does look like he wants a girl. He looks like a big softy thinking about it.

Mammy wails again.

'Won't be long now,' Hamish says.

'She's doing a fine job,' Mrs Lynch says, and she looks like she's in pain just listening. Maybe she's remembering and I feel sick thinking of a baby coming out of her.

33

The midwife starts chanting, as if Mammy's in a boxing match and she's the coach. Mammy's squealing like she's a pig being chased around with a carving knife.

'Final push,' Hamish says.

Mrs Lynch looks impressed with Hamish's knowledge. As the eldest he's sat through this five times; whether he remembers them all or not, he's definitely learned the way.

'Okay, let's finish this before she comes out,' Angus says, jumping up and wiping his jam face on his sleeve.

I know Angus wants to prove me wrong in front of everyone. He knows Hamish likes me and just because he's too weak to hit Hamish, he uses me to get at him instead. Hurting me is like hurting Hamish. And Hamish feels that way too. It's good for me but bad for the person who treats me bad: last week Hamish punched out a fella's front tooth for not picking me for his football team. I didn't even want to play football.

I stand up and take my place. Concentrating hard, my heart beating in my chest, my palms sweaty. I want that corkscrew.

The midwife is screaming about seeing the baby's head. Mammy's sounds are terrifying now. The piggy's being slashed.

'Good girl, good girl,' Mrs Lynch says, chewing on her nail and rocking back and forth on the step, as if Mammy can hear her. 'Nearly over, love. You're there. You're there.'

I throw the taw. It hits Duncan's marble just like I planned and it heads to Angus's. I want that corkscrew.

'A girl!' the midwife calls out.

Hamish stands up, about to punch the air but he stops himself.

My marble travels to Angus's corkscrew. It misses but nobody's looking, nobody's seen it happen. Everyone is frozen in place, Mrs Lynch goes still. Waiting; they're all waiting for the baby to cry.

Hamish puts his head in his hands. I check again. Nobody is looking at me, or my taw, which went straight past Angus's, it didn't even touch it.

I take a tiny step to the right but they're still not looking. I reach out my foot and push my marble back a bit so that it's touching Angus's Popeye corkscrew. My heart is beating wildly, I can't believe I'm doing it, but if I get away with it then I'll have the corkscrew, it'll actually be mine.

All of a sudden there's a wail, but it's not the baby, it's Mammy.

Hamish runs inside, Duncan follows. Tommy grabs Bobby from the dirt and carries him into the house. Angus looks down at the ground and sees his marble and my marble, touching.

His face is deadly serious. 'Okay. You win.' Then he follows the boys inside.

I pick up the green corkscrew and examine it, finally happy to have it in my hand, part of my collection. These are incredibly rare. My happiness is short-lived though as my adrenaline begins to wear off and it sinks in.

There's no baby girl. There's no baby at all. And I'm a cheat.

4

POOL RULES

No Jumping

'Sabrina, are you okay?' Eric asks me from across his desk.

'Yes,' I say, keeping my voice measured while feeling anything but. I have just fired my mug at the concrete wall because I missed a near-drowning. 'I thought there would be more pieces.' We both look at the mug sitting on his desk. The handle has come off and the rim is chipped, but that's it. 'My mum fired a teapot up at the ceiling once. There were definitely more pieces.'

Eric looks at it, studies it. 'I suppose it's the way it hit the wall. The angle or something.'

We consider that in silence.

'I think you should go home,' he says suddenly.

'Take the day off. Enjoy the solar eclipse everybody's talking about. Come back in on Monday.'

'Okay.'

Home for me is a three-bed end of terrace, where I live with my husband, Aidan, and our three boys. Aidan works in Eircom broadband support, though it never seems to work in our house. We've been married for seven years. We met in Ibiza when we were contestants in a competition that took place on the bar counter of a nightclub to see who could lick cream off a complete stranger's torso the quickest. He was the torso, I was the licker. We won. Don't for a moment think that was out of character for me. I was nineteen, and fourteen people took part in front of an audience of thousands, and we won a free bottle of tequila, which we subsequently drank on the beach, while we had sex. It would have been out of character not to. Aidan was a stranger to me then, but he's a stranger to that man now, unrecognisable from that cocky teenager with the pierced ear and the shaved eyebrow. I suppose we both changed. Aidan doesn't even like the beach now, says the sand gets everywhere. And I'm trying to stay off dairy.

It is rare that I find myself alone in the house; in fact I can't remember the last time that happened, no kids around asking me to do something every two seconds. I don't know what to do with myself so I sit in the empty, silent kitchen looking around.

It's ten a.m. and the day has barely started. I make myself a cup of tea, just for something to do, but don't drink it. I stop myself just in time from putting the teabags in the fridge. I'm always doing things like this. I look at the pile of washing and ironing but can't be bothered. I realise I've been holding my breath and I exhale.

There are things that I need to do all the time. Things that I never have the time for in my carefully ordered daily routine. Now I have some time – the whole day – but I don't know where to start.

My mobile rings, saving me from indecision, and it's my dad's hospital.

'Hello?' I say, feeling the tightness in my chest.

'Hi, Sabrina, it's Lea.' My dad's favourite nurse. 'We just got a delivery of five boxes for Fergus. Did you arrange it?'

'No,' I frown.

'Oh. Well, I haven't shown them to him yet, they're sitting in reception, I wanted to wait to speak with you first, just in case, you know, there's something in there that might confuse him.'

'Yes, you're right, thanks. Don't worry. I'll come get them now, I'm free.'

And that's what always seems to happen. Whenever I get a minute to myself away from work and the kids, Dad is the other person who fills it. I arrive at the hospital thirty minutes later and see the boxes piled in the corner of reception. Upon seeing them I know immediately where they've come from and I'm raging. These are the boxes of Dad's belongings that I packed after Dad's home was sold. Mum had been storing them, but she's obviously chosen not to any more. I don't understand why she sent them here and not to me.

Last year my dad suffered a severe stroke, which has led to his living in a long-term care facility, giving him the kind of skilled care that I know I could not have given with three young boys – Charlie at seven, Fergus at five and Alfie at three years old – and a job. Mum certainly wouldn't have taken on the role either as she and Dad are divorced, and have been separated since I was fifteen. Though right now they're getting along better than they ever have, and I even think Mum enjoys her fortnightly visits with him.

There are those who insist that stress does not cause strokes, but it happened during a time when Dad was the most stressed in his life, coping with the fallout of the financial crisis. He worked for a venture capital company. He scrambled for a while, trying to find new clients, trying to win old ones back, and all the while watching lives fall apart and feeling responsible for that, but it wasn't sustainable. Eventually he found a new job, in car sales, was trying to move on, but his blood pressure was high, his weight had ballooned, he smoked heavily, didn't exercise, and drank too much. I'm no doctor, but he did all of these things because he was stressed, and then he had a stroke.

His speech isn't easy to understand and he's in a wheelchair, though he's working on his walking. He's lost an enormous amount of weight, and seems like a completely different man to the man he was in the years leading up to his stroke. The stroke caused some memory problems, which enrages Mum. He seems to forget all the hurt he caused her. He has been able to wipe the slate clean of all of their problems and arguments, their heartache and his misdemeanours – of which there were many – throughout their marriage. He comes out of it smelling of roses.

'He gets to live like none of it happened, like he doesn't have to feel guilty or apologise for anything,' Mum regularly rants. She was obviously planning on him feeling bad for the rest of his life and he went and ruined it. He went and forgot it all. But even though she rants about the Fergus before the stroke, she visits him regularly and they talk like the couple they both wish they'd been. About what's happening in the news, about the garden, the seasons, the weather. It's comforting chat. I think what angers her most is the fact that she likes him now. This sweet, caring, gentle, patient man is a man she could have remained married to.

What has happened to Dad has been difficult, but we haven't lost him. He is still alive and in fact what we lost was the other side of him, the distant, detached, sometimes prickly side of him that was harder to love. The one that pushed people away. The one that wanted to be alone, but have us at the end of his fingertips, just in case, for when he wanted us. He is quite content where he is now; he gets along with the nurses, has made friends, and I spend more time with him now than I ever have, visiting him with Aidan and the boys on Sundays.

I never know what exactly Dad has forgotten until I bring something up and I watch that now all too familiar fog pass over his eyes, that vacant look as he tries to process what I've just said with his collection of memories and experiences, only to find it coming back empty, as if they don't tally. I understand why Nurse Lea didn't bring the boxes directly to him; an overload of too many things that he can't remember would surely upset him. There are ways to deal with those moments. I gently sidestep them, move on from them quickly as though they never happened, or pretend that I've gotten the details wrong myself. It's not because it upsets him – most of the time it goes by without drama, as if he's oblivious to it – but it upsets me.

There are more boxes than I remember and, too impatient to wait until I get home, I stand there in the corridor and use a key to pierce through the tape on the top of one of the boxes and slice it open. I fold back the box, curious to see what's inside. I expect photo albums, or wedding cards. Something sentimental that, far from conjuring beautiful memories, starts Mum spouting about everything that was taken from her by her own husband. The dreams that were shattered, the promises that were broken.

Instead I find a folder containing pages covered in handwriting: my dad's looping, swirling letters, that remind me of school sick notes and birthday cards. At the top of the page it says *Marbles Inventory*. Beneath the folder are tins, pouches and boxes, some in bubble wrap, others in tissue paper.

I open some of the lids. Inside each tin or box are deliciously colourful candy-like balls of shining glass. I look at them in utter shock and amazement. I had no idea my dad liked marbles. I had no idea my dad knew the slightest thing about marbles. If it wasn't for his handwriting in the inventory, I would have thought there was a mistake. It is as if I have opened a box to somebody else's life.

I open the folder and read through the list, which is not as sentimental as it first seemed. It is almost scientific.

The pouches – some velvet, others mesh – and the tin boxes are colour-coded and numbered with stickers, to save confusion, and adhere to the colours on the inventory.

The first on the list is a small velvet pouch of

four marbles. The inventory lists them as *Bloodies* and, beside that, *(Allies, Fr. Noel Doyle)*. Opening the pouch, the marbles are smaller than any others I can see offhand and have varying red swirls, but Dad has gone into detail describing them:

Rare Christensen Agate 'Bloodies' have transparent red swirls edged with translucent brown on an opaque white base.

There is a cube box of more bloodies, dating back to 1935 from the Peltier Glass Company. These are appropriately colour-coded red and are listed together with the velvet pouch. I scoop a few marbles into my hands and roll them around, enjoying the sound of them clicking together, while my mind races at what I've discovered. Pouches, tins, boxes, all containing the most beautiful colours, swirls and spirals, glistening as they catch the light. I lift some out and hold them up to the window, examining the detail inside, the bubbles, the light, utterly enchanted by the complexity within something so small. I flick through the pages quickly:

. . . latticinia core swirls, divided core swirls, solid core swirls, ribbon core swirls, joseph's coat swirls, banded/coreless swirls, peppermint swirls, clambroths, banded opaques, indian, banded lutz, onionskin lutz, ribbon lutz . . .

A myriad of marbles, all of them alien to me. What is even more astonishing is that in other pages of his handwritten documents he has included a table charting each marble's value depending upon how it measures up in terms of *size, mint, near mint, good, collectable*. It seems that his humble box of bloodies are worth $150–$250.

All of the prices are listed in US dollars. Some are valued at fifty dollars or one hundred, while the two-inch ribbon lutz has been priced at $4,500 in mint condition, $2,250 in near mint, $1,250 in good condition and collectable is $750. I know next to nothing about their condition – all of them appear perfect to me, nothing cracked or chipped – but there are hundreds of them packed away, and pages and pages of inventory. What Dad appears to have here are thousands of dollars' worth of marbles.

I stop and think. All around me are the sounds and smells of the care home and it transports me from the parallel marble world back to reality. I was worried about him being able to pay for his hospital costs but if his pricing is correct, then he has his nest egg right here. I'm always worried about those bills. We have no way of knowing when he might need another operation or new medicine, or a new physio. It's always changing, the bills are always climbing and the proceeds from the sale of his apartment didn't go far after paying his mortgage and numerous debts. None of us had known that he was in such a bad financial state.

His writing is impeccable, a beautiful flowing script; he hasn't made one mistake and if he did I imagine he started the page over. It is written with love, it has taken great time and dedication, research and knowledge. That's it: it's written by an expert. It's the writing of another man, not the one who now grasps the pen with great difficulty, but neither does it fit with the father I knew, whose only hobby seemed to be watching and talking about football. Wanting to take my time to go through the boxes at home, I pack everything away again and Gerry, the porter, helps me carry them to my car. But before locking them in the boot, I hesitate and take out the small bag of red marbles.

Dad is sitting in the lounge, drinking a cup of tea and watching *Bargain Hunt*. He watches the show every day: people searching for items at markets and then trying to auction them for as much as possible. Maybe there have been hints of his passion all the way along and I missed them. I think of the inventory and wonder if I should go back for it. As I watch him staring intently at the pricing of these old objects, I wonder if in fact he does remember exactly what is in those boxes after all. He sees me before I have time to think about it any further and so I go to him, to his smiling face. It breaks my heart how happy he is to receive visitors, not because he's lonely but because he could often be so irritated by others before, unless it was to convince them to buy something from him, and he now can't get enough of people's company, for nothing in return.

'Good morning.'

'Ah, to what do I owe this pleasure?' he asks. 'No work today?'

'Eric let me off early,' I explain diplomatically. 'And Lea called me. She said it was an emergency, that you were revving up the inmates, trying to organise a breakout again.'

He laughs, then he looks down at my hands and his laughter stops immediately. I'm holding the bag of red marbles. Something passes on his face. A look I've never seen before. As quickly as it arrived, it's gone again and he's smiling at me, the confusion back.

'What's that you've got there?'

I open my hand, reveal the red marbles in the mesh bag.

He just stares at them. I wait for him to say something but nothing comes. He barely blinks.

'Dad?'

Nothing.

'Dad?' I put my free hand on his arm gently.

'Yes.' He looks at me, troubled.

I loosen the drawstrings on the mesh purse and roll them into the palm of my hand. As I move the marbles in my hand they roll and click together. 'Do you want to hold them?'

He stares at them again, intently, as though trying to figure them out. I want to know what's going on inside his head. Too much? Everything? Nothing? I know that feeling. I watch for that sliver of recognition again. It doesn't come. Just bother and irritation, perhaps that he can't remember what he wants to remember. I stuff the marbles in my pocket quickly and change the subject, trying to hide my disappointment from him.

But I saw it. Like a flicker of a flame. The ruffle of a feather. The flash of the sea as the sun hits it. Something brief and then gone, but there. When he saw the marbles first, he was a different man, with a face I've never seen.

5

PLAYING WITH MARBLES

Picking Plums

I'm home from school, a fever, the first and only day of school I've ever missed. I hate school; I would have wanted this any day at all in the whole entire year. Any day but today. The funeral was yesterday – well, it wasn't a proper one with a priest, but Mattie's pal is an undertaker and he found out where they were burying our baby sister, in the same coffin as an old woman who had just died in the hospital. When we got to the graveyard, the old woman's family were finishing up their funeral so we had to wait around. Ma was happy it was an old woman she was being buried with and not an old man, or any man. The old woman was a mother, and a grandmother. Mammy spoke to one of her daughters who said that her ma would look after the baby. Uncle Joseph and Aunty Sheila said all the prayers at our ceremony. Mattie doesn't say prayers, I don't think he knows any, and Mammy couldn't speak.

The priest called round to the house beforehand and tried to talk Mammy out of making a show of herself by going to the grave. Mammy had a shouting match with him and Mattie grabbed the brandy from the priest's hand and told him to get the fuck out of his house. Hamish helped Mattie get rid of him, the only time I've seen them on the same side. I saw the way everyone looked at Mammy as we walked down the street to the graveyard, all dressed in black. They looked at her like she was crazy, like our baby sister was never really a baby at all, just because she didn't take a breath when she came out. Even though they're not supposed to, the midwife had let Mammy hold her baby after she was born. She held her for an hour, then when the midwife started to get a bit angry and tried to take her from Mammy, Hamish stepped in. Mattie wasn't there and he took over, he lifted the baby out of Mammy's arms and carried her down the stairs. He kissed her before he gave her back to the midwife, who took her away forever.

'She was alive inside of me,' I heard Mammy say to the priest, but I don't think he liked hearing her say that. He looked like it was a bit disgusting for him to think of things living inside of her. But she did it anyway, made up her own funeral at the graveyard, and it was cold and grey and it rained the whole time. My shoes got so wet, my socks and feet were soaking and numb. I sneezed all day, couldn't breathe out of my nose last night, the lads kept thumping me to stop me snoring and I spent the whole night going from hot to cold, shivering then sweating, feeling cold when I was sweating, feeling hot when I was cold. Crazy dreams: Da and Mattie fighting, and Father Murphy shouting at me about dead babies and hitting me, and my brothers stealing my marbles, and Mammy in black howling with grief. But that part was real.

Even though I feel like my skin is on fire and everything around me is swirling, I don't call Mammy. I stay in bed, tossing and turning, sometimes crying because I'm so confused and my skin is sore. Mammy brought me a boiled egg this morning and put a cold cloth on my head. She sat beside me, dressed in black, still with a big tummy looking like she has a baby in there, staring into space but not saying anything. It's kind of like when Da died but this is different; she was angry at Da, this time she's sad.

Usually Mammy never stops moving. She's always cleaning, cleaning Bobby's nappies, the house, banging sheets and rugs, cooking, preparing food. She never stops, always banging around the place, us always in her way and her moving us out of the way with her legs and feet, pushing us aside like she's in a field and we're long grass. Now and then she stops moving to straighten her back and groan, before going back to it again. But today the house is silent and I'm not used to that. Usually we're all shouting, fighting, laughing, talking; even at night there's a child crying, or Mammy singing to it, or Mattie bumping into things when he comes home drunk and swearing. I hear things that I've never heard before like creaks and moaning pipes, but there's no sound from Mammy. This worries me.

I get out of bed, my legs shaking and feeling weak like I have never walked before, and I hang on tight to the bannister as I go downstairs, every floorboard creaking beneath my bare feet. I go into the living room, joined on to the kitchen, tiny at the back of the house like they forgot it and added it on, and it's empty. She's not here. Not in the kitchen, not in the garden, not in the living room. I'm about to leave when I suddenly see her in black sitting in an armchair in the corner of the living room that only Mattie ever sits in; so still I nearly missed her. She's staring into space, her eyes red like she hasn't stopped crying since yesterday. I've never seen her so still. I don't remember it ever being just me and her before, just the two of us. I've never had Mammy to myself. Thinking about it makes me nervous: what do I say to Mammy when there's nobody around to hear me, to see me, to react, to tease, to goad, to impress? What do I say to Mammy when I'm not using her to get a rise out of someone else, to tell on someone, or know if what I'm saying is right or wrong because of their reactions?

I'm about to leave the room when I think of something, something I want to ask, that I would only ask if it was just me and her, with no one else around.

'Hi,' I say.

She looks over at me, surprised, like she's had a fright, then she smiles. 'Hi, love. How's your head? Do you need more water?'

'No thanks.'

She smiles.

'I want to ask you a question. If you don't mind.'

She beckons me in and I come closer and stand before her, fidgeting with my fingers.

'What is it?' she asks gently.

'Do you . . . do you think she's with Da?'

This seems to take her by surprise. Her eyes fill and she struggles to talk. I think if the others were here I wouldn't have asked such a stupid question. I've gone and upset her, the very thing Mattie told us not to do. I need to get myself out of it before she yells or, worse, cries.

'I know he's not her da, but he loved you, and you're her mammy. And he loved children. I don't remember loads about him but I remember that. Green eyes and he always played with us. Chased us. Wrestled us. I remember him laughing. He was skinny but he had huge hands. Some other das never did that, so I know he liked us. I think she's in heaven and that he's minding her and so I don't think you need to worry about her.'

'Oh, Fergus, love,' she says, opening her arms as tears run down her face. 'Come here to me.'

I go into her arms and she hugs me so tight I nearly can't breathe but am afraid to say. She rocks me, saying, 'My boy, my boy,' over and over again, and I think I might have said the right thing after all.

When she pulls away I say, 'Can I ask you another question?'

She nods.

'Why did you call her Victoria?'

Her face creases again, in pain, but she composes herself and even smiles. 'I haven't told anyone why.'

'Oh. Sorry.'

'No, pet, it's just that nobody asked. Come here and I'll tell you,' she says, and even though I'm too old, I squeeze onto her lap, half on the armchair, half on her. 'I felt different with her. A different kind of bump. I said to Mattie, "I feel like a plum." Says he, "We'll call her Plum, so."'

'Plum!' I laugh.

She nods and wipes her tears again. 'It got me thinking about my grandma's house. We used to visit her: me, Sheila and Paddy. She had apple trees, pears, blackberries, and she had two plum trees. I loved those plum trees because they were all she talked about, I think they were all she thought about – she wouldn't let those trees beat her.' She gives a little laugh and even though I don't get the joke, I laugh too. 'I think she thought it was exotic, that growing plums made her exotic, when really she was plain, plain as can be, like any of us. She'd make plum pies and I loved baking them with her. We stayed with her on my birthday every year, so every year my birthday cake was a plum pie.'

'Mmm,' I say, licking my lips. 'I've never had plum pie.'

'No,' she says, surprised. 'I've never baked it for you. She grew Opal plums, but they weren't reliable because the bullfinches ate the fruit buds in winter. They used to strip those branches clean and Nana would be crazy, running around the garden swatting them with her tea cloth. Sometimes she'd get us to stand by the tree all day just scaring them away; me, Sheila and Paddy, standing around like scarecrows.'

I laugh at that image of them.

'She gave the Opal more attention because it tasted better and it grew larger, almost twice the size of the other tree's plums, but the Opal made her angrier and didn't deliver every year. My favourite plum tree was the other tree, the Victoria plum. It was smaller but it always delivered and the bullfinches stayed away from that one more. To me, it was the sweetest . . .'

Her smile fades again and she looks away. 'Well, now.'

'I know a marble game called Picking Plums,' I say.

'Do you now?' she asks. 'Don't you have a marble game for every occasion?' She prods at me with her finger in my tickly bits and I laugh.

'Do you want to play?'

'Why not!' she says, surprised at herself.

I'm in such shock I run up the stairs faster than I ever have to get the marbles. Once downstairs she's still in the chair, daydreaming. I set up the game, explaining as I go.

I can't draw on the floor so I use a shoelace to mark a line and I place a row of marbles with a gap the width of two marbles in between. I use a skipping rope to mark a line on the other side of the room. The idea is to stand behind the line and take it in turns to shoot at the line of marbles.

'So these are the plums,' I say to her, pointing at the line of marbles, feeling such excitement that I have her attention, that she's all mine, that she's listening to me talking about marbles, that she's possibly going to play marbles, that nobody else can steal her attention away. All aches and pains from my fever are gone in the distraction and hopefully hers are too. 'You have to shoot your marble at the plums and if you hit it out of line you get the plum.'

She laughs. 'This is so silly, Fergus.' But she does it and she has fun, scowling when she misses and celebrating when she wins. I've never seen Mammy play like this, or punch the air in victory when she wins. It's the best moment I've ever spent with her in my whole life. We play the game until all the plums are picked and for once I'm hoping I miss, because I don't want it to end. When we hear voices at the door, the shouting and name-calling as my brothers return from school, I scurry for the marbles on the floor.

'Back to bed, you!' She ruffles my hair and returns to the kitchen.

I don't tell the others what me and Mammy talked about and I don't tell them we played marbles together. I want it to be between me and her.

And in the week that Mammy stops wearing black and bakes us plum pie for dessert, I don't tell anybody why. One thing I learned about carrying marbles in my pockets in case Father Murphy locked me in the dark room, and going out with Hamish and pretending to other kids that I've never played marbles before, is that keeping secrets makes me feel powerful.

6

POOL RULES

No Diving

Mid-morning and back home, I lug Dad's boxes into the middle of the living room floor and separate two I already know, boxes of sentimental and important items that we had to keep. I move them aside to make way for the three that are new to me. I'm mystified. Mum and I packed up his entire apartment, but I did not pack these boxes. I make myself a fresh cup of tea and begin emptying the same box I opened earlier, wanting to pick up where I left off. It is peculiar to have time to myself. Taking care and time, I start to go through Dad's inventory.

Latticino core swirls, divided core swirls, ribbon core swirls, Joseph's coat swirls. I take them out and line them up beside their boxes, crouched on the floor like one of my sons with their cars. I push my face up to them, examining the interiors, trying to compare and contrast. I marvel at the colours and detail; some are cloudy, some are clear, some appear to have trapped rainbows inside, while others have mini tornadoes frozen in a moment. Some have a base glass colour and nothing else. Despite being grouped together under these various alien titles I can't tell the difference no matter how hard I try. Absolutely every single one of them is unique and I have to be careful not to mix them up.

The description of each marble boggles my mind too as I try to identify which of the core swirls is the gooseberry, caramel or custard. Which is the 'beach ball' peppermint swirl, which is the one with mica. But I've no doubt Dad knew, he knew them all. Micas, slags, opaques and clearies, some so complex it's as though they house entire galaxies inside, others one single solid colour. Dark, bright, eerie and hypnotic, he has them all.

And then I come across a box that makes me laugh. Dad, who hated animals, who refused every plea for me to get a pet, has an entire collection of what are called 'Sulphides'. Transparent marbles with animal figures inside, like he has his own farmyard within his tiny marbles. Dogs, cats, squirrels and birds. He even has an elephant. The one which stands out the most to me is a clear marble with an angel inside. It's this that I hold and study for some time, straightening my aching back, trying to grasp what I've found, wondering when, what part of his life did this all occur. When we left the house did he watch us drive off and disappear to his 'farmyard animals'? Tend to them privately in his own world. Was it before I was born? Or was it after he and Mum divorced, filling his solitude with a new hobby?

There is a little empty box, an Akro Agate Company retailer stock box, to be precise, which Dad has valued at a surprising $400–$700. There's even a glass bottle with a marble inside, listed as a Codd bottle and valued at $2,100. It seems he didn't just collect marbles, he also collected their presentation boxes, probably hoping to find the missing pieces of the jigsaw as the years went by. I feel a wave of sadness for him that that won't happen now, that these marbles have been sitting in boxes for a year and he never knew to ask for them because he forgot that they were there.

I line them up, I watch them roll, the movement of colours inside like kaleidoscopes. And then when every inch of my carpet is covered, I sit up, straighten my spine till it clicks. I'm not sure what else to do, but I don't want to put them away again. They look so beautiful lining my floor, like a candy army.

I pick up the inventory and try once more to see if I can identify them myself, playing my own little marble game, and as I do so, I notice that not everything written on the list is on my floor.

I check the box again and it's empty, apart from some mesh bags and boxes which are collectable for their condition alone, despite there being no marbles inside them. I flip the top of the third box open and peer inside, but it's just a load of old newspapers and brochures, nothing like the Aladdin's cave of the first two boxes.

After my thorough search, which I repeat two more times, I can confirm that there are two missing items from the inventory. Allocated turquoise and yellow circular stickers, one is described as an Akro Agate Company box, circa 1930, the original sample case carried by salesmen as they made their calls. Dad has priced it at $7,500–$12,500. The other is what's called World's Best Moons. A Christensen Agate Company original box of twenty-five marbles, listed between $4,000–$7,000. His two most valuable items are gone.

I sit in a kind of stunned silence, until I realise I'm holding my breath and need to exhale.

Dad could have sold them. He went to the trouble of having them valued, so it would make sense for him to have sold them, and the most expensive ones too. He was having money troubles, we know that; perhaps he had to sell his beloved marbles just to get by. But it seems unlikely. Everything has been so well documented and catalogued, he would have made a note of their sale, probably even included the receipt. The two missing collections are written proudly and boldly on the inventory, as present as everything else in the inventory that sits on the floor.

First I'm baffled. Then I'm annoyed that Mum never told me about this collection. That objects held in such regard were packed away and forgotten. I don't have any memory of Dad and marbles, but that's not to say it didn't happen. I know he liked his secrets. I cast my mind back to the man before the stroke and I see pinstripe suits, cigarette smoke. Talk about stock markets and economics, shares up and down, the news or football always on the radio and television, and more recently car-talk. Nothing in my memory bank tells me anything about marbles, and I'm struggling to square this collection – this careful passion – with the man I recall from when I was growing up.

A new thought occurs. I wonder if in fact they're Dad's marbles at all. Perhaps he inherited them. His dad died when he was young, and he had a stepfather, Mattie. But from what I know about Mattie it seems unlikely that he was interested in marbles, or in such careful cataloguing as this. Perhaps they were his father's, or his Uncle Joseph's, and Dad took the time to get them valued and catalogue them. The only thing I am sure of is the inventory being his writing; anything beyond that is a mystery.

There's one person who can help me. I stretch my legs and reach for the phone and call Mum.

'I didn't know Dad had a marble collection,' I say straight away, trying to hide my accusatory tone.

Silence. 'Pardon me?'

'Why did I never know that?'

She laughs a little. 'He has a marble collection now? How sweet. Well, as long as it's making him happy, Sabrina.'

'No. He's not collecting them now. I found them in the boxes that you had delivered to the hospital today.' Also an accusatory tone.

'Oh.' A heavy sigh.

'We agreed that you would store them for him. Why did you send them to the hospital?'

Though I didn't recognise the marbles, I do recognise some of the other boxes' contents as items we packed away from Dad's apartment before putting it on the market. I still feel guilty that we had to do this, but we needed to raise as much money as possible for his rehabilitation. We tried to keep all the precious memories safe, like his lucky football shirt, his photographs and mementos, which I have in our shed in the back garden, the only place I could store them. I didn't have room for the rest, so Mum took them.

'Sabrina, I was *going* to store his boxes, but then Mickey Flanagan offered to take them and so I sent him everything.'

'Mickey Flanagan, the solicitor, had Dad's private things?' I say, annoyed.

'He's not exactly a random stranger. He's a kind of friend. He was Fergus's solicitor for years. Handled our divorce too. You know, he pushed for Fergus to get sole custody of you. You were fifteen – what the hell would Fergus have done with you at fifteen? Not to mention the fact you didn't even want to live with *me* at fifteen. You could barely live with *yourself*. Anyway, Mickey was handling the insurance and hospital bills, and he said he'd store Fergus's things, he had plenty of space.'

A bubble of anger rises in me. 'If I'd known his solicitor was taking his personal things, I would have had them, Mum.'

'I know. But you said you had no space for anything more.'

Which I didn't and I don't. I barely have space for my shoes. Aidan jokes that he has to step outside of the house in order to change his mind.

'So why did Mickey send the boxes to the hospital this morning?'

'Because Mickey had to get rid of them and I told him that was the best place for them. I didn't want to clutter you with them. It's a sad story really: Mickey's son lost his house and he and his wife and kids have to move in with Mickey and his wife. They're bringing all their furniture, which has to be stored in Mickey's garage, and he said he couldn't keep Fergus's things any more. Which is understandable. So I told him to send them to the hospital. They're Fergus's things. He can decide what to do with them. He's perfectly capable of that, you know. I thought he might enjoy it,' she adds gently, as I'm sure she can sense my frustration. 'Imagine the time it will pass for him, going down memory lane.'

I realise I'm holding my breath. I exhale.

'Did you discuss this walk down memory lane with his doctors first?'

'Oh,' she says suddenly, realising. 'No. I didn't, I . . . oh dear. Is he okay, love?'

I sense her sincere concern. 'Yes, I got to them before he did.'

'I'm sorry, I never thought of that. Sabrina, I didn't tell you because you would have insisted on taking everything and cluttering your house with things you don't need and taking too much on like you always do when it's not necessary. You've enough on your plate.'

Which is also true.

I can't blame her for wanting to rid herself of Dad's baggage, he's not her problem any more and ceased being so seventeen years ago. And I believe that she was doing it for my own good, not wanting to weigh me down.

'So did you know he had a marble collection?' I ask.

'Oh, that man!' Her resentment for the other

Fergus returns. The past Fergus. The old Fergus. 'Found among other pointless collections, I'm sure. Honestly, that man was a hoarder – remember how full the skip was when we sold the apartment? He used to bring those sachets of mustard, ketchup and mayonnaise home every day from whenever he ate out. I had to tell him to stop. I think he was addicted. You know they say that people who hoard have emotional issues. That they're holding on to all of those things because they're afraid of letting go.'

It goes on and I allow 90 per cent of it to wash over me, including the habit of referring to Dad in the past tense as though he's dead. To her, the man she knew is dead. She quite likes the man she visits in the hospital every fortnight.

'We had an argument about a marble once,' she says bitterly.

I think they had a fight about just about everything at least once in their lives.

'How did that come about?'

'I can't remember,' she says too quickly.

'But you never knew he had a marble collection?'

'How would I know?'

'Because you were married to him. And because I didn't pack them up, so you must have.'

'Oh please, I can't be called to account for anything he has done since we separated, nor during our marriage for that matter,' she spouts.

I'm baffled.

'Some of the items are missing,' I say, looking at them all laid out on the floor. The more I think about it, and hearing that they were in the possession of his solicitor, the more suspicious I am becoming. 'I'm not suggesting Mickey Flanagan *stole* them,' I say. 'I mean, Dad could have lost them.'

'What's missing?' she asks, with genuine concern. The man she divorced was an imbecile, but the nice man in rehabilitation must not be wronged.

'Part of his marble collection.'

'He's lost his marbles?' She laughs. I don't. She finally catches her breath. 'Well, I don't think your dad ever had anything to do with marbles, dear. Perhaps it's a mistake, perhaps they're not your father's, or Mickey delivered the wrong boxes. Do you want me to call him?'

'No,' I say, confused. I look on the floor and see pages and pages covered in Dad's handwriting, cataloguing these marbles, and yet Mum seems to genuinely know nothing.

'The marbles are definitely his and the missing items were valuable.'

'By his own estimation, I'm guessing.'

'I don't know who valued them, but there are certificates to show they're authentic. The certs for the missing marbles aren't here. The inventory says one item was worth up to twelve thousand dollars.'

'What?' she gasps. 'Twelve thousand for marbles!'

'One box of marbles.' I smile.

'Well, no wonder he almost went bankrupt. They weren't mentioned as assets in the divorce.'

'He mightn't have had them then,' I say quietly.

Mum talks like I haven't spoken at all, the conspiracy theories building in her head, but there's one question she's failed to ask. I didn't pack them and she didn't know about them, but somehow they found their way to the rest of Dad's belongings.

I take Mickey's office details from her and end the call.

The marble collection covers the entire floor. They are beautiful, twinkling from the carpet like a midnight sky.

The house is quiet but my head is now buzzing. I pick up the first batch of marbles on the list. The box of bloodies that I showed to Dad, listed as 'Allies'.

I start to polish them. Kind of like an apology for not ever knowing about them before.

I have a knack for remembering things that people forget and I now know something important about Dad that he kept to himself, which he has forgotten. Things we want to forget, things we can't forget, things we forgot we'd forgotten until we remember them. There is a new category. We all have things we never want to forget. We all need a person to remember them just in case.

7

PLAYING WITH MARBLES

Trap the Fox

I was supposed to be keeping my eye on Bobby. That's exactly what Ma said when she left the house, in her usual threatening tone. 'You keep your eye on him, you hear? Don't. Take. Your. Eye. Off. Him.' Every word a prod in the chest with her dry, cracked finger.

I promised. I meant it. When she's looking at you like that you really mean whatever you're saying.

But then I got distracted.

For some reason Ma trusted me with keeping my eye on him. It might have been something to do with the little chat we had about Victoria when the others were at school and we got to play the marble game together. I think she's been different with me since then. Maybe not, maybe it's all in my head, maybe it's just that it's different to me. I'd never seen her play like that before; a bit with the babies, but not down on the floor like she was with me, skirt hooshed up, her knees on the carpet. I think Hamish has noticed it too. Hamish notices everything and maybe that makes me a bit more cool to him too – Ma trusting me with things and not slapping the head off me as much as she usually would. Or maybe she's like this with me because she's grieving. I learned about grieving from a priest. I might have done that after Da died but I can't remember. I think it's just for adults.

Ma hates priests now. After what he said to her when Victoria died, after Mattie and Hamish chased him out of the house. She still goes to Mass though, she says it's a sin not to. She drags us to Gardiner Street Church every Sunday to ten o'clock Mass, in our best clothes. I can always smell her spit on my forehead from when she smooths down my hair. Sunday morning smells of spit and incense. We always sit in the third row, most families stick to the same place all the time. She says Mass is the only time she can get peace and all of us will shut the fuck up. Even Mattie goes, smelling of last night's drink and circling in his chair like he's still pissed. We're always quiet at Mass because my first memory of Mass is Ma pointing up at Jesus on the cross, blood dripping down his forehead and nails sticking out of his hands and feet, and her saying, 'If you say one word in here, embarrass me, I'll do that to you.' I believed her. We all do. Even Bobby sits still. He sits with his bottle of milk in his hand as the priest drones on, his voice echoing around the enormous ceilings, looking at all the pictures on the walls of a near naked man being tortured in fourteen different ways, and he knows this isn't a place to fuck about.

Ma is at school with Angus. He's in trouble because he was caught eating all the communion wafers when he was doing his altar boy duties, locking them away after Mass. He ate an entire bag of them, three hundred and fifty to be precise. When they asked if he had anything to say for himself, he said he asked for a drink because there were dozens stuck to the roof of his mouth. 'My mouth was dry as a nun's crotch,' he'd whispered late at night when we were all in bed and we'd almost pissed ourselves laughing. And then when we were all almost asleep, the giggles finally gone, Hamish whispered, 'Angus, you know you haven't just eaten the body of Christ, you've eaten the whole carcass.' And that set us all off again, forcing Mattie to bang on the wall for us to shut up.

Angus loves being an altar boy; he gets paid for it, more for funerals, and when he's in class the priest passes by his window and gives him the thumbs up or down to let him know what he's needed for that weekend. If it's a thumbs up it's a funeral, and he'll get more money, if it's a wedding, he gets less. No one wants to be an altar boy at a wedding.

Duncan is at Mattie's butcher shop, plucking feathers off chickens and turkeys as punishment for cheating in a school exam. He says he wants to leave school like Hamish did but Ma won't let him. She says he's not as smart as Hamish, which doesn't make much sense to me because I thought it was the smart ones that do better at school, it's the dumb ones that should leave.

Tommy's playing football outside and so it's my job to look after Bobby. Only I wasn't watching him. Not even God could watch Bobby all the time, he's a tornado, he never stops.

While he's playing on the floor with his train, I take out my new Trap the Fox game that I got for my eleventh birthday. It's from Cairo Novelty Company and the hounds are black and white swirls and the fox is an opaque marble. I don't see Bobby grab the fox but from the corner of my eye I see him suddenly go still; he's watching me. I look at him and see the opaque in his hand, close to his mouth. He does it while giving me that sidelong cheeky look, his blue eyes twinkling mischievously like he'd do anything just to get a rise out of me, even if it means his death.

'Bobby, no!' I shout.

He smiles, enjoying my reaction. He moves it closer to his mouth.

'No!' I dive at him and he runs, the fastest little fucker you've ever seen on two legs. All chub and no muscle at one hundred miles an hour, weaving in and out of chairs, ducking, diving. Finally, I have him cornered, so I stop. The marble is against his lips.

He giggles.

'Bobby, listen.' I try to catch my breath. 'If you put that in your mouth, you'll choke and die, do you understand? Bobby all gone. Bobby. Fucking. Dead.'

He giggles again, tickled by my fear, by the power he has over me.

'Bobby . . .' I say, warning in my voice, moving slowly towards him, ready to pounce at any moment. 'Give me the marble . . .'

He puts it in his mouth and I dive on him, squeezing his pudgy cheeks, trying to push the marble back out. Sometimes he just holds things there. Stones, snails, nails, dirt . . . sometimes he just puts stuff in his mouth like it's a holding room then spits it out. But I can't feel a marble in his mouth, his cheeks are all squidge, all flesh, mixed with his spit and snotty runny nose. He makes a choking sound and I prise open his mouth and it's empty. Just little white milky fangs and a squishy red tongue.

'Fuck,' I whisper.

'Uck,' he repeats.

'HAMISH!' I yell. Hamish is supposed to be out working, or looking for a job, or doing whatever it is that Hamish does now that he's out of school, but I heard him come home, bang the door closed and bang his way up the stairs to our room. 'HAAAYYY-MIIIIIISH!' I yell. 'He ate the fox! Bobby ate the fox!'

Bobby looks at me, startled by my reaction, by my fear and he looks like he's about to burst into tears any second. That's the least of my worries.

I hear Hamish's boots on the stairs and he bursts into the room. 'What's wrong?'

'Bobby swallowed the fox.'

Hamish looks confused at first but then sees my game on the table and understands. As Hamish goes towards Bobby, Bobby really looks as if he's going to cry. He tries to run but I grab him and he squeals like a pig.

'When?'

'Just now.'

Hamish picks Bobby up and turns him upside down. He shakes him as if trying to shake the coins from his pockets like I've seen him do with lads before. Bobby starts to laugh.

Hamish puts him back on his feet again and opens his mouth, sticks his fingers inside. Bobby's eyes widen and he starts retching, vomits up some foul-smelling porridge.

'Is it there?' Hamish asks, and I don't know what he's talking about until he gets down on his knees and looks through the vomit for the marble.

Before Bobby has a chance to cry, Hamish takes hold of him again and starts squeezing him and shaking him, poking him in the belly and ribs. Bobby giggles again, despite the lingering smell of vomit, trying to dodge Hamish's finger, thinking it's a game, as we both get increasingly annoyed.

'Are you sure he ate it?'

I nod, thinking he'll turn me upside down next.

'She's going to kill me,' I say, my heart pounding.

'She won't kill you,' he says, unconvincingly, like he's amused.

'She told me not to play marbles with Bobby around, he always tries to eat them.'

'Oh. Well then, she might kill you.'

I picture Jesus on the cross, the nails through his hands, and wonder why nobody ever wondered if Mary had done it. If maybe the biggest miracle of all wasn't Mary getting pregnant without ever touching a mickey, but Jesus's ma getting away with nailing him to a cross. If I ever end up on a cross, the first person anyone will suspect is my ma and she won't bother with the fourteen stations, she'll just get straight to it.

'He seems grand though,' Hamish says as Bobby grows bored of us inspecting him and resumes playing with his train.

'Yeah, but I have to tell her,' I say nervously, heart pounding, body trembling. I'm thinking of thorns in my head, nails in my hands, a rag around my mickey and my nips out for everyone to see. She'd do it somewhere public too, like Jesus on the hill, for everyone to see. Maybe my schoolyard or on the wall behind the butcher counter. Maybe hanging me off one of those giant meat hooks, so everyone who comes in for their Sunday roast can see me. *There he is now, the lad who took his eye off his baby brother. Tsk, tsk, tsk. Two pork chops, please.*

'You don't have to tell her,' Hamish says calmly, going to the kitchen and grabbing a rag. 'Here, clean up his puke.'

I do.

'What if the fox gets trapped somewhere inside of him?' I ask. 'And he stops breathing?'

He considers that. We look at Bobby playing. Blond and white pudge crashing a train into the leg of a chair over and over, talking to himself in his own language where his tongue's too big for his mouth and the words won't come out properly.

'Look, we can't tell Ma,' Hamish says finally. He sounds all grown up, and sure of himself. 'Not after Victoria, she'll go . . .' He doesn't need to say what Ma will do, we've seen enough to guess.

'What will I do?' I ask.

It must be the way I ask. I hear the baby in my voice, which he sometimes hates and wants to thump out of you, but instead he goes soft. 'You don't worry. I'll sort it out.'

'How?'

'Well, it went in one way, only one way it can come back out. We'll just have to keep an eye on his nappy.'

I look at him in shock and he laughs, that chesty cigarette laugh that's already starting to sound like Mattie even though he's only sixteen and Mattie is ancient.

'How are we going to get it out?' I ask, following him around like a little dog.

He opens the fridge, scans it, then closes it, unimpressed. He taps his finger on the worktop and looks around the small cubby kitchen, thinking, his brain in full action. I'm shitting myself but Hamish thrives on this stuff. He loves trouble, he loves it so much he wants my trouble to be his trouble. He loves finding solutions, spurred on by a countdown of how many minutes remain till our lives will be made hell. Most of the time he doesn't find the solutions, he causes bigger problems trying to fix things. That's Hamish. But he's all I've got right now. I'm as useless as tits on a bull, as he tells me.

His eyes settle on the freshly baked brown bread that Ma has left to rest on the bread board, covered in a red-and-white checked tea cloth. She baked it fresh this morning and it filled the house with the best smell.

'Ma told me not to touch it.'

'She also told you not to take your eyes off Bobby.'

That's me told. That nervous flutter again in my tummy, visions of a crown of thorns and being forced to carry a cross through the street, though maybe in Ma's case it would be a load of dirty washing. That's her cross to bear she always says. That and the six of us boys.

'And just in case the bread's not enough to flush it out . . .' Hamish says, taking a bottle of castor oil from the cupboard and grabbing a spoon. He throws off the towel and picks up the bread. 'Oh, Bobby,' he sings, dancing the bread in the air in Bobby's face. Bobby's eyes light up.

An hour later I've changed two of the most indescribably wettest shits I've ever seen and there's still no sign of the fox.

'You've really trapped that fox, haven't you, buddy?' Hamish says to Bobby and laughs hysterically.

He offers another slice of brown bread and spoon of castor oil to Bobby and Bobby says, 'No!' and runs away. I don't blame him and I'm glad. I'm literally up to my elbows in shitty terry cloths. I don't know how Ma cleans them but I've boiled up some water and have steeped them for as long as I could, burning my hands in the process, and have tried rubbing the parts together to get the stains off but nothing. I still think I get the better end of the deal as it's Hamish that sifts through the poo first with a knife before handing it to me to deal with. If I wasn't so terrified about Ma coming home and finding the bread gone and a marble stuck inside her precious baby then I'd be able to laugh like Hamish is.

It is when Hamish is looking through Bobby's third crappy nappy that I hear the key in the door. Ma's home and my world ends. My heart thuds and my throat closes up like it's the end of my world.

'Hurry up,' I whisper and Hamish sifts through the poo faster.

The front door opens, Hamish dashes out the back door, and Ma and Angus are greeted by a naked-from-the-waist-down Bobby who's demonstrating tumbles on the floor, his pudgy legs crashing into everything as he follows through.

'Everything all right?' Ma asks, stepping into the room.

Angus is behind her, quiet, one red cheek like he's been slapped, hands in his pockets, shoulders hunched, and I can tell she's had a good go at him. He looks at me suspiciously. Hamish is in the back garden sifting through the poo. Or at least I hope he is; part of me thinks he's nipped out the backyard door into the alleyway and left me to deal with this mess on my own.

A grin works its way onto Angus's face; he knows that I've done something, I must look guilty. He'd love it if I got caught out. Convinced I'm about to get it, that the spotlight will be taken off him for a while, he grins at me.

'What's wrong, Tick?'

'What on earth?' Ma asks, looking at Bobby who's on tumble hyper-drive. Then she sees the empty bread plate on the table, crumbs everywhere and out the window I see Hamish with a shitty hand in the window, a white marble between his fingers and a great big smile on his face. My relief is immense but now I've to deal with the brown bread situation.

'Bobby ate some, I'm sorry,' I say quickly. Too quickly. She suspects there's more to it.

'My brown bread!' Ma shouts. 'That was for tea. I told you not to touch it!' she yells. Hamish appears beside me and dumps the soiled terry cloth in my hands, slips the marble in my pocket, his hands now clean.

'Sorry, Ma, that was my fault,' Hamish pipes up. 'I told Fergus I'd watch Bobby for him, but I must have taken my eye off him because he ate it. You know what he's like with putting things in his mouth.' When Ma's not looking, when she's staring at her half-eaten loaf, devastated, he looks at me and winks.

Ma shouts a tirade of angry abuse at Hamish and all the time I think I should interrupt and confess to it all but I don't. I can't. I'm too chicken.

Ma sees the nappy in my hand, and the boiling water outside filled with cloths, and her expression changes so I can't read it. 'How many did you change?'

'Three,' I say nervously.

She surprises me then by laughing. 'Oh, Fergus,' she laughs, then ruffles my hair and kisses the top of my head. She goes outside to the toilet to flush the faeces, laughing as she goes, and I see Hamish watching her sadly.

I ask him later when the others are asleep why he did that for me, why he helped me and then took the blame.

'I didn't do it for you. I did it for her. She doesn't want to be disappointed in you, she's used to it with me.'

Ma was right about Hamish being smart because when he gave me a calculating look in the eye and said, 'You owe me one,' I knew that he meant it and that he had me over a barrel. I don't know if he always had what we did next planned, and that's why he took the blame for the brown bread, knowing I'd have no choice but to do what he'd ask me to do, or if he thought about it after. Either way that was the beginning of our marble adventures, or misadventures, and brown bread incident or not, I would have gone anywhere with him.

But that pretty much describes Hamish. He was willing to go through any amount of shit to save my arse.

8

PLAYING WITH MARBLES

Eggs in the Bush

It's three a.m. and I'm out with Hamish. He often comes to get me during the night, but these days it's different, no nudging, kicking, or hand across the mouth so I won't scream with fright as I used to do when he woke me in the middle of the night. Instead he has to throw stones against the window to wake me up. He hasn't been living at home for a few months now since Ma threw him out. She found out he was working for The Barber, but that's not why she threw him out. Mattie and him had a massive fight, where they thrashed the house walloping each other. Hamish even put Mattie's head through the glass of the good cabinet – glass everywhere and he had to get three stitches.

Tommy pissed his pants even though he said he hadn't.

So Hamish is out of the house. At twenty-one years of age Ma says he should be out of the house anyway, married and working. Even though he's out I still see him. We can't hustle people any more like we used to, I'm fifteen now and everyone knows I'm the best marble player around, or one of them; there's a new fella on the scene, Peader Lackey. People like to watch us play against each other, The Barber sets it up in his barbershop at night. He likes to entertain his people; he has meetings in the back, in his office and while that's going on he has drinks and smokes in the shop, cards, marbles, women, you name it. Hamish says The Barber would bet on a snail race. Not to his face, obviously. You don't want to piss off The Barber. If you do, and you go in for a cut and a shave, you can end up with a lot more damage done.

The Barber gives me a few bob for showing up, Hamish takes most of it. Still it's the same as with the caramels when I was ten: I'd do it for free then and I'd do it for free now. People place bets on who'll win and Hamish is the tote. You'd better watch out if you don't pay up, Hamish commands a lot of respect, with him being close to The Barber, and the ones who don't pay are looking for trouble, which they get.

But Hamish didn't wake me up tonight, I find

him in the alleyway behind our house, bent over and looking for pebbles. I sneak up on him and kick him in the arse and he jumps like The Barber has a hot blade to his neck.

I break my shit laughing.

'What the fuck are you doing up?' he says, trying to play it all cool but his pupils are all wide and black.

'None of your business.'

'Ah, that's how it is, is it?' he grins. 'Heard you've been getting fresh with one of the Sullivan girls. Sarah, is it?'

'Might have been.' It always surprises me how Hamish knows everything. I haven't told anyone about Sarah, kept it right to myself – not that there is anything to tell, she won't do much till her wedding day, said as much herself. She's sweet enough, but I didn't meet her tonight. I was meeting her sister Annie, who's a lot less sweet. Two years older and she caught me up on what her baby sister wasn't sharing. My legs are still shaking from it, but I feel alive, like a man, like I can do anything. Which is probably a bad place to be in when Hamish is involved.

He motions for me to follow but doesn't tell me about what we're out to do. I figure it's a game of marbles somewhere that he's set up with an audience to bet, which is what it usually is. On the times it's not, it's about visiting the lads who haven't paid up.

We go to the school, climb over the back wall and get to the dorms easy. Hamish already knows a way in, and when we climb in a window I send a jar of marbles on a desk spilling all over the floor. I expect Hamish to clock me one but instead he pisses himself laughing. None of the brothers come, thankfully. It's one thing getting a clatter on school time, it's quite another to get it when you shouldn't even be there. Hamish is laughing like a maniac, and slips on the marbles, and that's when I smell the drink on him. I get a bit worried then.

Two boys sit up in their beds, sleepy. They're fifteen, same age as me, but I look younger.

'Get up, you faggots,' he says, hitting them both over the heads. He uses shoelaces and school ties, anything he can find, to tie their hands behind their backs, their ankles to chair-legs and tells them we're going to play a little game.

While he's messing around with them I tidy the marbles up from the floor, and take a look at them. The collection has no value, just a bunch of opaques, cat's eyes, swirls and patches, nothing mint, nothing collectable. This surprises me because I know one of the lads is a rich boy. Daddy's a doctor, drives a fancy car, I would have been expecting a little bit better than this. I root through the jar and find gold. It's a two-colour, peerless patch made by Peltier. It stands out because the edges are curved instead of straight and it's my lucky day because he has three of them with picture marbles on, that's with black transfers of one of twelve different syndicate comic characters fired on the marble. I've never seen these before. The young lad watches me studying it. He's right to be worried. He's got three of them, Smitty, Andy and, can you believe it, Annie. Annie is red on white with the black transfer. It's kind of like fate. I'm not a cruel bastard, I only pocket one: Annie.

Eggs in the bush, Hamish tells them we're playing. It's a guessing game, which requires no skill whatsoever. The kind of game we play when the family go on a long journey, not that we go anywhere much. It's too expensive and Ma says we're a bloody nightmare and that she can't take us anywhere. We usually end up getting split up and going to different members of her family for a week. Two years in a row I've gone to Aunty Sheila, who has two girls and only lives around the corner. Back sleeping on her floor again, I have no good memories of being there and they're the worst summer holidays ever, except cousin Mary was friends with Sarah Sullivan and that's how I met her. It was worth pretending to be the nice kind gentleman cousin for a week.

Back to the game, and a player picks up a number of marbles and asks the other players to guess a number. If they guess correctly they get to keep the marbles, if they get it wrong, they have to pay the questioner the difference between the number guessed and the number held. Except Hamish puts his own spin on the game. Every time they get it wrong, the difference in the amount guessed and the amount held is how many times he lands a punch to their face and body. It stops being fun really quickly. We've gone collecting money a few times before, scared lads a few times, usually it's just enough for them to see Hamish in their room at night, knowing he's been sent by The Barber, but never this – or at least, never this bad. Hamish is wired. He punches too much, too hard, those boys are bleeding and crying and tied to the chairs.

I try to tell him that's enough and he fires himself at me, pulls my hair so hard I think my scalp's about to come off. The alcohol from him smells worse now, and his eyes are bloodshot, like it took a while to hit him. What I mistook in the alley for a fright and then joy at seeing me was something else. He roughs them up a little more and one of the boys cries really loudly for help, his nose bleeding, his eye all shut up. I don't get any satis-faction from it, they're only kids, and it's not even that much money. Hamish gets his hands on their savings and takes it all, then we're out of there. We walk back to the house in silence; he knows I disapprove and Hamish hates that. Although he tries to be the big man, what he really wants is for everyone to like him. But he has never known how to make that happen.

He doesn't walk me back to the house, just leaves me at the alley entrance. I think he's going to walk away without a word, but he's got more to say.

'So, The Barber told me to tell you not to win tomorrow night.'

'What?'

'You heard me. Don't win.'

'Why?'

'Why do you think? He's got something going with someone. You lose, he wins a packet. You might get a bit of it.'

'Who am I playing?'

'Peader.'

'I'm not losing to Peader, no way.'

'Lookit, you have to.'

'I don't have to do anything. I don't work for The Barber, you do, and I'm not losing for anyone.'

He grabs my collar and pushes me hard up against the wall, but I'm not afraid, I just feel sad. I see a bully, my brother, where I once saw a hero.

'You be here at eleven tomorrow night, okay? Or else.'

'Or else what? You won't be my brother any more, Hamish?' All of a sudden, I'm furious. Furious with the way Hamish hit those boys, furious with the way he's implicated me in it, furious that he thinks he can still tell me what to do and I'll do it, no questions asked. 'You going to slap me around like you did with those lads tonight? I don't think so.

You think Ma will ever let you set foot in the house again if you do that?'

He shifts uneasily. I know he wants to come home more than anything. He's a homebird, though he has a funny way of showing it. He's the kind of fella that teases a girl senseless if he fancies her, who treats you bad if he wants to be your friend, who hangs around his family and acts the prat when really he wants to be invited inside.

'The Barber will come after you,' he threatens me.

'No he won't. The Barber's got better things to be doing than worrying about me and a marble game. He just uses it as a distraction from whatever he's doing in that room. He uses you to cause a distraction, Hamish, that's all. Has he ever asked you into that back room? He won't even bother coming after you, he'll get someone else to do it for him. He doesn't care about you. I'm not losing for him, I'm not losing for you. I'm never losing, full stop.'

It must be the way I say it because he gets it straight away, he believes me, he knows he's nothing to The Barber, has always tried to make himself more important than he is, like pulling the stunt he pulled tonight. I've revealed him and he hates it. He knows there's nothing he can do to talk me out of it, or into it.

When I walk down the alleyway and get close to the house I suddenly feel a slap on the side of my head. It stings. I think it's The Barber at first, not him but one of his boys. Instead it's Sarah and she's crying.

'Jesus, Sarah, what are you doing out here at this hour?'

'Is it true?' She's crying. 'Did you and Annie . . . do it?'

By the next day I can forget about Annie, I can forget about Sarah and I can forget about Hamish.

The guards come round looking for Hamish, but Hamish has already legged it. He's luckier to have escaped the wrath of Ma than anything the guards would have done to him. Everyone thinks I know where he is but I don't. I tell them I don't and that I don't care either. It's true too. He went over the line last night and I can't back him up on that one. For the first time, I can't. It should make me feel sad but it doesn't, it makes me feel tougher, stronger, like if I can *think* I'm better than Hamish then that practically gives me superpowers. I've never thought of myself as better than Hamish and I spend the day puffed up with something like pride.

That night in bed the lads and I are whispering, we have to because Ma is so close to the edge any one of us will get it over nothing. Duncan says a lad he knows who works on the docks saw Hamish getting on a boat going to Liverpool.

And now I feel less like a superhero. I didn't think our meeting would be the last. I wanted a chance for us to make it up, for him to say sorry, for him to see what a big man I was. The lads talk about what Hamish will do in England, having a laugh picturing him in situations, but all I do is lie in the dark and see him working his way through England to Scotland, some old-fashioned image of him climbing across the land with a stick, finding some of Da's family to settle down with, living on the farm I can't remember any more, working the land like Da did. The thought helps me drift off to sleep, but no less worried, no less guilty, and feeling none of the superpowers I'd felt only moments earlier.

I get a warning from the guards for being a stupid kid in the wrong place at the wrong time, being influenced by my older brother. As a gesture I give the rich boy that Hamish beat up his Annie marble, much as it pains me to do it. But I win it back off him a few weeks later. That and the whole comic collection. Whenever I see those marbles they remind me of the night I became a man with Annie and the night that I went one way and Hamish went another. And sometimes when I really want to go the other way, Hamish's way, when life is just begging me to do it, I take them out as a reminder and it quietens the voice.

I don't see Hamish for a long time, and when I do, the sight of him is enough to tell me never to cross to the other side, ever. But seeing a dead body will do that to most people.

9

POOL RULES

No Ball Games

Armed with the new information from Mum, I hop in the car and drive to Virginia. I get parking on the street, outside Mickey Flanagan's office, which is between a closed-down DVD rental store and a not-yet-open Chinese takeaway. The window onto the street is covered in frosted glass and his name stencilled in black on the front. Mickey's secretary – her name badge says Amy – sits behind a protective screen, with holes punched in the glass in a circular design either for her to breathe or for us to talk. It's only when I go to speak that I realise I've been holding my breath. I must have been doing that all the way to Virginia because my chest feels tight.

'Hello, I'm Sabrina Boggs.' I made an appointment

as soon as I hung up the phone to Mum and they kindly squeezed me in, though now that I look around the empty waiting room I'm not sure much squeezing was necessary.

'Hello.' She gives me a polite smile. 'Please take a seat, he'll be with you as soon as he can.'

The waiting area is beside the frosted glass. I sit between a water cooler and a waxy-looking potted plant. The radio is on to hide the usual uncomfortable silence in a waiting room, more talk about today's total solar eclipse, which has commanded every news station and talk show for the past week: what can we expect to see, where can we expect to see it, how to look at the sun, how not to look at the sun, where best to look at the sun. I'm all eclipsed-out. Aidan is taking a half-day this afternoon to collect the boys from school, then they're going to a campsite, one of the official areas for watching the total eclipse. He'll be joining his brother and his kids, whose new money-making scheme has been to invest his savings in solar eclipse glasses, which he's been selling the past few weeks at hiked-up prices. My boys have been so excited about it all week, wearing the glasses, making versions of solar eclipses with cereal boxes, Styrofoam and balls of string, decorating their bedrooms with glow-in-the-dark moons. It helps that it's a Friday night in May and we're having good weather so everyone can show interest and actually be able to see the sky. I'm not disinterested in sky-gazing but I'm not a camper and so I have a night to myself.

'I'm just not a camper,' I'd said to Aidan when he'd told me of his plans last week.

'You're not a *happy* camper,' he'd replied, watching me. I knew he was watching me though I pretended I didn't, continuing to make the school lunches. His comment had irritated me, but I didn't want to let it show. Count to five in my head, butter, ham, cheese, bread, slice. Next. He was still watching me when I jammed the raisins into the lunch boxes.

'This is a natural phenomenon,' a scientist is saying on the radio. 'In some ancient and modern cultures, solar eclipses have been attributed to supernatural causes or regarded as bad omens. It was frightening for people who were unaware of the astronomical explanation, as the sun seems to disappear during the day and the sky darkens in a matter of minutes.'

'I totally believe in all of that,' Amy says suddenly from behind her screen. 'I had a boyfriend once who used to go totally mental when there was a full moon.' She screws her finger into her temple. 'Locked me in a wardrobe, threw my shoes in the toilet. Accused me of saying things when I hadn't even opened my mouth, of moving things I didn't even know he owned, like "*Me*, did you touch my chessboard?" and I'd be like, What chessboard? And I hated being called *Me*. It's Amy. Isn't it weird that

97

he called me *Me*, like he wanted *me* to be a part of *him*? Weird stuff. If I'd stayed, I'm sure he would have killed me like he killed that rat.' She looks at me to explain. 'He kept it for three days in the basement, torturing it.'

I picture a rat being waterboarded.

'Days like today scare me. Especially when dealing with the public. You wouldn't believe the calls we get. Freaks. The word lunatic comes from it, did you know that?'

I nod but she continues anyway. 'Lunar. Lunatic. It brings out the worst in people: violence, mentalness, you name it. I have a friend who works as a paramedic and she says full moon days and nights are her busiest. People just flip out. It's to do with the tidal effect and the water in our bodies,' she says. She's quiet for a moment, thinking. 'Though I think there really was something wrong with George. He was mental on days when you couldn't even see the moon.'

I think of me throwing the mug against the wall at work. Of saying to Eric, '*The moon made me do it.*' It would be ridiculous of course but not so far out for me. I've always had difficulty sleeping during full moons. Not so much pounding headaches as too many thoughts. Too many thoughts too quickly, all together, like the moon acts as a signal tower for my brain. Everything flowing all at once instead of slowly filtering. I think of me sitting here today, on a quest to find Dad's marbles, and wonder if this is lunacy after all. The moon made me do it. But I don't care what's making me do it. I'm doing it and if I need the moon to urge me on, then I'll take it.

I think of how excited the boys will be if the day actually darkens. If the clouds don't cover the perfect sky first and ruin everyone's chances of witnessing it. I wonder where I'll be, what I'll be doing during it, and hope it will coincide with my discovery of Dad's marbles, Scooby-Doo style, in Mickey Flanagan's house, using the veil of darkness to sneak in unnoticed and steal them back from his safe behind the oil painting in the walnut-panelled study.

'It's a new moon today,' Amy continues. 'Also known as a dark moon, because it's just a black circle. You know how crazy people go when it's a full moon, now imagine a black full moon. I mean, we should really have just stayed inside today and locked the doors. Who knows what will happen?'

She leaves us hanging on that thought.

The phone rings and we both jump, and then laugh. 'He'll see you now.'

I enter Mickey Flanagan's office, feeling anxious about what I'm here to do, and am faced with a short, bald Humpty-Dumpty-like man with a welcoming face. We met just after Dad's stroke, to discuss how to manage Dad's affairs, but we've had nothing but the occasional electronic correspondence since. Each time I see an email from Mickey I worry that the money's run out, that Dad's rehabilitation will have to come to an abrupt end. I've avoided every type of meeting with him since to avoid discussing that inevitability. Mickey struggles to his feet, bumping his belly off the edge of the desk, and comes round it to shake my hand warmly, before returning behind it.

I'm nervous. I pull the plastic folder with Dad's inventory out of my bag and prepare myself for my questioning. If he has taken the marbles, I know that he won't admit his theft right away, maybe he won't admit it at all, but I'm hoping my appearance will rattle his conscience at least. I've thought of every possible scenario, I've heard his every possible answer: *I had to sell them, he hadn't paid me for months, do you expect me to work for free? Or of course I sold them, we had an arrangement, see this contract here, he is paying me through the sale of his marbles.* I've thought about it all, but my answer will be the same. Get them back.

'Nice to meet you, Sabrina, how's your dad doing?' he asks, concerned.

'How's he doing?' I ask, feeling my legs starting to tremble, my whole body in fact, including my tongue. My lip starts to twitch, which irritates me and makes me even more frustrated and angry. I want to be able to say what I want to say without impediment. I need to be emotion-free but it has bubbled up inside of me so quickly, the mere question *How's he doing?* acting as the trigger, that my emotion clouds my clarity. This feeling reminds me of the dream I have when I'm trying to explain myself to someone, always a different person, but chewing gum gets stuck in my mouth and the more I pull it out the more it keeps forming, stopping the words.

I clear my throat. 'Sometimes he doesn't even remember yesterday. But then he'll tell you a story with pinpoint accuracy from when he was a child, so clear and vivid, it's like you're back there with him. Like today, this morning he told me about being at the All-Ireland final in 1963 when Dublin beat Galway, when he was a boy. He remembered every single little thing, explained in so much detail I felt like I was there with him.'

'Well that's a day to remember,' he says politely, good-natured.

'And then he'll forget something that is or once was apparently incredibly important to him.' I clear my throat again. Make the segue, Sabrina. 'Like his marbles. Up until today I didn't even know he had marbles. But he has hundreds of them. In fact, probably thousands if I was to count. Some of them are valuable, but regardless of the price all of them are important, or otherwise why would he have taken the time to do all this?' I fumble to pass over the inventory with trembling fingers. He goes through each page, from the page to my face, up and down, over and over again.

'Mickey,' I start, 'there's no way for me to say this politely. You had these marbles in your possession until yesterday. There's a part of his collection missing. Do you know what happened to my dad's marbles?'

He looks surprised, freezes with the inventory still in his hand. 'Goodness, no!'

'Mickey. I really need to know. I'm not accusing you of stealing them, I mean, obviously there could have been an arrangement with someone, with Dad maybe, where you were given permission to take them. Whatever happened, I don't need to know. I just want to find them so I can get them back and complete the collection.'

'No. No, I didn't take them and there was no arrangement with anyone, nor your dad.' He straightens up, and is firm. 'As you know, the boxes were delivered to me *after* his stroke and, as you say, he doesn't remember owning them so he couldn't have instructed me to do anything with them, nor would I have so much as laid a finger on them.' He is genuine, also clearly annoyed to be accused of such a thing, but he is being professional about it. 'You have my word on that, Sabrina.'

'Could anyone have had access to them in your house? Was there ever a break-in?' I try to soften the accusation of his nearest and dearest. 'The marbles that were taken were the most expensive marbles. It seems somebody went through the inventory and chose them.'

He gives me the courtesy of appearing to think about it before answering. 'I can assure you that neither I nor anybody who was in my home is responsible for the missing marbles. I never opened the boxes. They were sealed on arrival and still had the same seal when they left. They were kept in the garage for the past year and they were out of sight and out of reach in all that time.'

I believe him. But I'm stuck because I don't know where else to go after this.

Mickey hands me back the inventory and I just stare at it, at Dad's lovely loopy handwriting, seeing, *Sabrina could not come to school today because she had a doctor's appointment.* I see handwritten birthday cards. I see scribbled notes around the house.

I purse my lips, my cheeks still a little pink with embarrassment for the accusation, no matter how politely I tried to put it.

'Well, there's one other thing. Apart from wanting to find them, it would help to know who brought them to you. Mum and I packed up everything from the apartment and we never saw these boxes before.'

He frowns, genuinely confused. 'Is that so? You didn't have help? Movers or family members?'

I shake my head. 'It was just the two of us.'

He takes his time thinking about it. 'I'm not sure if you know how I came to store your dad's things.'

'Mum said that you kindly offered. I didn't have the space for them and she . . . well, she's obviously moved on.'

'The thing is, I didn't kindly offer,' he says politely, a twinkle in the blue eyes that glow from his big moon face. 'Your mother hasn't been entirely honest with you, but I'm going to be, particularly as you have come here with these . . . concerns, and rightly so, as the boxes were in my possession for the past year.'

I squirm in my chair, embarrassed now, when before I was determined.

'Your uncles, Fergus's brothers, expressed dissatisfaction with Gina keeping your dad's things. They felt that the boxes weren't safe in Gina's hands, given her feelings towards your dad. But Gina was suspicious of why they wanted the boxes, as they and Fergus weren't close in her opinion, and so we all came to the arrangement that the boxes would be kept safe by a third party. Both parties were satisfied that I was neutral enough to be trusted with them. It's not the usual thing for me to do, but I was fond of Fergus and so I did. Unfortunately my personal circumstances have changed and I no longer have the space to store his things.'

I nod along quickly, trying to kill my earlier embarrassment and surprised that Mum didn't share this with me. Did she think he wouldn't tell me? I was oblivious to all of this family drama while setting up Dad in the rehab. I was just focused on him getting better, going from the hospital to his apartment, to work, taking care of the kids, completely exhausted, like a walking zombie. I took photos of Dad's furniture and sold it all online, delivering couches across the city, meeting people on George's Street at five a.m. to hand over a coffee table. I think of the days it took to sort the items to keep from the items to sell, seeing how my dad lived, his private things, all of it so simple really, apart from the sickening stashes of chocolate bars, the disturbing collection of DVDs that you never want to imagine your dad watching, but no grand revelations. No sign of any person other than my father in the whole place.

I went through every room, every cupboard, every drawer and I sold every single one of those cupboards that wasn't stuck to the floor or wall. Of all the boxes I taped shut, I never came across these marbles. Somebody else packed them, and sent them to Mickey's home, and if it wasn't me or Mum, then who?

'I don't know how else I can help you, Sabrina.'

Me neither.

'My only thought is that they weren't in the boxes before they were delivered to me, but of course if it was just you and your mam who packed everything up then I don't know what to think.'

But it's glaringly obvious. He's being polite, but if it wasn't me then it had to have been Mum, who has already lied to me about why the boxes ended up with Mickey in the first place.

So many secrets, so many things I didn't know. What else don't I know?

10

PLAYING WITH MARBLES

Bounce About

I see Hamish again when I'm nineteen years old. It's the last thing I would have expected: to get on a plane and leave Ireland for the first time in my adult life, since arriving on a boat when I was five, for this reason.

Ma receives a visit from a garda, who received a phone call from the Irish embassy to say that Fergus Boggs has been found dead in London, and that somebody needs to go and identify the body.

'London? But Fergus is here!'

Ma shouts and yells the house down, everybody runs to her, everybody that doesn't run to her runs looking for me. I'm sitting in the pub having a pint and playing Bounce About when I should be at work in Mattie's butcher shop with the other lads. I've just started and they have me doing the worst jobs, like washing away guts, which when hungover on the first week sent me racing to the toilet to vomit. It doesn't make me queasy now, just bored, and I find a few pints at lunchtime gets me through it in the afternoons. I'm more interested in the kind of meat that Mattie's buying; I'd like to get into that side of things, sourcing better kinds of meat. It's something I want to talk to him about, but I know he won't listen until I do at least a year of stinking, stenching time in the back.

Angus finds me at the pub and grabs me, tells me to say nothing, he doesn't want to hear it, and drags me down the road to the house. I think I'm in trouble for stepping out of the shop for a pint when I should have been having a sandwich in the backyard. Duncan meets us at the front door, which is wide open. Mammy is holding court in the living room, surrounded by worried women, tea and scones. Three-year-old Joe is on her knee, bouncing up and down, big eyes worried and scared by Ma's hysterics. Everyone parts for me like I'm the prodigy child she's always wished for. She looks at me coming towards her like I'm an angel, with so much tenderness and love, I'm shitting myself and don't know what the fuck is going on.

She puts Joe down and stands up. He clings to her leg. Ma reaches out to my face, her hands hot from the gallons of tea, her skin rough from a life-time of cleaning and scorching. Her face is softer than I've ever seen it, her eyes piercing blue. I suppose I've seen it when she looks at her babies, when I caught her when I was younger when she didn't know anyone was looking as she breastfed, as her eyes and the baby's connected to each other like they were having a silent conversation. I just never remember her looking at me like this.

'My son,' she says tenderly, flooded with relief. 'You're alive.'

Which brings a sudden snigger out of me because I have no idea where this is coming from, all I know is I was dragged out of the pub for this nonsensical drama. Mrs Lynch tuts and I want to deck her because this spurs Ma on.

Ma's look of serenity fades and she slaps me hard across the face. I mustn't look sorry enough because she does it again.

'Okay, Ma,' Angus says, pulling me away. 'He didn't know. He didn't know.'

'I didn't know what?'

'A garda called by—'

Ma is helped to her seat, the grieving queen bee.

'He said that Fergus Boggs was found dead. In London,' Angus says. He slaps me hard on the shoulder, squeezes me. 'But you're not dead, you're grand. Aren't ya?'

I can't reply, my heart is hammering. I know it

then, I just know it. Hamish. No one else would have picked my name and he wouldn't have picked anybody else's name either. It was always me. Me and him. Him and me. Even if we didn't know it at the time, I know it the moment I think he's dead, feel his loss now more than when he upped and left.

'Lighten up, everybody, will you?' Duncan says and the women relax, get the joke, suddenly see the funny side in what has happened.

But Ma doesn't laugh. And I don't laugh. Our eyes meet. We both know.

I fly over on my first flight. Windy conditions and we bounce about the place, my mind completely off Hamish as I hang on for dear life and think about what a strange fate it would be, me dying going over to see if a fella who called himself me is dead.

Mrs Smith's son Seamus is living in London and it's been arranged that I can stay with him for a few nights. I don't know what Seamus told his ma about his new life but I don't imagine it's this. Sharing one damp Victorian room with six other lads isn't my idea of making it big in London, so I stay out as late as I can on the first night to avoid having to sleep on that floor. I avoid the Irish bar they all tell me to go to in case I'm forced to join up, and instead, after asking around in an English accent, I find a place called the Bricklayer's Arms that advertises marble games. But first I walk the streets for hours knowing that every minute that passes is a minute closer to seeing Hamish, and sometimes I want the time to slow down, and other times speed up.

I strike up a game of marbles with some locals, just a game of Bounce About, like I'd been doing earlier, as if I was picking up where I left off. I can't believe it's the same day and I'm in a different country waiting to identify the body of someone claiming to be me, feeling like a different person.

The game is for two to four players but three of us play until the third guy vomits on himself and then falls asleep in the corner with his own piss leaking down his leg. It's just me and a fella named George then, who calls me Paddy like he doesn't know it's an insult. It's okay because I beat him hands down. It doesn't involve huge skill – you throw marbles, not shoot them. The medium-sized marbles are called bouncers; the first player throws his forward, the second player tries to hit it, and so on. It's about as much as he can handle, he's had so much to drink. If a bouncer is hit, the owner pays the thrower one marble, but you can't take the bouncer, which is a problem because George's bouncer is the only marble I'm interested in. Bouncers get away with murder that way.

It's a Czechoslovakian bullet-mould marble, it has a frosty finish to it. George tells me something about an acid bath. I ask him if I can buy it and he says no, but he gives it to me instead. I've told him about why I'm here and who I think I'm going to see and he feels sorry for me, says he had to view a body once that had been chopped up into bits and I wonder if it was an official identification at all, or something to do with his lifestyle. I even wonder if he was the one who had to chop it up into bits. His story doesn't scare me off, though; oddly, the gift of the marble does make me feel a little better. I pocket the bullet and after getting lost for almost two hours, fall into Seamus Smith's shithole bedsit at four a.m., stepping over bodies to reach my space, one guy going at himself till all hours thinking nobody can hear him.

Four hours later I'm at the morgue looking at Hamish's dead naked body on a slab. The coroner just shows me his face but I pull the sheet down more. Hamish has a birthmark on his belly button shaped like Australia; nothing really like Australia, but then that would have ruined the joke. 'Want to see down under?' I hear Hamish say to the girls, so clearly, like his lips could have moved. I smile, remembering him, everything good about him and the coroner looks at me, angry, like I'm smiling because I'm glad he's dead.

'I was just thinking of something funny he used to say,' I explain.

Then he looks at me like he doesn't care, he's just here for the scientific part, not the emotional bit.

I feel the Czech bullet-mould in my pocket.

'Was he shot?' I ask. I always thought if Hamish was going to go before old age, that's what he'd prefer. Like a cowboy, he loved those films.

'No. Do you see a bullet hole?' he asks, like he's defending himself, like I'm accusing him of missing the evidence.

'No.'

'Well then.'

'What happened to him?'

'The police will tell you.' He covers Hamish's face again. I haven't seen Hamish for four years but I'll never know how much he changed in that time because he was so bloated and bruised I could barely recognise him. I know it's him all right, but I couldn't begin to tell what he looked like as an older Hamish. They think he'd been in the water for two days, probably more, because his body floated to the surface, and decomposition had begun. The police officer that I talk to afterwards says something about the skin on his foot falling off like a sock, but that's when I tune out. The part I remember more than anything else is that nobody had reported him missing.

Fergus Boggs was drunk. He had drunk far too much when he bothered the two bouncers of Orbit nightclub on Saturday night. When they turned him away they say he got aggressive. I have no reason not to believe them, it sounds like any of the Boggs boys so far, even little Joe has a meltdown when you tell him no, lying on his stomach and kicking his shoes off regardless where we are. As the youngest, Ma rarely tells him no. One bouncer got so frustrated with Fergus that he told him he'd let him in the side door so the boss wouldn't see him get in so drunk, and without paying. Instead he took him to the dark alley and beat the lights out of him. With a broken nose and a broken rib, Fergus Boggs stumbled along until he tripped, fell into a river and drowned. He was twenty-five.

Seamus Smith is waiting for me when I come out of the morgue. He's smoking a cigarette and looking shifty, his hands shoved into tiny pockets in a leather jacket.

'Is it him?' he asks.

'Yeah.'

'Fuck.'

He takes out a packet of cigarettes and hands me one. I appreciate him bringing me to the pub from there because I don't remember anything from the cigarette onwards. The next day me and Hamish get the boat together for the second time as I bring him home.

The police officer wasn't pressing charges against the bouncer who 'bounced him about a little' because the police agreed Fergus was being a nuisance and the bouncer didn't mean to kill him, it was Fergus's inebriation that led to his drowning. Bouncers get away with murder that way.

11

POOL RULES

No Pushing

When I opened the box of marbles, I opened up a can of worms.

I don't know if I sensed it when I looked at them, when I held them in my hands and my eyes scanned the inventory, but I knew it when I saw the way Dad's face changed as soon as he set eyes on the bloodies. And it's confirmed even further by learning of the messiness my family created simply by the decision of where to store boxes. I don't know what to do next. It's the moon, I've too many thoughts, can't process them all at once. Breathe.

Once outside Mickey's office I call Mum, fuming inside.

'How's Miss Marble getting on?' She laughs at

her own joke. 'Did you see Mickey Flanagan yet?' I hear the anxiety in her voice and I wonder if she's afraid of me discovering her lie.

'Which of Dad's brothers didn't want you to store the boxes?' I ask.

She sighs. 'Mickey told you. Oh, love, I didn't want him to tell you.'

'I appreciate that, Mum, but if I'm going to find these marbles, I need the truth?'

'You're really going to look for these missing *marbles*? Sabrina, love, is everything okay? With you and Aidan? Are you still going to counselling?'

'Yes, we're fine,' I say, as if on autopilot. I should never have mentioned the counselling to Mum, now she thinks everything I say and do is a result of our couple counselling, which I'm going to for Aidan's sake. I'd be perfectly content not to bother. But I've been saying that a lot lately without really thinking about it. Are we fine? I change the subject back. 'Tell me what happened with the boxes and Dad's brothers.'

She sighs, knowing she has no choice but to address it, and as she speaks I hear the anger. Not at me but at him, at the situation last year. 'Angus called me, but it was really all of them that had the problem. They'd heard we'd been around at Fergus's apartment. They didn't want me with his belongings. They were fine with you having them, but I told them you had no space. You know the rest.'

I try to picture Angus. I was never particularly close to my uncles and aunts, I never saw them much because Dad didn't. While growing up I saw them at the odd family event but we never stayed long, Dad was always uptight, somebody would always say something to annoy him and we'd leave early. Mum never protested, she hated his family events too, somebody would always end up in a fight, a drunken cousin flipping over a table of drinks in a fight with a girlfriend, or sisters-in-law who couldn't keep their sharp tongues to themselves. There was always drama at a Boggs–Doyle event and we rarely went. We spent most of the time popping in, or as Dad would say, 'Let's show our faces.' That's all he ever wanted to do with his family, show his face. Perhaps that's all he did with us too, because who is this man I'm learning about?

Angus is the oldest of the brothers, a butcher, so not the one with a van. I think Duncan has the van, but that's not to say they weren't all in on it. It's been a long time since I've seen them all. I haven't been dragged to a family do since I was eighteen, and I didn't invite them to my wedding. Aidan and I had a small one in Spain with twenty guests.

Do I really want to visit Angus to ask him what happened last year? Why didn't you want my mum to store Dad's things? Did you want them for yourself so you could steal Dad's marbles? What a

117

ridiculous line of questioning. And do I really blame the brothers for not wanting Mum to keep their brother's things? They were absolutely right and I only see that now. At any moment Mum could have decided to throw them on a bonfire, fuelled by wine and a bitter memory of something Dad did to her to make her life a misery, even though she's now happily remarried.

'Did you know about him having a marble collection?' I ask her again firmly. 'Did you pack them away in his apartment?'

'Not at all. I told you that yesterday.'

There is enough annoyance and hurt in her voice for me to believe her.

'And if I had come across them when we were packing them up, I would have thrown them straight in the skip,' she says defiantly. 'A grown man with marbles, honestly.'

I believe her, but it makes me wonder what she came across in the apartment that I didn't, that she considered not worth keeping. Maybe she wasn't the right person to help me out at the time. And why am I only thinking of all this now? Guilt is eating away at me. I was busy, I was stressed, I was worried. I should have handled it all better. Perhaps I should have invited his brothers to join us, see if there was anything they'd like, from his past. Perhaps that's why they were angry with Mum, I didn't include them in anything. I just took over, thinking I knew everything there was to know about him.

'Mum, have you remembered what your marble fight with Dad was about?' I refuse to let that one go. I know she was holding out on me and I need to know as much as I can right now. No more secrets.

'Oh, I can barely remember now . . .' She goes quiet for a moment and I think that's the end of her answer, when she suddenly continues. 'We were on our honeymoon, that much I remember. He went wandering off on his own, like he always did, no explanation, then came back after spending months' worth of our savings on some ridiculous marble.'

I slide the inventory out of the folder as I'm driving, keeping a close eye on the road. I cast my eyes over the list.

'Was it a heart?'

'I can't remember the design.' She goes quiet. 'Actually, yes, I think it was. It drove me insane that he would spend all of our money on it. We spent three days in Venice unable to eat a thing. I remember sharing a can of Coke one day because we hadn't the money for anything else. Silly eejit,' she says softly. 'But that was your father all over. By the way, how did you know it was a heart?'

'Oh. I just . . . guessed.'

I run my finger over Dad's handwriting: '*Heart – damaged. Condition: collectable. Venice '79.*'

So it wasn't Mum who packed up the marbles, or took from them. I think I've established she would have wanted nothing to do with them.

Access. I have to think who had access to the boxes. It wasn't Mickey, it wasn't his family. There's no way of me ever really knowing that for sure, but I have to trust him. Access. Contacting the delivery company from last year seems a long shot: Excuse me, did you ever happen to steal some items you were delivering last year? Maybe Mickey is wrong about the marbles not being in the box when they arrived at his house. Maybe they were taken yesterday, and yesterday's delivery driver isn't a long shot.

'Can I help you, Sabrina?' Amy asks gently as I walk back into the waiting room.

I try to compose myself. *The moon made me do it.* 'I received a delivery from Mickey yesterday, from his home to my dad's hospital, and I was trying to figure out who delivered it. Do you know anything about it?'

'Know about it? I spent an entire weekend in that garage, unpaid, arranging deliveries. Not my job, but tell that to Mickey.'

My heart leaps a little, feeling a bit of hope. 'Were the boxes sealed before you sent them?' I ask lightly, not wanting to offend her.

'Oh God,' she groaned. 'Yes, they were and they were very carefully stored, I can tell you that, but don't tell me something was broken, or missing.'

'Well, yes, actually something was missing.'

'Oh, Looper.'

'Pardon?'

'Sorry, it's Looper. The delivery guy. To explain, yes, absolutely the boxes were sealed when I got to them, and I was under strict orders not to open them either. Mickey wouldn't want me seeing in his stuff – yours weren't the only ones in there, by the way. There was a bunch of stuff that had to go. Old furniture, clothes, all in storage that hadn't been touched in years, covered in dust. Anyway, I used Looper to deliver them, Mickey's nephew. He's had so many complaints, but I have no choice but to use him. Mickey's trying to help out family, you know how it is. It's between you and him, I'm afraid, I can't get involved, but I can give you his contact details.'

'Yes please,' I say happily, feeling that perhaps all is not lost. I'm getting places.

'Do you know your way around here?' she asks, handing the address over reluctantly.

'No, but I have satnav.'

Amy bites her lip. 'Satnav won't even know where you're going,' she says. 'It's pretty remote.'

'It's okay, I have time,' I say, moving towards the door. For the first time in I don't know how long, I feel a surge of excitement.

'Just be careful, he's not really a people person, and particularly on a day like today –' she gestures towards the sky – 'days like today are made for people like him,' she adds before I close the door.

I drive to the address Amy has provided, and I look up at the sun and wonder if there's anything in what Amy said. Is today the day we're doomed? Or is today the day I've finally lost it myself, going on a hunt for some lost marbles that I've no real proof ever really existed in the first place. Just a handwritten inventory from I don't know how many years ago. About to approach a man named Looper in the middle of nowhere and accuse him of stealing.

After driving up and down a few random streets, satnav giving up almost as soon as I pass the town limits, much as Amy warned, I find the right place. Looper, a concerning name in itself, lives in a small bungalow, a Seventies-style build, which has been badly maintained and looks completely run-down. The front yard is covered in car parts, tyres, engines, car hoods, random items strewn about the place. There's a white van on the front drive, beneath it a pair of legs stick out wearing filthy stone-washed jeans and workman's boots. A nearby radio blares AC/DC. I pull up outside the front gate and can't get any further as it's heavily padlocked with a sign saying 'No Trespassing – guard dogs on duty', alongside a picture of two snarling dogs.

I get out of the car and stand at the gate wondering if I have finally lost it.

'Excuse me,' I call to the pair of legs, loudly. 'Looper!'

The legs finally move and slide from under the van. A young man climbs up. He's got long greasy hair that grows from a well-receded hairline, despite his youth, and he's wearing a white vest covered in oil, sweat and grease and who knows what else. He's more chunky than muscular but he's tall and big, like an oaf, something that wouldn't look out of place in Middle-earth.

He stares at me, wiping a tool on his T-shirt, taking me in, slowly, bit by bit. He stares at the car, then back at me and then slowly saunters towards me with the wrench in his hand, as though he's got all the time in the world and he's giving great academic thought as to whether to whack me with it. He doesn't come to the gate, stops a few strides short. He licks a snake-like tongue over his lips as he looks me up and down. Smacking sounds like I'm his next meal.

'Are you Looper?' I ask.

'Maybe. Maybe not. Depends on who's asking.'

'Well . . . I am.' I smile. A wobbly one.

Looper doesn't like this hint of a smile, he thinks he's being made fun of, doesn't like this, isn't sure why, doesn't understand. Confusion makes him feel less of a man so he behaves like more of a grunt. He hacks up a golly, spits it on the ground in clear protest.

123

'You're the delivery man around here?'

'The one and only. You got a job for me? 'Cos I've got a job for you . . .' He gropes his crotch and sneers.

I step back, revolted. 'Are you Mickey Flanagan's nephew?'

'Who's asking?'

'Me. Again,' I say flatly. 'I'm a client. He sent me here.' *He knows I'm here, I will be missed. Don't kill me!* 'Did you do a delivery yesterday to Dublin for your uncle?'

'I do a lot of deliveries to Dublin.'

I sincerely doubt that. 'Specifically, a hospital.'

'That where you live?' he sneers, revealing that the few teeth he has are a greenish colour. He looks me up and down, like a cat would a mouse. He wants to play. His eyes are unusual, a murky colour with not much going on in them or behind them. The thought of this man in possession of my dad's precious marbles makes me sick. I wouldn't trust this guy with anything. I look around, mostly for help, for a witness in case it all goes wrong, for a rescuer in case Looper does what I'm thinking he wants to do. There are acres upon acres surrounding the house. A burned-out car sits in the middle of one unfarmed field.

Looper follows my gaze to the fields that stretch into the distance. 'Pain in my hole. Spuds is all it was ever good for. Daddy was a farmer. Them developers offered him a fortune, he said no, says he's a farmer what else would he do? Then he went and fucking died and left it to me and no one is interested in buying it now. It's a waste of space.'

'Why don't you farm it?'

'I've my own thing going on here. My garage and delivery business.'

Nothing in this yard vaguely resembles a business.

'Want to come inside? I'll show you around.'

I look in the open front door and see mayhem in the house, dirty, piled-up, cluttered mess. I shake my head. I don't want to pass the gate.

'You brought five boxes from Mickey's garage to my dad's home. Some things are missing from the box and I'm wondering if you could . . . help me.'

'You calling me a thief?'

'No, I would like your help,' I stress. 'Did you stop off anywhere? Anybody else have access to your van?'

'I put them in the van and drove them to Dublin. Simple as.'

'Did you open the boxes? Could something have fallen out?'

He smiles. 'Tell you what, I'll answer your question if you give me a kiss.'

I back away.

'Okay okay!' he laughs. 'I'll answer your question if you shake my hand.'

That's bad enough, but I'll play along. I want him to answer my question.

Looper steps forward. Hand extended. He puts the wrench in his back pocket and raises his hand to show he's weapon free.

'Come on. If you shake my hand, I'll answer your questions. I'm a man of my word.'

I look at the hand suspiciously. I reach out and as he takes my hand, he pulls my arm roughly, pulling me towards him and grabs the back of my neck, and pulls my head close for a kiss. His lips touch mine and I'm stuck in that position. I close mine tight, not letting a part of him get into me. I try to move but I can't, his hand stays at the back of my neck. I lift my hands to his chest to push him away but he's too strong and I feel panic rising. Finally he pulls back and licks his lips and howls with laughter.

I wipe at my face furiously, wanting to run to my car. My heart pounding, I look around for help, but he's not coming after me for any more, he's standing back laughing.

'You didn't answer my question,' I say angrily, wiping my lips roughly. I refuse to leave now without an answer, or even better, without the marbles. This will not be a wasted trip.

Looper looks at me, wrench back in hand, amused. 'I picked up your boxes from Mickey's, pulled over on the motorway and had a look through them.

Nothing good in it so I sealed them up again and drove to Dublin.' He shrugs unapologetically. 'Papers and some kids' marbles don't do it for me. I didn't take a thing. I suggest you look elsewhere.'

And I actually believe him. He wouldn't have the brains to have looked through the inventory. It's a book and I doubt he's ever read a book in his life. He also wouldn't have the common sense to recognise or link the items on the list to the marbles in the boxes. The person who picked the two most expensive items spent time going through the list, and the marbles, not just a quick pull-over on the road. They took the two most expensive, which would have taken time to discover as the list does not go from low to high, it is categorised by the names of the marbles.

'Was it worth it?' he winks as I storm back to the car. 'Did I help?' he calls after me.

I start up the engine and drive away. Yes, he helped.

Looper didn't take the marbles. Those marbles weren't in the box when they left Mickey Flanagan's house. I'm absolutely sure of that now. And they weren't in the boxes when they reached Mickey's house. So I have to go back. Back to last year. Maybe even further than that.

12

PLAYING WITH MARBLES

Moonie

'Fergus, it's time!' Nurse Lea says brightly as she enters my room with a great big smile on her face. She's always smiling, she has two big dimples in her cheeks, like holes, big enough to fit marbles in; maybe not average-sized marbles, but miniature ones would slot in there quite nicely and never budge. She's a young girl, a country girl, from Kerry. She sings everything and you can hear her laugh from the nurses' desk all the way down the corridor to my room at the end. My spirits are usually up but she has the ability to lift them even higher. If I've had a tough day in physio – and there are plenty of those – she always arrives with a smile on her face, a steaming mug of coffee and a cupcake. She makes them herself and hands them around to everyone. I tell her if she put as much effort into her boyfriends she'd have them eating out of her hand, but she's single and always has stories of disastrous dates to share with me.

I have a soft spot for her. She reminds me of Sabrina. Or how Sabrina used to be before she had the boys. Now she's distracted, obviously, by three little boys on hyper drive. We start a conversation and never finish it, a lot of the time we barely get the chance to finish the sentence. She's scattier than she used to be; she used to be sharp, like Lea. She's always tired, she's put on weight too. My ma was always as tough as old boots, the only time I recall her softening is when she'd had more than one brandy, which was rare, maybe twice a year. She was rake thin, always running after the seven of us, and after her pregnancies she always managed to get her figure straight back. Maybe if I'd known my ma before she'd had us I'd have seen a change in her too; maybe she had a carefree spirit before us and the pressures of life and motherhood changed that. God knows I changed in my life; I'm in here now. I can't imagine her ever carefree, not even in photos, they're posed rigid and uptight-looking. Arms down by your sides, no physical contact, glum faces to the camera, which I expect was felt to be the best face forward. There is one photograph though, one which I keep close to me at all times, of Ma, on the beach, taken by Da, in Scotland. She's sitting on a towel on the sand, leaning back on her elbows, her face lifted to the sun, her eyes closed. She's laughing. I don't know how many times I've studied it and wondered what she's laughing at. It's a sexy pose, provocative, though I'm sure she didn't intend it to be so. Hamish is a baby and sits by her toes. She's probably laughing at something Hamish has done, or something Da said, something innocent that resulted in this look. It's odd, I know, to keep provocative photos of your ma, psychotherapists would have a field day with it, but it lifts me.

When I picture Sabrina in my mind I see a screwed-up face, worried.

'Are we watching a 3-D film?' I ask Lea, teasing her about the funny glasses that she's wearing.

'I have a pair for you too,' she says, taking a pair out of her pocket and handing them to me. 'Pop them on.'

I put them on and stick out my tongue and she laughs.

'Did you forget, Fergus, the solar eclipse is today?'

I'm not sure if I'd forgotten it, as I don't remember ever knowing it.

'We have a perfect sky to see it, not a cloud anywhere. Of course we're not in the perfect place, they keep going on on the radio about the best path to stand in, but the sun is the sun, sure wherever you stand you'll see it. I've made cupcakes for everyone.

Vanilla cupcakes. I wanted to make chocolate but Fidelma, my new flat mate – remember I told you about her, the Donegal nurse? She's a pig, she ate all the Cadbury bars in the fridge,' she fumes. 'Four of them. The large ones. I've put Post-its all over the flat now, "Don't touch this", "Don't eat this". Just looking at her makes me mad. And remember that new plasma TV I got from my neighbour who was throwing it out? She hasn't a clue how to use it, keeps feckin' using the wrong remote controls. Found her pointing the gas fire remote control at the TV screen.'

We both laugh at that. She gives out but not in an angry way, it's humorous, it's all with a smile on her face, and that strong sing-song voice. It's lovely, like a bird chirping outside your window on a sunny May day. She tells this story while she helps me up out of my reading chair and into the wheel-chair. Lea is with me most days, but when she's not the others have a different style, which is difficult to adjust to. Some are quieter, trying to be respectful, or lost in their heads with whatever's going on in their own lives, or they're too bossy and talk at me, reminding me of my ma barking at me when I was a boy. They're not rude, but Lea just has the magic touch. She knows to talk me through it, talks about other things like what we're doing isn't happening. You want that from a person who has had to wipe your arse and clean your balls. The silence with the others makes me realise it's really happening. Tom next door can't stand her. 'Does she ever shut up?' he grumbles. He says it so loud I'm sure she's heard, but it doesn't stop her. But that's Tom, he wouldn't be happy unless he had something to complain about.

She wheels me out into the sunshine, to the small lawn that we sit out on on sunny days like today. Everyone is gathered outside and looking up at the sky with these ridiculous plastic glasses. The radio is on, Radio One, a live commentary of what we're about to see, like they've been doing all week. I've never heard so much about numbras and penumbras and then fellas on talking about voodoo stuff with the full moon, though that I believe. Sabrina could never sleep as a little girl whenever there was a full moon. She'd always come into our room, crawl into our bed, curl up in the middle of me and Gina, and lie there awake, sighing loudly, tapping on my shoulder, my face, anything to wake me up to have some company. Once I brought her downstairs and made her a hot chocolate and we sat in the dark kitchen, lights off, and watched the moon, her wide awake, staring at the moon as though hypnotised by it, as though having a silent conversation with it, me falling asleep in the chair. Gina came down and shouted the head off me, it was a school night, it was three a.m., what did I think I was doing? That was that.

I think of her now on nights when I see the full moon, wonder if she's up, sitting in her kitchen having a hot chocolate, long curls down her back, though the curls are gone now of course.

Everyone is in flying form, excited about the natural phenomenon. Lea is telling me about the date she was on last night as she applies sun cream to my face and arms. My legs are covered up. She went to the cinema with a garda from Antrim. I tut.

'You can't talk at the cinema,' I say. 'Never go to the cinema on a first date.'

'I know, I know, you told me that when he asked me and you're right, but we went for drinks afterwards and believe me I was glad of the two hours not talking, he was such an eejit, Fergus. My ex-girlfriend this, my ex-girlfriend that. Well, tell you what, fella, you can have your ex-girlfriend. I'm off.'

I chuckle.

'I'll get you a cupcake, which one do you want? I've some with jellies, marshmallows, I had Maltesers but Fidelma ate them too,' she says with a grin.

'Surprise me,' I say. While she's gone I look around and see that there's lots of visitors today. Children run around the grass, one has a kite, though no matter how fast he runs it won't take off from the ground, no wind today. There's not a cloud in the sky, it's a beautiful indigo blue, with wispy white swirls. This triggers something and I try hard to remember but I can't. This happens sometimes. A lot. And it frustrates me.

'Here you go.' She returns with a plate of two cupcakes and a soft drink.

I look at them, feeling a bit confused.

'Don't you want them?' she asks.

'No, no, it's not that,' I say. 'Is my wife coming?'

She stiffens a little, but pulls up a chair and sits down beside me.

'Do you mean Gina?'

'Of course I mean Gina. My wife, Gina. And Sabrina, and the boys.'

'Remember the boys are going off camping with their dad today? Aidan was to bring them to Wicklow with their cousins.'

'Ah.' I don't remember that. Sounds like fun for them. Alfie will no doubt go hunting for worms, he likes that. Reminds me a bit of Bobby when he was little, except instead of eating them like Bobby did, he likes to name them. He once made me keep Whilomena worm in a cup for an entire day. 'But what about Sabrina? Where is she?' I picture that screwed-up, worried face, frowning in concentration like she's trying to solve a problem, or remember the answer to something that she's forgotten. Yes, that's what it is. Always as though she has forgotten something. If the boys are all off on their jaunt then she must be alone. Unless she's with Gina, but Gina is very busy these days, with Robert, her new husband. Of course, that's why Lea looked at me in that way, I must stop calling Gina my wife. I sometimes forget these things.

'Sabrina was here this morning, remember? I think she had some stuff to take care of, but she'll be back in to visit tomorrow as usual, I'm sure.'

I feel around my pockets.

'Can I help you, Fergus?'

Lea again, always at the right time.

'My phone, I think I left it in my room.'

'I think it's getting close to the eclipse now. Will I get it for you after? I don't want you to miss it, being on the phone.'

I think of Sabrina and I have an overwhelming feeling for her not to be alone. I see her as a little girl again, her serious, pale face lit up by the white light.

'Now, please, if you don't mind.'

I feel like I've blinked and Lea is back. I was lost in a thought but now I can't remember what that thought was. Lea's breathless and I feel bad for nearly making her miss the eclipse. Of course she's excited about a thing like that. She should have gone on a date to watch it, if she could have got the time off, and I'm selfishly glad she didn't. The others would have waited until after the eclipse to get my phone.

I dial Sabrina's number.

'Dad,' she answers immediately, on the first ring. 'I was just thinking about you.'

I smile. 'I picked up on your thoughts. Is everything okay?'

'Yeah, yeah,' she says, distracted. 'Hold on, let me move away for a minute so I can talk.'

'Oh. You're not alone then?'

'No.'

'Good. I was hoping you weren't. I know Aidan and the boys are camping.' I feel foolishly proud of myself for sounding like I remembered such a fact, when I didn't. 'Where are you?'

'I'm sitting on the hood of a car in the middle of a field in Cavan.'

'What on earth?'

She laughs and it's light.

'Are you there with friends?'

'No. But there's plenty of people around watching it. It's one of those official viewing places.'

Silence. There's more to it, and she's not telling me.

'I'm just travelling around a bit, looking for something.'

'You lost something?'

'Yes. In a way.'

'I hope you find it.'

'Yeah.' She sounds distant again. 'So how are you? Are you in a good spot to see the eclipse?'

'I'm great. I'm sitting outside on the lawn with everyone eating cakes and drinking fizzy drinks, watching the sky. I don't think we're in the correct path, whatever it's called, but it's keeping us all busy.

I was thinking though while waiting, something today reminded me of an incident when you were two.' It was Lea's smile that triggered the memory, Lea's dimples that would fit miniature marbles, and I thought of the marbles because of the pouch in Sabrina's hand this morning. 'Don't think I ever told you about it.'

'If I did something bad then I'm sure Mum told me.'

'No, no, she never knew about this. I didn't tell her.'

'Oh?'

'She had to go out on an errand one day, a doctor's appointment, or maybe it was a funeral, I can't quite remember, but she left you with me. You were two. You managed to get your hands on some marbles that you found in my office.'

'Really?' she sounds surprised, interested, so eager, surprisingly so as that isn't the high point of the story. 'What kind of marbles were they?'

'Oh, tiny ones. Miniature ones. It's getting darker here, is it happening there too?'

'Yes, it's happening here. Go on.'

'Is that a dog I hear howling?'

'Yes, the animals are getting nervous. I don't think they're happy with the situation. Tell me more, Dad, please.'

'Well, you put the marble up your nostril. Right or left, can't remember which.'

'I what?' she asks. 'Why would I do that?'

'Because you were two years old, and why not?'

She laughs.

'Well, I couldn't get the bloody thing out. I tried everything I could, so eventually I had to bring you to A&E. They tried tweezers, tried to make you blow your nose, which you couldn't do, you kept blowing out through your mouth until eventually Dr Punjabi, an Indian man that I subsequently had a few dealings with, did a kind of CPR. He blew into your mouth and pressed your nostril closed and pop, out it came.'

We both laugh. It is dusk now, everyone around me is looking up, glasses on and looking like wallies, me included. Lea sees me and gives me an excited thumbs up.

'When your mam got home that day you told her that an Indian man kissed you. I pretended I had no idea what you were talking about, that you'd seen it on a cartoon or something.'

'I remember that story,' she says, breathless. 'Our next-door neighbour Mary Hayes said that I told her I kissed an Indian man. I never knew where it came from.'

'You told the entire street I think.'

We laugh.

'Tell me more about the moonie,' Sabrina says.

I'm taken aback by her question. It unsettles me and I don't know why. I feel uncomfortable and a bit upset. It's all very confusing. Perhaps it's got to do with what's happening up there in the sky. Maybe everybody feels like this right now. I gather myself.

'The moonie marble,' I say, conjuring up the image in my mind. 'An appropriate story for today, perhaps that's why it came to mind. I was looking for a particular type, but couldn't find it, could only get the miniature ones. A box of two hundred and fifty of them, like little pearls, and they came in a wonderful glass jar, like an oversized jam jar. I don't know how you got your hands on one. I left you for a moment, I suppose, or wasn't watching when I should have been.'

'What did the marble look like?'

'You don't want to know about this, Sabrina, it's boring—'

'It's not boring,' she interrupts, voice insistent. 'It's important. I'm interested. Tell me about it, I want to hear.'

I close my eyes and picture it, my body relaxing. 'A moonie marble is a translucent marble, and I suppose what I like about it is that when a bright light casts a shadow on it there's a distinct fire burning at its centre. They have a remarkable inner glow.'

And it's odd, and I feel so odd, in this unusual moment when the sun has faded, disappeared behind the moon in the middle of the afternoon, that I realise why it is exactly that I hold on to my ma's photograph. It's because, just like the moonie, you can see her fire burning at her centre, and that in anything and anyone is something to behold, to collect and preserve, take it out to study when you feel the need of a lift, or reassurance, maybe when the glow in you has dimmed and the fire inside you feels more like embers.

'Dad? Dad, are you okay?' she's whispering and I don't know why she's whispering.

The moon has passed the sun entirely and the daylight has returned again. Everyone around me is cheering.

I feel a tear trickle down my cheek.

13

POOL RULES

No Peeing in the Pool

I'm sitting on the hood of my car, in a field where I've pulled over to view the eclipse. A clever local farmer has charged two euro to everybody to effectively park and view the eclipse on his land. Every car hood is filled with people wearing ridiculous glasses. I've just hung up the phone to Dad and there is a lump in my throat but I'm ignoring that and flicking manically through the pages of Dad's marble inventory. I stop suddenly.

Moonies.

He has many but I run my finger down the list and find what I'm looking for.

Miniature moonies (250) and there is the mention of the glass jar too, in mint condition. Below that is 'World's Best Moon' a Christensen Agate Company single-stream marble and Dad's description: *A translucent white opalescent marble, has tiny air bubbles inside and a slightly bluish tinge to it. Courtesy of Dr Punjabi.*

Everyone is cheering around me as the sun has appeared again in its total form. I don't know how long the entire thing took, a few minutes maybe, but everyone is hugging and clapping, moved by the event and on a natural high. My eyes are moist. It was the tone of Dad's voice which startled me and moved me the most. It had completely altered, it sounded like another man was talking to me. Somebody else shone through and told a story, a secret story about him and me as a child, but it wasn't just that, it was a marble story. In the thirty years of my life I don't recall that word passing his lips and now, while I'm on this . . . quest and while I watch a natural phenomenon, I feel overwhelmed. I take my eclipse-viewing glasses off to wipe my eyes. I must drive directly to Dad now, talk to him about the marbles. It didn't feel right to raise the issue before when he clearly didn't remember, but perhaps the bloodies triggered more memories today.

I exhale slowly, deliberately, and hear Aidan's voice from a previous conversation.

'What's wrong?'

'Nothing,' I snap.

144

'You sighed,' he says, demonstrating it. It's heavy and slow, and sad. 'You do it all the time.'

'I wasn't sighing, I was just . . . exhaling.'

'Isn't that what sighing is?'

'No, it's not. I just . . . doesn't matter.' I continue making the school lunch in silence. Butter, ham, cheese, bread, slice. Next.

He bangs the fridge closed. I realise I'm not communicating again.

'It's just a habit,' I say, making an effort to communicate, not to snap, not to be angry. I must follow the counsellor's rules. I don't want to be in the spotlight again this week for all of my bad faults. I don't want to be at counselling at all. Aidan thinks it will help us. I, on the other hand, find that silence and tolerance is the best way forward, even if the tolerance is on the edge, particularly when I don't know what the problem is, or even if there is one. I'm just told that my behaviour points to the fact that there is. My behaviour being one of silence and tolerance. It's a vicious circle.

'I hold my breath and then I release it,' I explain to Aidan.

'Why do you hold your breath?' he asks.

'I don't know.'

I think he's going to get in a huff again, because he'll think I'm holding something back, some enormous secret that doesn't exist but which he thinks does. But he doesn't say anything, he's thinking about it.

'Maybe you're waiting for something to happen,' he says.

'Maybe,' I say without really thinking it through, adding the raisins to the lunch box, just happy he's not in a huff any more. Argument avoided, I don't have to worry about the eggshells that surround him. Or maybe they're around me.

But I think about it now. Yeah, maybe I am waiting for something to happen. Maybe it will never happen. Maybe I will have to make it happen myself. Maybe that's what I'm doing now.

My phone rings and I don't recognise the number. 'Hello?'

'Sabrina, Mickey Flanagan here. Can you talk?'

'Yes, of course. I'm just on my way home, I pulled in to watch the eclipse.' I wonder if he knows about my trip to his nephew. I hope not. Accusing him was one thing, accusing a nephew would be a double insult. Even though it turns out he did open the boxes.

'Ah, a remarkable thing, wasn't it? I went home to watch it with my better half, Judy. We were talking about you and the marbles.' He pauses and I know something is coming up. 'We were talking about your boxes and Judy remembered that they didn't all come together on the same day in a single delivery.'

'No?' I sit up straighter, slow the car down.

'The first boxes came in one van with my delivery fella, just like I arranged with the family. But Judy reminded me just now that a few days later a few more boxes arrived, I forgot about it but Judy didn't. She remembers because I hadn't told her that I was storing anything for anyone and she only found out when a woman arrived to the house with three more boxes. Judy had to call me at the office to check. Wasn't sure if the woman was a loo-lah making it up.'

'A woman?'

'That's right.'

'A delivery woman?'

'No, Judy doesn't think that she was. And Judy's good like that. Even though it was a year ago, she's perceptive. Sharp memory. She wasn't driving a van, just a car. She doesn't know anything about the woman at all, they didn't talk much. She thought maybe she was a neighbour, or a colleague.'

'And this woman delivered *three* boxes?'

'She did.'

Which would have to make it the boxes of marbles. Wouldn't it? Again I think of Mum, and wonder if for some reason she's holding back, if she hadn't wanted me to see these three boxes.

'One other thing,' he adds in a rush and sounds embarrassed by the minor detail. 'Judy said she was a blonde woman.'

My mother is not blonde. I think of my aunts but dismiss it quickly; I haven't seen them for years, they could have purple hair for all I know, or had blonde hair last year and no hair now. I have more questions, but really it's all he can help me with.

'Good luck, Sabrina,' Mickey says. 'I hope you find them. It sure would put my mind at ease.'

14

PLAYING WITH MARBLES

Steelies

Commies. The poor boy's marble. They were the first kind of marble. Made of clay, not always round and perfect but they were cheap and common, and they were what got every child playing outside during World War I. Then the aggies and porcelain came along, and glass marbles that were prettier, no two alike. Glass is my preference. But there are also steelies. I have a few of them too. Steelies are chrome-coated solid metal, like knights in battle, and they make deadly shooters. They're heavy and fast and send opponents' marbles flying out of the ring. That's me today. I'm surrounded by glass and porcelain, maybe even a little clay, but I'm the steelie. I'm twenty-four, it's my wedding day and I'm sending all the men in Gina's life out of the ring.

Iona parish church is the venue for the big day. Gina's local church where she was baptised, received first confession, first communion as a little bride, was confirmed and took the pledge and now finally is getting married. The same priest who carried out all those landmark events in her life marries us today and looks at me in the same way he has since the moment we met.

He fucking hates me.

What kind of family has a priest as a family friend? Gina's kind of family. He buried her dad, comforted her ma on many late nights of free whiskey and advice and he looks at me now like the bastard who's taking his place in the family clan. I said it to Gina. Told her he was looking at me oddly. She said it's because he's known her since she was born, he's protective, he's fatherly. I didn't say so but I think it's the look of a father who needs to be locked up and given a good beating.

Gina says I'm paranoid about most of her friends not liking me. Maybe I am. I think they look at me funny. Or maybe it's the fact they're so polite, like I can't figure out who they really are, because they're not shouting across from me at the table or pinning me down and telling me what they really think, that makes me suspicious of them. There was no politeness in my family, no smokescreens. Not in my house, not in my school, not on my street. I know where I stand with them, but the priest doesn't like me and I know it. I know it from the way that he looks at me when Gina's not looking. Two men, two stags who at any moment want to crash heads, tear each other's antlers off. I was glad Gina's dad is dead, so I wouldn't have to deal with that male-ownership bullshit, the fella who's 'stealing' the daughter away, but I didn't expect to have the issue with the family priest.

And the family doctor.

Jesus, him too. What kind of family has a family doctor? Gina's kind of family.

When we were sick, Ma had her own ways of getting us better. Baking soda and water for sunburn, butter and sugar for a cough, brown sugar and boiling water for constipation. I remember I'd a lump on my knee so Mattie dipped it in boiling water then hit it with a book; simple, it disappeared. A pimple on Hamish's nose was cut off with scissors then treated with aftershave. Iodine for cuts. Gargled salt water for throats. Rarely were we on antibiotics. Rarely were we with a doctor for enough time as to strike up the friendship Gina and her ma have with their GP. No family doctor and definitely none that would care who the fuck we marry. But that's Gina's family. Even worse, or better, I'm not sure, I'll be part of their family. I can hear Hamish chuckling. I hear it as I fix my tie in the toilet and prepare for the reception that Gina's grandda is paying for.

'Best day of your life?' Angus asks cheekily, taking a piss beside me in the urinal, disturbing my thoughts.

'Yeah.'

I'd asked Angus to be my best man, wished Hamish was here to do it even though he'd be a thousand times more risky and send every family anything running from the reception with his speech. No, that's wrong. Hamish was subtle. He wasn't like the rest, he observed, knew how to hustle, judge the atmosphere and then make his move. It didn't mean he wouldn't do anything wrong, but at least he'd think about it beforehand, not shoot out the first thing that came into his head like the others. Five years since he died and he's still alive in my head. But Angus was the closest thing to Hamish and if I didn't involve my family in the wedding in some way there'd be blue murder. If I'd really had the choice I'd have asked my mate Jimmy, but it's complicated there. Shame, really, seeing as he's the person I most enjoy talking to.

I talk to him more than anyone else. We're always talking about something, as long as the something is about nothing. I could do that all day with him. He's the same age as me, he's into marbles too, that's how we met, and we play marbles a few times a week. Only grown man I know who does. He says he knows a few others, and we joke about putting a team together, going for the international title. I don't know. Maybe we actually will some day.

It felt odd, not telling Jimmy about today. Friends would do that, wouldn't they? Not us though. He doesn't exactly spill the beans on himself though either; just enough for me to figure it out eventually, but he can be so bloody cryptic. I like it this way. Why? I've asked myself that a lot. I like it when I can keep myself to myself. I can control what people know about me. The boy from Scotland who moved to Dublin for everyone to talk about, slept on the floor for a year with everyone talking, before moving to Mattie's house after a quick marriage with everyone talking – and they were right to, Ma's baby Tommy came 'early'; then us as kids, wild as anything; and then, much later, after Hamish died, the talk, everybody talking about what he did or didn't do. Everyone summing him up in one phrase or one word or one look like they knew him, but they never did and never could. Not like I did. I don't even think my other brothers knew Hamish like I did. And I wanted to get away from all that. All that talk. I wanted to be who I wanted to be, because I wanted to. No reasons, no talk. Hamish did it, but he left the country, I don't know if I could do that.

Get me away from all of them but not too far. They drive me crazy but I need them. I need to see them at least, from afar, know that they're all right.

If I'd wanted to marry a girl I'd fingered when I was fourteen I'd have stayed put but I didn't. I was twenty-three years old, ready for marriage, and leaving my home turf to meet the likes of Gina was better. Not that I travelled far. Fifteen minutes' walk away. Just a new community is all. And we didn't come from nothing either. Lived on a farm in Scotland till the age of five, Ma met Da when she moved there to be a nanny, then after sleeping on Aunty Sheila's floor, we moved to a nice house too, terraced house on St Benedict's Gardens, around the corner from our stomping ground Dorset Street, Mattie's family home that he got to keep when his ma and da kicked the bucket. Mattie does grand with the butcher's, all of us working there now, giving every penny that we earn to Ma, until marriage. But it's not where you're raised, it's how you're raised, and Gina's ma raised her differently to how Ma raised us. Raising men is different, I've heard Ma say when her and Mrs Lynch were talking about her girls.

I wanted someone better than me. I didn't know until later that was because *I* wanted to be better, like she'd rub off on me. Not more money but the politeness, the fucking genuine way she cared about what absolute tosspots were saying. We both lost our das at a young age so you can't say she had a sheltered life, no child should have to live through that, but everything she did was within three streets of her house. The same for her friends. School, shops, work. Her da ran a button factory, they lived in one of those big houses in Iona, plenty of room for lots of children that they didn't get to have because he died, dropped dead of a heart attack one day. Her ma turned their house into a guest house, they do well on match days with Croker nearby, and Gina works there with her. Always the perfect hosts. Polite. Welcoming. Every time I meet them it's as if they're standing at their guest desk, no matter where they are.

I knew Gina's da had died and I used that to chat her up. I used my da dying to get her, making up a load of old crap about how much I missed him, felt him around me, wondered if he was looking down on me and all that type of thing. I've learned that women love that stuff. It felt kind of nice to be that lad talking like that but I've never felt Da around me. Not once. Not ever. Not when I needed him. I'm not bitter about that, Da's dead, dead's dead, and when you're dead you'd think you'd want to just enjoy being dead without having to worry about the people you left behind. Worrying is for the living.

Hamish, though, I don't know, sometimes I think it with him, about him hanging around. If I'm about to do something that maybe I shouldn't, I hear him, that smoker's laugh that he had at sixteen, or I hear him warning me, the sound of my name coming through teeth clamped tight together, or I feel his fist against my ribs as he tries to stop me. But that's just my memory, isn't it? Not him actually meddling, helping me out, like he's a ghost.

I could have talked to Gina about Hamish but I didn't. I chose Da. Easier to make stuff up that way. It doesn't make me a liar, or a bad person. I wouldn't be the first lad to get a girl just out of saying things she wanted to hear. Angus got Caroline when he pretended for six weeks to have a broken leg after she ran into him on her bicycle. She kept visiting, feeling all guilty, and every time she was coming he'd run in from playing football in the alley and leg it to the couch and put his leg up on cushions. We all had to go along with it. I think Ma thought it was funny, though she didn't smile. But she didn't tell him to stop either. I think she liked Caroline visiting. They used to talk. I think Ma liked having a girl in the house. Angus got her in the end. Duncan, too. He pretended to like Abba for an entire year. Him and Mary even had it as their first dance on their wedding day before he told her that night, drunk, that he hated them and never wanted to hear them again. She ran to the toilet crying and it took four girls and a make-up kit to get her out.

On our first proper date I took Gina to an Italian restaurant on Capel Street. I thought she'd like something exotic like that even though pasta wasn't my thing. I told her about playing marbles then and she laughed, thinking I was messing.

'Ah, come on, Fergus, seriously, what do you really play? Football?'

It was then. I didn't tell her, for a few reasons. I was embarrassed that she'd laughed. I felt uncomfortable in the restaurant, the waiters made me nervous, were watching me like I was going to rob the knife and fork. The prices on the menu were more than I thought they'd be and she'd ordered starter *and* main course. I was going to have to think of something before she went for dessert. Anyway when she laughed, I thought, yeah, maybe she's right, maybe it's stupid, maybe I won't play any more. And then I thought, I can still play and have her, and that's the way it went, thinking it's no big deal keeping them separate, it's not as if I'm cheating on her, though I had a few times by then. Waiting for a virgin wife, I had to be relieved a few times by Fiona Murphy. I swear she knew how desperate I was as soon as she'd see me. I didn't bring Gina to my local, too many reasons, Fiona Murphy being one of them, and every other girl I was with. Fiona literally had me in the palm of her hand. Her da had a job in the Tayto factory and she always had cheese-and-onion breath. But now that I'm married I'll have to change all that. A vow's a vow.

I've been with Gina for one year and she hasn't

met my family much in that time. Enough times to not cause outrage on either side, but I know it's not enough. Short visits, quick visits. Pop into the house, drop by a party. Never let her get to know them, because then she'd get to know me, or the me she might think I am. I want her to know me through being with me.

'There's some drama going on with one of Gina's bridesmaids,' Angus says. 'The one with the kegs for tits.'

I laugh. 'Michelle.'

'She says her boyfriend just got up and left the church, saw him leaving before she'd made her grand entrance.'

I make a face. 'That's a bit harsh.'

'All the girls are in the toilet trying to fix her make-up now.'

I make a face again. But I'm not really listening to Angus, I'm concentrating more on what I'm about to say. The right thing in the right way.

'Angus, you know the speech.'

'Yep, got it right here.' He takes it out of his pocket, a few pages, more pages than I was hoping for, waves it in my face proudly. 'Spent all summer writing this. Spoke to a few of your old school friends. Remember Lampy? He had a few tales to tell.'

Which made sense as to why Lampy apologised to me after the ceremony.

Angus tucks it back into the inside of his pocket. He taps it to make sure it's safe.

'Yeah, well . . . just remember that, er, Gina's family and friends are . . . well, you know, they're not like us.'

I know they're the wrong words as soon as I say them. I know from the look on his face. It has been glaringly obvious they are not 'like us' all day. They're quieter for a start. Every second word isn't a swear word. They use other words to express themselves.

I try to backtrack. 'It's just that, they're not *exactly* like us. You know? They've a different humour. Us Boggs and Doyles, we have a different way. So I was just wondering if you could go easy in the speech. You know what I mean? Gina's grandparents are old. Very fuckin', you know, religious.'

He knows. He looks at me with absolute contempt. The last time I saw this look on his face, it was followed with a head butt.

'Sure,' he says simply. Then he looks me up and down like he has no idea who I am, as though it's not his own brother standing in front of him, in a puddle of piss. 'Good luck, Fergus.' Then he walks out of the toilet leaving me feeling like absolute shit.

His speech is boring. It is the most mind-numbingly boring speech in history. No jokes, just all formality. He didn't reach into his pocket for his speech, all those handwritten pages that I know he spent weeks on and probably practised all night. It is hands down the worst speech ever. No emotion. No love. I could have asked a stranger on the street to do a better job. Which maybe is his point. A stranger, who doesn't even know me.

Gina's ma, the family doctor and the family priest all think he is 'terrific'.

Ma's dressed in the same outfit she wore to Angus's wedding. Something else to Duncan's wedding a few months ago and then back to this dress for mine. It's pea green, a coat, a shift dress and low heels. A sparkly clip in her hair. Her best brooch. Da gave it to her, I remember it. A Tara brooch with green stones. She's wearing make-up, powder that makes her paler and red lipstick that's stuck to her teeth. She isn't dancing. I remember her dancing all night at Angus's. Her and Mattie do a good jive, the only time I ever see them physical with each other. At Duncan's we had to carry her home. Here, she's sitting down, stiff back, a glass of brandy in front of her, and I'm wondering what Angus said to her. Mattie's watching the girls dancing, tongue running along his lips, like he's choosing from a menu. Ma and Mattie are alone at the round table. All of my brothers and their other halves headed off early with Angus; I assume he'd told them what I said. Something like telling him not to be a Boggs, pretend to be someone else. But that wasn't exactly what I'd said, was it?

That's fine with me though. I can relax more without them. No one is going to go flying across the room and smashing into a table because of a funny look or an intimated tone.

I go over and sit with Ma and we have a chat. Then as we're talking she slaps me hard across the cheek.

'Ma, what the . . . ?' I hold my stinging cheek, looking around to see who's seen. Too many people.

'You're not him.'

'What?' My heart starts to pound. 'What are you talking about?'

She slaps me again. Same cheek.

'You're not him,' she says again.

The way she looks at me.

'Come on.' She throws her purse at Mattie, and he jumps to action, eyes off the dancing girls, tongue back inside. 'We're going.'

By midnight my family are all gone.

'Long way to get home,' Gina's ma says politely, as if trying to make me feel better, but it doesn't.

I tell myself I don't care, I can dance, I can chat, I can relax with them all gone. The hard man, the unbreakable, unbeatable steelie.

15

PLAYING WITH MARBLES

Hundreds

She's never been for a massage before and so as soon as we arrive at the hotel in Venice she goes straight to the spa. She's glowing, excited, I can tell she feels grown up. We were married yesterday and we still haven't had sex. We partied hard until three a.m., in spite of all the Boggs and Doyles leaving early. The sing-song was in full swing when we left and then we both collapsed in a heap on the bed and had to get up an hour later for a six a.m. flight. Definitely no time for sex, particularly sex for the first time. For her obviously, not me. I sit on the double bed and bounce up and down. I've waited for her for a year, I suppose I can wait for the length of a massage. She thinks I'm a virgin too, I don't know what got it into her head, I never claimed I was, but that's how all the people in her life are. They're the following-those-rules type of people and she got it into her head that I am too. I just went along with it, save myself the trouble.

I know how I want to do it with her. The first time. I've thought about it. I want to play Hundreds with her. You draw a small circle on the floor. Both players shoot a marble towards the circle. If both or neither marble stops in the circle then we shoot again. If only one stops in the circle that player scores ten points each time the marble stops in the circle on subsequent throws. Gina never wears a bra, she doesn't need to, and always wears a tight tank top and flares. She doesn't wear make-up, freckles across her nose and cheeks, freckles on her chest bone. I think about kissing them all. Most of them I've kissed already. The first player to reach one hundred points is the winner and the loser hands over a predetermined number of marbles. Only in our game, which will involve white wine because now we're married and grown up, whoever doesn't make it to the circle will have to strip off an item of clothes. She's never played marbles before, she'll keep missing, I'll miss just enough times too to make her comfortable. By the time I reach one hundred, I want her in the circle, naked. But this won't happen, I know. This is just what's kept me going this year while I do the gentlemanly thing and wait. I've never mixed marbles and sex before, and although Gina laughed the first time I told her I played marbles, I want to do this with her, with my wife.

Gina is worth the wait. She's gorgeous, any fella I know would do the same. She's too good for me of course. Not too good for the me that she knows, but for the me that she doesn't know. The part of me she knows is some man I've concocted over time. He's good with people, patient, polite, interested. He doesn't think everyone she introduces him to is up themselves and he wouldn't prefer to top himself than have a conversation with them. It's better being him, he makes life easier for him and me. But he's not me. I try to keep her away from my family as much as I can; whenever her and Ma talk I break out in a cold sweat. But Ma will never say anything, she knows the deal, knows that I'm in way over my head, but she wanted me to marry her just as much as I did so she could tick me off her list, another of her boys taken care of. Gina's only met Angus briefly, at the wedding; he's living in Liverpool and he can stay there, but Duncan, Tommy, Bobby and Joe are okay in small doses. She just thinks they're always busy. Good enough.

She knows one of my brothers died, thinks Hamish drowned. Well, he did, but she thinks it was some freak accident. I plan on keeping it that way. Hamish's problems were his own but I don't want him bringing that into my new life. Gina's sweet, she's naïve, and she judges people. She'd hear a thing like that and she'd look at me different. She'd probably be right. Not that I'm trouble, I'm always on the right side of the law, but I'm not the lad who promises to play croquet with her granddad. Thank God her dad's dead and her granddad's not far from it.

I chose Venice for the honeymoon. I've wanted to come here since I saw a documentary about the Murano glass factory, an entire island dedicated to making glass is an island I want to if not live on, at least visit. I don't have much money, in fact we have very little to spend here at all, but I'm not leaving this country without a pocket full of marbles one way or another, whether I have to beg, borrow or steal. This honeymoon is being funded by Gina's granddad who couldn't help but step in when he heard we were going to Cobh for our honeymoon. *Pick anywhere you want*, he said. *Anywhere in the world.* Gina was hoping for a week in Yugoslavia because that's where one of her friends went on honeymoon, but I managed to talk her into three days in Venice instead. Yugoslavia we could maybe some day afford by ourselves, Venice we couldn't. Venice is a real escape, an adventure in another world. She bought it, because I meant it. I don't care about her grandda helping me out, giving me money. I'll take any helping hand offered, it doesn't hurt my pride. If I don't have it, I don't have it; if someone wants to give it, then I'll take it.

I pace the small room; it's not the most luxurious hotel, far from it, but I appreciate being here at all. I'd sleep anywhere and I can't wait to get out and explore.

I thought I'd be knackered from last night but I'm hopping. I'm eager to get moving. I don't know how long a massage is but I'm not sitting here in this room when there's a world out there waiting for me. I don't think Gina will want to spend much time looking at marbles, not in the way I want to, so I take my moment now and slip away. I don't have to go far before I see the most incredible marbles I've ever seen in my life. They're contemporary art marbles, definitely not for playing with, they're for collecting. I'm in such awe that I can't move from the front window. The salesman comes outside and practically pulls me in, he can see the lust written all over my face. Problem is I have the lust for them but not the money. He answers question after question that I throw at him about every aspect, allows me to examine the works of art under a 10x loupe so I can see the skill of the artist. They are clear handmade glass marbles with elaborate designs captured inside. One is clear with a green four-leaf clover trapped deep inside, another is a goldfish that looks like it's swimming in bubbles, another has a white swan in a swirl of blue sea. There's a vortex, a swirl of purple, green, turquoise, green storms that corkscrew to the very centre of the marble. It's hypnotising. Another is of an eye. A clear marble with an olive green eye and black pupil, red veins trickle around the sides. I feel like it's watching me. Another is called 'New Earth' and it's the entire planet, every country created inside, with clouds on the outer layer. It's a work of pure genius. The entire planet captured in a four-inch marble. This is the one I want but I can barely afford one, let alone the collection. The cost of one is the amount of money I have for the entire three days.

It takes everything I have to walk away and it's the walking away that fires the salesman into action. The best negotiator is the one who is always willing to walk away and he thinks I'm hustling him, which I'm not, I would sell my house for this collection if I had a house. We have to live with Gina's mother for a year while we save up for a deposit for a house. To even be thinking about buying any of these marbles is pure lunacy and I know it. But. I feel alive, the adrenaline is rushing through my body. This is the only good side of me, the best side of me, and she doesn't know it. Looking at these marbles, I vow right here to be faithful to her and I don't mean not sleeping around, but to let her see the real me for the first time. Show her this marble, show her the biggest and best part of me.

I buy a clear marble with a red heart inside. It has corkscrew swirls of deep red, like drops of blood captured in a bubble. I bargain hard and pay almost half of what he was asking for. It's still too much money but it's not just a marble for me, it's for Gina, an offering of who I truly am. It means more to me than the ceremony yesterday and words that I didn't feel in my heart. This means something to me. This is the scariest, bravest thing I have ever set out to do in my adult life. I'm going to give her this heart, my heart, and tell her who I am. Who she's married.

The seller wraps the heart in bubble wrap, then places it in a burgundy velvet pouch, pulled closed by a gold plaited tie and glass beads that I can't help but admire. Even the beads on the pouch are beautiful. I push it deep into my pocket and return to the hotel.

When I get back to the room I can see she's been crying but she tries to hide it. She wears a bathrobe which is tied tightly at her waist.

'What's wrong? What happened?' I'm ready to punch someone.

'Oh, nothing.' She wipes her eyes roughly with the sleeve of her towel until the skin around them is red raw.

'It wasn't nothing, tell me.' I feel the anger pumping through my veins. Be calm or she won't tell you. Be the patient, understanding fella who listens, don't go thumping people. Not yet.

'It was just so embarrassing, Fergus.' She sits on the bed and looks tiny on the big bed. She's twenty-one years old. I'm twenty-four. 'She touched my . . .' Her eyes widen and the anger leaves me and I feel a laugh rising.

'Yeah? Your what?' My fantasy game of Hundreds comes to mind. She's on that bed, in the robe, my wife.

'It's not funny!' She throws herself down, covers her face with a pillow.

'I'm not laughing.' I sit down beside her.

'You look like you're going to,' she says, voice muffled. 'I just didn't know a massage was so invasive. I didn't wait all this time to have sex to have a four-foot Italian mama maul me before you.'

And on that I have to laugh.

'Stop!' she whinges, but I can see her smile buried beneath the pillow.

'Did you like her hands on you?' I tease her, my hand travelling up her leg.

'Stop it, Fergus.' But she means the teasing, not the touching, because for the first time she's not stopping me. I have to do it now though, I have to show her the marble now, so that it's me that she meets, it's me that she makes love to for the first time, not him.

I stop my own hand from travelling and she sits up, confused, hair all in her face.

'I want to give you something first.'

She moves her hair away from her face and she looks so sweet and so innocent right at that moment that I take a mental picture of it. I don't know it now but I'll try to recall it in the future at the moments when I feel like I've lost her, or hate her so much I can't help but look away from her.

'I went for a walk around. And I found something special for you. For us. It's important to me.' My voice is shaking and so I decide to shut up. I take the pouch out of my pocket, remove the heart from the pouch, my fingers trembling. I feel like I'm giving a part of myself to her. I've never felt like this before. You married me yesterday but today is the first time you've met me. My name is Fergus Boggs, my life is marked by marbles. I unwrap the bubble wrap and I hold it out in my palm. Her reaction first, then my explanation. Let her take it in, drink in her drinking it in.

'What is this?' she says, her voice flat.

I look at her in surprise, heart pounding in my throat. I immediately start to backtrack, back-pedal, hide in my shell. The other me starts warming up in the wings.

'I mean, how much was it? We said we wouldn't buy each other anything here. We can't afford it. No more gifts, remember? After the wedding? We agreed.' She's barely looked at it, she's so annoyed.

Yes, we did agree, we promised each other, but this is more than a piece of jewellery, it means more to me than the ring she loves so much on her finger. I want to say that but I don't.

'How much did this cost?'

I stutter and stammer, too broken and hurt to reply honestly. I'm caught between being him and being me, I'm unable to focus on being one.

She is holding it too roughly, too harshly, she moves it from one hand to the other too carelessly, she could easily drop it. I feel tense watching her.

'I can't believe you wasted your money on this!' She jumps up from the bed. 'On a . . . on a . . .' She studies it. 'A toy! What were you thinking, Fergus? Oh my God.' She sits down again, her eyes filling up. 'We've been saving for so long. I just want to get away from living with Mum, I want it to be just you and me. We budgeted for this trip so carefully, Fergus, why would you . . . ?' She looks at the marble in her hand, confused. 'I mean, it's sweet, thank you, I know you were trying to be kind, but . . .' Her anger starts to calm but it's too late.

She places her hands on my cheeks, knows that she has hurt my feelings though I don't admit to it. I will take it back, I tell her, I will gladly take it back, I never want to see it again ever in my life, to be reminded of this moment when I offered my real self and I was rejected. But I can't bring it back because she drops it, by accident, and its surface is scratched, meaning it will never have a perfect heart again.

16

POOL RULES

No Bombing

On my journey back from Cavan to Dublin I can't help myself slipping into my mind. My driving is clumsy, I have to apologise to other drivers too many times, so I lower the window for the fresh air and sit up.

Aidan is on loudspeaker in the car. I needed to call him, to root myself with my life. Talk to somebody real.

'So you're looking for the missing marbles now?' he asks after I fill him in on everything that's happened so far today, apart from the mug-throwing incident, and I hear the squeals of delight as the kids have a water fight in the background.

'I don't even know if it's about the missing marbles

any more,' I say, suddenly deciding. 'Finding out about Dad seems to be much more important than finding the actual marbles. It started with them and it opened up more questions, big gaping holes that I need to fill. There is a side to Dad that I never knew, there is a life he led that he kept from me and I want to discover it. Not just for me. But if *he* can't remember it, how can he ever know that part of himself again?'

Aidan leaves a long silence and I try to read it. He thinks I'm crazy, I've finally lost it, or he's jumping around with jubilance that I'm newly energised. But his response is calm, measured.

'You know best, Sabrina. I'm not going to tell you not to. If you think it will help.'

He doesn't need to say any more, I understand what it means. If it will help me and, as a consequence, us.

'I think it will,' I reply.

'Love you,' he says. 'Try not to let any more men kiss you.'

I laugh.

'Seriously. Be careful, Sabrina.'

'I will.'

The kids shout down the phone to me, *love you, miss you, poo poo, wee wee head*, and then they're gone.

A blonde woman delivered the marbles. I will delay my visit to Dad for now. I need to find the blonde woman who delivered the marbles, the woman who knows the man that I don't, and there is only one woman I can think of who fits that description, who agreed to meet me as soon as I called.

She's sitting in the darkest corner, away from the window, the light, the buzz of the rest of the café. She looks older than I remember, but then she is older than I remember. Nearly ten years have passed since we've seen each other, almost twenty since I saw her first. She's still blonde, her hair one week over its last needed colour, the greys and brown showing at the roots. Ten years older than me, she is forty-two now; I always thought she was so young, but so much older than me. Too young for him, but still much older than me. Now we could look the same. She looks bored as she waits and I wonder is the boredom hiding the nervousness beneath, the same anxiety that I feel as soon as I see her. She sees me walking towards her and she fixes her posture, lifts her chin in that proud move and I hate her all over again like I always did. That self-right-eous bitch who thought everything she wanted was automatically supposed to be hers. I try to calm myself, not allow the anger to bubble over.

I saw her with Dad when I was fifteen years old. It was before my parents separated. He introduced me to her less than a year later. I was supposed to think they'd just met, that this was the beginning of a beautiful new relationship for him, that I was to be supportive and happy but I knew that he'd been with her all along. For how long I don't know, but I never said a word. He hadn't just lied to Mum, he had lied to me too, because he looked at me and said the same words. Lies.

They were drunk at lunchtime when I saw them and every time I pass that restaurant to this day I get the same feeling in my stomach and see them all over again. People don't know that they do that to people when they do the things they shouldn't. Hurtful things are roots, they spread, branch out, creep under the surface, touching other parts of the lives of those they hurt. It's never one mistake, it's never one moment, it becomes a series of moments, each moment growing roots and spurting in different directions. And over time they become muddled like an old twisted tree, strangling itself and tying itself up in knots.

I was off school early to go to the dentist, one of my many train-track appointments to try to get to the bottom of my internal cheek bleeding as they scratched and scraped as I talked and chewed. I remember my mouth throbbing as I walked down the road, tears in my eyes from frustration because another cruel boy made another cruel joke at school that day and I was tired of laughing and pretending I didn't care. It was then that I saw Dad. In a fancy restaurant in town, one of the expensive ones with tables outside that I was too embarrassed to walk by. At fifteen, feeling eyes on me from every corner of the street, my head was bowed, my cheeks already pink, my walk self-conscious, but I couldn't help it. When you try hard not to look at something it means you'd have to poke your own eyes out to stop you from looking at that something. So I looked up at all the eyes that I was afraid were looking at me and laughing, and I saw him. I actually stopped for a moment and somebody crashed into the back of me. It was only for a second and I moved again, but I saw enough. Him and her at a table by the window, drunk face, drunk eyes, quick kiss, hands groping under the chair. I didn't say anything to Mum about it because, well, they were so bad at that stage I thought maybe she knew, thought that the woman was the reason, or at least one of the reasons for things being so bad. I never said a word about seeing them together, even when I was intro-duced to her months later in that fake, made-up, rehearsed introduction as if they'd just recently met. I always hated her.

Regina.

It made me think of the word Vagina. She was just that. Every time I heard her name, every time I had to say her name, I was all the time hearing and saying Vagina. I called her it once by mistake. She laughed and said, 'What?' but I pretended she'd misheard. She giggled to herself thinking her hearing odd and funny.

And now here I am face to face with Vagina. And I have to ask her for her help, something I hate to do but it's necessary. She is the only lead I have, she is the only woman I know that was in Dad's life for the longest amount of time who could have had access to his personal belongings, his apartment, the blonde woman who delivered the marbles to Mickey Flanagan's house, who could help solve this mystery.

We don't hug or kiss when greeting, we're not old friends, not even acquaintances, not even enemies. Just two people who got twisted together.

She works at the hair salon next door to the café we're in, the same hair salon that Mum and I have avoided going to for almost twenty years. I called her from the car, after Mickey's phone call, and don't know what I was expecting but I'd come up with a few guesses. She could straight out tell me to never call her again. She could politely pawn me off, suggest a date in the future that kept changing. I didn't expect the instant agreement to meet. She was about to take a coffee break, she could meet me in thirty minutes. I wasn't prepared for that. Twenty minutes on the phone with Aidan explaining it all and I'm still not prepared.

'I really appreciate you agreeing to meet with me on such short notice,' I say, as I sit down and take off my coat, feeling like that awkward fifteen-year-old again with her eyes on me as I clumsily hang up my coat on the back of the chair. 'I'm sure it came as a bit of a surprise to you.'

'I was waiting for you to call,' she says, matter-of-factly. 'No, not waiting. Expecting,' she says. She's wearing an oversized black cardigan pulled down past her hands like she's cold, but it's not cold, it's a beautiful day and I realise she's nervous.

'Why's that?' I ask, picturing Mickey Flanagan's wife on the phone, grasping the receiver in two hands in her house, in urgent hushed tones telling her, *She knows, Regina, Sabrina knows that you were here and that you delivered the marbles. She's on her way to you now.*

'I don't know,' she says thoughtfully, taking me in. 'You were always an interesting little one. You always looked like you had a lot of questions but never asked any of them. I used to wait for you to ask, but you never did.'

'I don't think I was looking at you in any particular way because I wanted to ask you questions,' I say, and her smile drops a little. 'I knew you and Dad were together before they separated, I saw you both in a restaurant long before . . .' I pause for her reaction. 'I had a hard time listening to your lies. I could tell you both enjoyed it.'

This gives her a surprise, a little jolt, and she sits upright. Then she smiles. 'So is that what this is about? Letting me know I didn't pull the wool over your eyes?' She asks it as though she's amused, not an ounce of apology or disgust with herself. I don't know why I expected there should be.

'No, actually.' I look down, add a sugar to my cappuccino, stir it, take a sip. Centre myself. I'm here for a reason. 'As you know, there are a few things that Dad doesn't recall.'

She nods, genuinely sad.

'So sometimes I have to contact people in his life to see if I can fill the holes.'

'Ah,' she says, humble now. 'Anything I can do to help.'

Breathe. 'Did you know about his marble collection?'

'Did I know about his, what now?'

'Marble collection. He had a collection. And he played marbles too.'

She shakes her head, her forehead wrinkled in a frown. 'No. I never, we never . . . marbles? The things that children play with? No. Never.'

My heart drops. I thought. I really thought . . . 'Did you deliver boxes to a house in Virginia last year?'

'Last year? Virginia? Cavan? No, why would I? I haven't seen Fergus for almost five years, and even when we were together we were more off than on. We weren't exactly platonic. We just met up occasionally when, you know . . .'

I don't want to know their reasons for meeting, I don't need to hear it, it's clear already. I'm so disappointed, I just want to grab my coat and go. There is no point to the remainder of this conversation, no point in finishing my coffee.

Maybe she senses this. Tries her best to be useful. 'Do you know one of the reasons why Fergus and I broke up for good?'

'Let me guess,' I say wryly. 'He cheated on you.'

She takes it well. It makes me not want to throw any more at her as I feel it cheapened me and not her.

'Probably. Though that wasn't the reason. He was so secretive. I never quite knew exactly what he was doing or where he was. And not because he didn't answer a question but because he'd answer it and somehow I'd realise that, after listening to him, I still didn't know. He was vague. I don't know if it was deliberate, but to pin him down was to confuse him, annoy him, seem like a nag, which I never wanted to be, but he had the ability to make a person a nag, because he never answered, he never really explained. He didn't understand why I needed to know so much. He thought there was something wrong with me. I did wonder if he was cheating on me. And the thing is, I didn't care, we didn't have that kind of relationship, but it bothered me that I couldn't get answers. So I started following him.' She takes a timely sip of her tea, enjoying it as I hang on her every word. 'And I realised after a very short time that he was not as exciting as he seemed. He was going to the same place all the time, or at least most of the time.'

'Where?'

'He was going to a pub.' She arches her eyebrow. 'He loved to drink. Boring, isn't it? I was hoping it was something else. I followed him for two weeks. And one time . . . oh my God, it was so funny, he almost caught me!' She starts laughing and I can tell she's settling down for a long chat. But I don't have the time.

I finish my cappuccino.

'Regina,' I say, hearing Vagina in my head. 'Which pub was he going to?'

She stops, realising I'm not here to listen to her detective stories into my father's behaviour. She's back to how she was when I entered. Bored. Unhappy. Disappointed nothing in her life lived up to anything it could have been. Waiting for the people she hurt in the past to make an appearance and spice up her life, make her feel powerful.

'One on Capel Street.'

'My dad wasn't an alcoholic,' I say to her, though I don't really know this. I don't know his life in detail but I think I'd have known that, wouldn't I?

'Oh, I know that,' she laughs, and I feel stupid, my cheeks burn. 'My daddy was an alcoholic. Believe me, I couldn't spend two minutes with one. But they had some things in common. Fergus lied about most places he went to. About visiting his mother, about going to the pub, about going to watch matches, about being at meetings, or being away for a weekend. He didn't lie because he was going somewhere more exciting or more daring, or to be with another woman. The life he escaped to was not exotic. He was sitting in a pub. He didn't even need to lie to me, I wasn't trying to pin him down.' She leans in, hands clasped, matter-of-fact, eyes alight like she's enjoying every moment of the revelation. 'Sabrina, your dad lied *all the time*. He lied because he wanted to, because he liked to, because he got some kind of buzz out of it. He lied because that's the kind of person he chose to be, and that was the kind of life he chose to live. And that's it.'

'What was the name of the pub?' I ask, refusing to believe her explanation. I know that Dad lied, but he lied for a reason. And I want to find out what that reason was.

Regina looks as though she's trying to decide whether to tell me or not, like a cat playing with a mouse, one last game with me before she knows I'll never see her again. 'The Marble Cat,' she says finally.

'Aidan,' I say loudly, pulling the car out of my parking space.

'How are you doing?' he asks.

'Just met with Regina,' I say confidently, feeling like I'm flying now.

'Vagina? I didn't think you'd go through with it. I thought that woman gave you nightmares?'

'Not any more,' I say confidently. 'Not any more.'

'So where to next?' he asks.

'A pub on Capel Street. The Marble Cat. I think I'm close to something.'

He pauses. 'Okay, baby, okay. If you think it will help.'

He sounds so uncertain, so nervous but too afraid to express it, that we both laugh.

17

PLAYING WITH MARBLES

Cabbaging

I'm lying on a picnic blanket though I can still feel the bumpy ground beneath me, earth and broken rock. I'm roasting in my suit. My tie is off, my sleeves rolled up, my legs feel like they're burning in my black pants beneath the heat of the summer sun. There's a bottle of white wine beside us, half of it already drunk, I doubt we'll make it back to the office at all. Friday afternoon, the boss probably won't return from lunch as usual, pretending to be at a meeting but instead sitting in the Stag's Head and downing the Guinness, thinking nobody knows he's there.

I'm with the new girl. Our first sales trip together, this one took us to Limerick. I'm helping her to settle in, though she's currently straddling me, and slowly opening the buttons on her silk blouse. I'd say she's settling in just fine.

No one will see us, she insists, though I don't know how she can be so sure. I'm guessing she's done this before, if not here, somewhere like this. She leaves the blouse on, a salmon peach colour, but undoes her strapless bra which falls to the blanket. It topples off the blanket and onto the soil. Her panties are off already. I know this because my hands are where the fabric should be.

Her skin is a colour I've never seen before, a milky white, so white she glows, so pale I'm surprised she hasn't sizzled under the sun's blaze by now. Her hair is strawberry blonde, but if she'd told me it was peach I would have believed her. Her lips are peach, her cheeks are peach. She's like a doll, one of Sabrina's china dolls. Fragile. Delicate looking. But she's not fragile, nor angelic; she is self-assured and has a glimmer of mischief in her hazel-brown eyes, an almost sly lick of her lips as she sees what she wants and takes it.

It is ironic that we are lying in this cabbage field on a Friday afternoon, the day when my ma would serve us up cabbage soup. The word soup was an exaggeration, it was hot water with slithery slimy over-boiled strips of cabbage at the bottom. Salty hot water. The money would always run out by Friday and Ma would save for a big roast on a

Sunday. Saturday we would be left to our own devices, have to fend for ourselves. We would go to the orchard and laze in the trees eating whatever apples we could, or beg and bother Mrs Lynch next door, or we'd rob something on Moore Street, but they were quick catching on to us so we couldn't go there much.

It is doubly ironic that we're lying in this cabbage field because in a game of marbles the banned practice of moving your marble closer to the target marbles is called 'cabbaging', which is cheating. This is no great coincidence, of course. I tell her this fact as we pass the fields; not of my involvement, no, only the men I play with know this and nothing much else about me. I simply share the term with her as we pass fields of cabbage, me in the passenger seat, her driving – on her insistence, which is fine with me as I'm drinking from the wine bottle, which she occasionally reaches for and takes a swig from. She's wild, she's dangerous, she's the one who will get me in trouble. Maybe I want this. I want to be found out, I don't want to pretend any more, I'm tired. Maybe the mere mention of a marble term is the beginning of my undoing. She looks at me when I say it, then slams her foot on the brake, spilling my wine, then does a U-turn and heads back the way we came. She pulls in beside the cabbage field, kills the engine, gets out of the car, grabs a blanket from the back seat and heads for the field. She hitches her skirt up to climb over the wall, high up on her skinny pale thighs, and then she's gone.

I jump out of the car and scurry after her, bottle in hand. I find her lying on the ground, back to the soil, looking up at me with a satisfied grin on her face.

'I want a part of this cabbaging business. What do you think, Fergus?'

I look down at her, drink from the bottle of wine, and look around the field. There's no one around, passing cars can't see.

'You know what it means?'

'You just told me: cheating.'

'No, no, what it means exactly, is when you shoot from an incorrect spot.'

She arches her back and spreads her legs as she laughs. 'Shoot away.'

I join her on the blanket. Gina's at home in Dublin, at Sabrina's parent–teacher meeting, but despite the thought of her, this opportunity really doesn't offer much of a challenge to me and my morals. This electric peach girl isn't the first woman I've been with since I married Gina.

Apart from the day baby Victoria was stillborn and I cheated at Conqueror to win Angus's cork-screw marble on the road outside of our house, I have never since cheated in a game of marbles in my whole life. I don't need reminding from anyone, not even as I enter her and she cries out, that in the marble world I am a man of my word, a perfect rule-abiding man, but the man without the marbles? His whole life has been about cabbaging.

18

PLAYING WITH MARBLES

Foreign Sparkler

'Hello,' I hear a woman say to me suddenly. She's in a chair beside me. I wasn't aware of her before now, not even of an empty chair, but all of a sudden there she is.

The sun is back out again, eclipse over, everybody's eclipse glasses are off, mine too though I don't recall doing that either. I feel like my ma, in her final years, dithery and forgetful with her glasses, when she was always previously spot on. I don't like this part of ageing, I always prided myself on my memory. I'd a good head for names and faces, could tell you where and how I knew them, where we first met, the conversation we had and, if it was a woman, the clothes that she was wearing. It works sometimes like this, my memory, but not always. I know that comes with age and I know the stroke contributed to it too, but at least I'm here being looked after, not at work having to remember things and not being able to. That happens to people and I wouldn't like that.

'Hello,' I say to her politely.

'Are you okay?' she asks. 'I notice you seem a bit upset. I hope you didn't get a bad phone call.'

I look down and see I'm still holding the mobile phone. 'No, not at all.' But was it? Who was it? Think, Fergus. 'It was my daughter. I was worried about her, but she's okay.' I can't quite remember what we talked about, I got lost in a daydream after that, but my feeling is that it's fine, she's fine. 'Why do you think I was sad?' I ask.

'You had tears on your cheeks,' she says softly. 'I sat here because I was concerned. I can leave if you like.'

'No, no,' I say quickly, not wanting her to leave. I try to remember why I would have been so sad speaking to Sabrina. I look over at Lea, who's watching me, worrying, and then up at the sky and I remember the moon, the miniature marbles that would fit in her dimples and then I remember the marble up Sabrina's nose and tell the concerned lady the story. I chuckle, picturing Sabrina's bold face as a two-year-old, red cheeks, stubborn as anything. No to everything and everyone. She could do with learning that word now, running around after three boys all the time.

The lady's eyes have widened as though in fright.

'Oh, don't be alarmed, we got the marble out. She's fine.'

'It's just that . . . the marble story . . . do you . . .' She seems flustered. 'Do you have any more marble stories?'

I smile at her, amused; what an unusual question, but it's kind of her to show interest. I wrack my brain for marble stories, not imagining that I will have any, but I'd like to please her and she seems eager to talk. There it is again, the haze, the shutters of my mind firmly down. I sigh.

'Did you grow up with marbles, as a boy?' she prompts.

And then a sudden memory pops up, just like that. I smile. 'I'll tell you what I do remember: growing up with my brothers. There were seven of us, and my ma, who was a tough woman, introduced a marble swearing jar. Any time someone swore they had to put a marble in the jar, which in our house was the worst kind of punishment. We were all marble mad.' Were we? Yes, we were. I laugh. 'I remember my ma lining us up in the room, wooden spoon in her hand and pointing it in our faces. "If one of you fucking swears, you'll have to put one of those fucking marbles in here. Do you hear?" Well, sure, how could we keep a straight face to that? Hamish started laughing first, then I went. Then it was all of us. I don't remember Joe there, if Joe was born at all, I don't remember him around much. Probably too young. And that was it, in the first minute of its inception there were six marbles in the jar. They were our least favourites, of course, clearies that were chipped and scratched; Ma hadn't a clue. And even though we didn't own those marbles it would still bother us, me anyway, seeing them sitting up high on a shelf so that we couldn't touch them.'

'What did your mother do with them?' she asks, eyes glistening like there's tears in them.'

I study her for a bit. 'Your accent. It's peculiar.'

She laughs. 'Thank you very much.'

'No, not in a bad way. It's nice. It's a mix of something.'

'Germany. And Cork. I moved there in my twenties.'

'Ah.'

I look down at her hands. No wedding ring, but a ring on her engagement finger, that she keeps playing with. Rolling it back and forth on her finger.

She sees me looking and stops fiddling with it.

'What did your mother do with the marble jar? Did you ever get them back?'

'We had to earn them.' I smile. 'Every month we'd have the chance to earn them back. One person would win them all, which was a game in itself, though I don't think Ma saw it like that. I wouldn't be surprised if a few of us swore a few times on purpose just to up the stakes of the game. We would have to help out around the house. Do the washing, cleaning, and then Ma would decide who deserved to win.'

'Controversial,' she laughs.

'It was. We had some terrible scraps after those days. Sometimes it wasn't worth winning or you'd get your head kicked in, you'd end up giving back the marbles they owned in the first place. But if you could tough it out, they were yours.'

'Did you ever win them?'

'Always.'

She laughs. A musical laugh.

'I won them every month for the first few months because Ma used to give me a note; I'd bring it to the chemist, and then I'd carry a brown paper bag back to the house. Never knew what was in it till my brothers told me I was carrying lady pads. They ripped into me so much I never did anything to help again.'

'You lost out on your marbles.'

'Not mine. I figured out I should just not swear in front of Ma.'

We both laugh.

'We've talked before,' I say, suddenly realising.

'Yes,' she says, a sad smile that she tries to hide. 'Several times.'

'I'm sorry.'

'That's okay.'

'You're visiting someone here,' I say.

'Yes.'

We sit in silence, but it's a comfortable silence. She has her shoes off, and she has nice feet. Bright pink toenails. She fidgets with her ring.

'Who are you visiting?' I ask. It's not grumpy Joe, I never see her with him. It's not Gerry or Ciaran or Tom. It's not Eleanor or Paddy. In fact I don't recall seeing her speaking with anyone other than me and the nurses. Though my recollection of that doesn't count for much. Not these days.

'You've never asked me that before. You've never asked who I'm visiting.'

'I'm sorry.'

'Don't be.'

'You're visiting me, aren't you?'

'Yes.'

Her eyes are bright, she's almost breathless. She's beautiful, there's no doubt about that, and I study her hard, her green eyes . . . Something in my mind stirs, then stops again. I don't even know this lady's name. To ask now would feel rude, because she looks at me so intimately. She's still fiddling with her ring, looking down. I look at it more closely.

There's a piece of what looks like a marble embedded in a gold band, a transparent clear base with a ribbon of white and bright-coloured stripes on white in the centre. It is a machine-made marble from Germany. I know this instinctively. I know this and nothing else. No wonder she asked about the marble story. She has a fascination with them.

'Did I tell you the marble-swearing-jar story before?' I ask.

'Yes,' she says softly, with a big beautiful smile.

'I'm sorry.'

'Stop saying sorry.' She places her hand over mine, the one with the ring. Her skin is soft, and warm. Another stir. 'You never told me it here, though.'

I run my finger over her fingers and over the marble. Her eyes fill with tears.

'I'm sorry,' she says, swiping quickly at her eyes.

'Don't be. It's incredibly frustrating to forget, it must be an entirely other thing to be the forgotten.'

'You don't always forget, and those days are the most wonderful days,' she says, and I see a sweet woman who holds on to the smallest hope.

'Foreign sparkler,' I say suddenly, and she gasps. 'That's what this marble is.'

'That's what you called me sometimes. Fergus,' she whispers, 'what is happening to you today? This is wonderful.'

We sit in silence for a moment.

'I loved you, didn't I?' I ask.

Her eyes fill again and she nods.

'Why don't I remember?' My voice cracks and I become agitated, frustrated, I want to stand up from my wheelchair and run, stride, jump, move, for everything to be the way it was.

She turns my face to her, one hand below my chin, and she looks at me with warmth and I remember my ma's face when I was summoned to her one day when she thought I was dead, and I think of Bounce About and I think of a pub in London and a man named George who called me Paddy and handed me a Czech bullet and of seeing Hamish dead. All in a flash.

'Fergus,' she says, her voice bringing me back, calming me. 'I'm not worried about you not remembering. I'm not here to remind you of anything. The past is the past. I have just been hoping that I will be lucky enough that you will fall in love with me again, a second time round.'

This makes me smile, instantly stops my agitation because, of course, it's beautiful. I don't know her and I know everything about her at the same time. I want to love her and for her to love me. I take her hand, the one with the ring, and I hold it tight.

19

PLAYING WITH MARBLES

Slags

I arrive home from the airport feeling rough but exhilarated, still on a high, the adrenaline racing around my veins shouting for 'more!'; a night of partying preceded an early morning flight to get back in time for Sabrina's thirteenth birthday party. Her first year as a teenager. Gina has arranged a marquee and private catering for forty people, mainly her family, thankfully none of mine could come. Or at least that's what I told Gina; I only asked Ma to come but after Mattie's recent heart operation she's afraid to leave his bedside. Gina didn't mind, I think she's happy none of my family could make it, and she wasn't surprised either, it's nothing new. We're not the closest of brothers. We were until I met Gina, then I separated her from my family, always thinking she was too good for them. After sixteen years I'm beginning to see that was a stupid idea; there are times, occasions when I'd like them to be here. When Sabrina did something, or said something and I wished they'd been there to see. Or a family day out when the waiter trips up, or a twat friend of Gina's says something and nobody but me can see he's a twat. I know they'd agree with me and I wish they were there. I could imagine a wisecrack from Duncan, the intensity from Angus, the way he took over at protecting me after Hamish went, as if he knew something, as if he knew he had to. Little Bobby's charm, attracting all the ladies – we called him our 'bit bait'. I think of Tommy looking out for Bobby all the time, still watching out for the slugs and snails in his path, and Joe, the baby, the one who came long after we lost Victoria, sensible Joe, who looks at me, Angus, and Duncan like we're somebody else's family, not his, never fully able to connect with us, as we'd all moved out of the house as he grew up. He listened to stories from locals about Hamish and thought of him as a monster, the boogie man: if he wasn't careful, Hamish would come and get him; if he wasn't careful, he'd end up like Hamish. Hamish, the ghost in our home that was always there, sleeping in our room, eating at our dinner table, the echoes of him in every single room, his energies absorbed into everything around us, into all of us.

We didn't talk like that about him though, neither did Ma. Hamish was funny, Hamish was strong, Hamish was brave. The best way to be the best you can be is to be dead. Ma mollycoddled Joe, made him a bit soft. Not in a sweet way, like most younger kids are, but in a way that made him worry, that made him fragile, that made him think he should be looked after more. She was afraid he'd hurt himself, she was afraid he'd get lost, get sick, die at any moment. Too dark out, too wet out, too hot out, too far away, too late, too early – No, Joe, just stay in with Ma and you'll be grand. He's a worrier, serious, thinks about everything twenty times before he thinks about it again. Safe. Has a boyfriend and lives with him in a new apartment on the quays, pretends to us he doesn't, walks around with a coffee cup and a briefcase. I see him sometimes if I'm driving to town in the mornings. Gina would like Joe, he's doing well for himself, something with computers, but Joe doesn't like me. I miss them sometimes, when I least expect it, but I'm glad they're not here today.

Sabrina greets me at the door, appearing happy, wearing too much make-up in a too short skirt with heels on for the first time. She's letting her top fall off her shoulder, showing off her bra-strap – the new bra that Gina bought her a few weeks ago. She doesn't look good, not to me, not even to me and I'm her dad, I'm supposed to think she's perfect in everything, blinded by fatherly love. Not today. It's a birthday lunch, the weather's not great for April, it's a grey day and Sabrina looks dressed for a garden party in Spain. The material of her skirt is flimsy and nearly see-through, a cheap silk of some sort, I can see the goosebumps on her skin.

When she smiles at me it's a full mouth of metal and my heart melts. My goofy, awkward, beautiful daughter looks better in her pyjamas and spot cream all over her face curled up on the couch and watching *Family Fortunes* than this yoke.

'You look like crap,' she says, giving me a hug. I freeze. If she thinks that then Gina will most definitely think it too. She'll analyse it, dissect it, ask me a thousand paranoid questions with her claws dug into me, and I'll have to deny everything. I have to get to the shower before she sees me. I can hear her in the kitchen, busy talking about prawn cocktails, her voice louder than everyone else's. The marquee has taken over our tiny back garden, the side of it pushed up against the garden wall so that a corner of the shed roof is digging through the canvas, looking like it will pierce it, and somebody's skull, at any moment. Gina is dressed and ready and beautiful as always, still, after all this time, talking and organising everybody like she lives in the Hollywood Hills. We don't. I couldn't give her what I know she longed for, which was the upbringing she had. Now that Sabrina is thirteen

Gina's talking about going to work. I don't think she will, in fact I know she's bluffing, it's all just to say to me, 'You're not giving me what I need. You're not making enough money.'

I'll have to sit in that tent for the next few hours listening to people ask me, 'What are you doing now, Fergus?' like I change jobs faster than my underwear. I haven't found it easy staying put anywhere, but think I'm on to something now. Truth be told I'm not the best at managing my own money, but I know that now and I've copped on. I'm a good salesman, a great one; it all came from Mattie's butcher's shop, when I did my best to get out of cleaning guts and odd jobs that nobody else wanted to do. I started looking into getting better meat, I started advising Mattie on how best to sell it too. And it worked. Quickly found myself out of the back of the butcher's and upstairs in the office, focusing on sales. Then when I married Gina I felt it was time for me to leave Mattie, take my skills elsewhere, which I did to much success. Mobile phones, mortgages, and now a friend wants to hire me for this new company. I just need to understand the markets, which I do. I'm not good at managing my own money, doesn't mean I'm not good at making it for other people. I just need a qualification to convince people to believe me. I've enrolled in an evening course in town twice a week and then I'll be a bona fide venture capitalist.

'What's in there? My present?' She jabs at the bag in my hand and I pull it away sharply from her.

'Sorry,' she says, face suddenly serious, a little afraid, and steps back.

'Sorry, love, I didn't mean to, I just . . .' I keep my bag behind my back. I need to hide it somewhere fast before Gina wonders the same thing. A night away from her and she'll be in her element of paranoia.

I rush upstairs to the spare bedroom that's also used as my home office. From the way it looks I assume her ma is staying over, a multitude of candles, flowers, shampoo, shower gels, everything she'd need for a night away, she's just short of adding a chocolate to her pillow. I pull the desk chair over to the wardrobe and stand up. The marbles are at the top, at the back, deep in the wardrobe. I can barely reach them myself I've hidden them so well and it's exactly where I'm going to stuff this bag until I have time to empty it later.

I hear footsteps on the stairs and I literally can't get the bag in there fast enough. I'm pushing it but to no avail. If I'd used my common sense I would take the offending objects out separately, but I'm panicking. I'm sweating, can smell the black coffee smell from my armpits, feel the alcohol seeping from my pores from a night of partying. She's too close. I close the wardrobe and jump down from the chair, travel bag still in my hand, chair still beside the wardrobe.

The door opens.

Gina stares at me, looks me up and down. I know it, feel it in my gut, more than any other time and it's come close a lot of times, but I know the moment has come.

'What are you doing?'

'Just want to check up on something for work.'

I'm sweating, my chest is heaving with panic and I try to control it.

'For work,' she says flatly.

Her eyes are dark, her face fierce, I have never seen her look like this before. I feel it slipping away and I'm almost relieved but at the same time I don't want it to go.

'Where did you stay last night?'

'The Winchester.'

'Where?'

'King's Cross.'

'For the Strategic Technology Forum.'

'Yeah.'

'Yes, that's what I thought you told me. So I called. Looking for you. There was no booking in that hotel under your name, no forum. No nothing. Unless you were at an Indian wedding, Fergus, you weren't there.'

She's shaking now, voice and body trembling.

'You were there with one of your slags, weren't you?'

This throws me. She's never accused me of that before. Not directly. She has hinted as much with questions and uncertainty but has never come right out and said it. It makes me feel disgusting, the way she looks at me, the way I've made her feel, reduced her to this version of a woman I've never met. It's over, it's over, she's got me. I give up – or do I? I never give up. One more try. Don't go without a fight.

'No, Gina, look at me . . .' I take hold of her shoulders. 'I was there all right, the conference was in another hotel. It wasn't booked under my name because work booked it through a travel agency and it's probably under their name. I don't know which one, but I can find out.' My voice is too high-pitched, it's weak, it's breaking, it's giving me away. With marbles you never have to speak, your voice can't deceive you.

'Get your hands off me,' she says, voice quiet and threatening. 'What's in the bag?'

I swallow. 'I can't . . . nothing.'

She looks at it and I'm afraid that she's going to grab it, open it, reveal the truth. She's right, I wasn't in The Winchester. I wasn't at a work forum. I was in the Greyhound Inn, Tinsley Green in West Sussex, but I wasn't with another woman. It is where I've been on the same day for the past five years for the World Marble Championships. In my bag are two trophies, the first trophy I've won with my team, and the second is for best individual player. The team is Electric Slags, named after the Christensen Agate transparent-coloured base marbles with opaque white swirls. 'Electric' because Christensen Agate slags are much brighter than those produced by any other manufacturer, the rarest colour being peach. I named the team this because it's a marble that I bought after my liaison in the cabbage field. The marble reminded me of the cream of her skin, her peach hair and lips and the moment in the cabbage field five years earlier, a reminder that my marble life was my secret, my way of cheating. Naming the team after that was branding myself, I think, with a mixture of pride and detestation, recognition and acknowledgement of who I am, a cheat with a title, who wanted to take his secret marble-playing further. It was an instant hit with my teammates, they'd no idea of the real meaning. The marble world is no different to the world of people, it too has its reproductions and fakes, and slags were an attempt to mimic hand-cut stones. Gina is my hand-cut stone, always was, always will be, while my cabbage-field lover and I were only ever slags and we both knew it.

It was a coincidence that Gina used the word slag. She had no idea, I'm certain. My teammates, five other men, know nothing about my personal life, nothing beyond the games we play together and the banter that allows men to avoid any real personal discussion. We've got together five years in a row to win the world championships; this is the first time Ireland have ever won and I can't tell anyone about it. There's a small article in the paper today about the Irish win, accompanied by a grainy photo of the team, me deliberately hiding at the back, you can't make me out. *Electric Slags win for Ireland*. And then of course mention of the best individual player, me, who scored the winning throw.

The game we played was Ring Taw, where forty-nine target marbles are placed on a six-foot raised ring. The surface is three inches off the ground and is covered in sand. The marbles are half an inch in diameter and can be glass or ceramic. Of course we used glass. Two teams of six players get a point each for each marble they knock out of the ring. The first team to knock out twenty-five marbles from the ring is the winner. Electric Slags beat Team USA to become the world champions; apart from Sabrina's birth, the second greatest day of my life. A moment I will no doubt remember forever.

How can I tell Gina now? What would I say? For the past sixteen years I've been lying to you about a hobby of mine. It's been a huge part of my life, but you know nothing about it. Women or no women, that in itself is a betrayal. It's also weird, embarrassing. If I'm hiding a hobby, what else am I hiding? It's gone on too long to explain, to go back. Why is it easier to lie? Because I promised

Hamish. Sneaking out into the night from the age of ten, it was our secret. A secret kept from Ma that we were hustling, a secret from players that I was good. I don't know why, but I kept that secret, like a pact with Hamish, a connection to him. We're the only two, of people who matter in our lives, who know. Just you and me, Hamish. But Hamish is gone and Gina is here and I can't carry on like this for the rest of my life. It will drive me mad, it is already starting to. I feel the pressure more than ever before. I'll tell her. It will be difficult for a while, she won't trust me, but she hasn't for some time anyway. But I'll tell her. Now.

'I'll show you,' I say, taking the bag from behind my back and unzipping it, my fingers shaking like you wouldn't believe. Even in the final moments of the most important game of my life, my fingers were rock steady.

'No!' she says suddenly, afraid, stopping me, hand held out.

I want to tell her it's not what she thinks it is, though I don't know what she thinks it is, but it can't be this.

'No. If you say you were there, you were there.' She swallows hard. 'Everyone will be here in fifteen minutes, please be ready.' She leaves me, the zip open on the bag, the metal of the trophy shining for me to see. If she'd just looked down.

Later that evening, mask back on, sweat washed

off, prawn cocktail and chicken Kiev polished off, pavlova waiting to be eaten, I go in search of Sabrina. I find her curled in a ball on the couch, crying.

'What's wrong, love?'

'John said I look like a slag.'

I take her in my arms, the tears washing away the too much make-up. 'No, you're not that. You'll never be that. But all of this –' I look down at her outfit. 'It's not you, love, is it?'

She shakes her head miserably.

'Remember,' I feel a lump in my throat, 'just always remember to be you.'

20

POOL RULES

No Outdoor Footwear

The Marble Cat is a smart black-framed pub on Capel Street with Kilkenny flags suspended on beams from the frame. It's inviting, advertising its daily specials – root vegetable soup and Guinness brown bread and Dublin Bay prawns – on a blackboard outside, unlike some of the others which wish to shut out the world and light and lock the door behind. It's four p.m. on Friday and it's not yet bustling with end-of-day workers ready to let their hair down and unload their stress for the weekend. The pub is separated into the pub and lounge. I choose the lounge, always less intrusive. Three men sit up at the bar, staring deeply into their pints, with a few empty stools between each of them; they are not together but occasionally converse. Two other men in suits, eating soup and bread rolls, talk shop but there is no one else in the place.

A young barman stands behind the bar, watching the racing on TV. I approach the bar and he looks at me.

'Hi.' I keep my voice down and he comes closer. 'Could I speak to the manager, please? Or anybody who has worked here a long time?'

'Boss is here today, in the bar. I'll get him.'

He disappears through the opening to the pub next door and after a few moments the space is filled by an enormous wide man.

'Here's the marble cat himself,' one man at the bar says, suddenly coming alive.

'Spud, how are ye?' he says, shaking his hand.

He's enormous, over six feet and broad, and it's then when I look around the walls of the pub that I realise who he is. Photographs, trophies, framed jerseys, newspaper articles of All-Ireland finals and wins cover every inch of the walls. Black-and-yellow stripes – the cats – and I realise suddenly what the pub name refers to, part of it at least. Kilkenny hurlers are famously called The Cats, a term which refers to anyone who is a tenacious fighter. I can see him smashing into other players, hurley in hand, before helmets and protective gear, pure solid. A marble man. He leans on the bar to get closer to my level though he's still towering, elbows on the varnished wood.

'They call you the marble cat?' I ask.

'They call me lots of things. Glad it was that one that stuck.' He returns the smile.

'You don't know this fella?' Spud pipes up. 'Six All-Ireland medals in the seventies. Kilkenny's star player. Nothing like him before, nothing like him since.'

'How can I help you?' he asks, turning away from Spud to end the chat.

'My name is Sabrina Boggs.' I watch his face for recognition, Boggs isn't a common name, but there's nothing. 'My dad is having memory problems, and I wanted to help fill in the gaps for him. He used to drink here. He was a regular.'

'Well, you're in luck, because I know every single person that comes through that door, especially the regulars.'

'He played marbles, I thought that's why he chose to come here, but you're not a marble pub.' I laugh at myself.

'Kilkenny is called the Marble City,' he explains kindly. 'The footpaths of the city streets were paved with limestone flagstones and on wet winter evenings they glistened. Hence the name.'

I bet he's told this countless times to American tourists.

'A very dark grey limestone was quarried just outside of the city at a place called the Black Quarry. Between you and me,' he speaks out the side of his mouth and looks around, 'I wanted to give the pub that name, but the money men reckoned the Marble Cat would be better for our pockets.'

I smile.

'But we did play marbles here at one time, you'll be pleased to know. A small group used to come in. What is his name?'

'Fergus Boggs.'

He frowns immediately, then shakes his head. He looks at the men at the bar. 'Spud, you know a fella named Fergus Boggs, played marbles here?'

'Not here,' Spud says, without thinking about it, eyes back in his pint.

'He would have been here five years ago,' I explain, wondering if Regina's story is to be trusted.

I've piqued his curiosity, I can tell. 'Sorry, love, we only had a small marble team in here. Spud, who's here, Gerry, who's in there,' he points to the bar, 'and three other fellas. No Fergus.'

'Show her the winners' corner,' Spud shouts proudly.

The Marble Cat chuckles and lifts the bar counter. He towers over me. 'Let me give you a tour. I don't think Spud wants me to show you any of my walls of fame, but down here is the Electric Slags' corner.'

Feeling disappointed that they've never heard of Dad, I follow him through the bar to the far corner. Spud hops off his stool and follows us.

There is a glass display cabinet on the wall, inside

are two trophies. 'This is the trophy they won at the World Marble Championships back in . . .' he searches his pockets for his glasses.

'Ninety-four,' Spud says immediately. 'April.'

The Marble Cat rolls his eyes. 'The second trophy is for Best Individual Player. Spud didn't win that – I can tell you that without needing my glasses,' he teases, still patting down his pockets.

'And over here is where we got a mention in the paper.' Spud points to the framed newspaper cutout and I move closer to view the photograph.

'If you look close you'll see Spud has hair,' the Marble Cat says.

To be polite I move closer. I follow the line-up and suddenly my heart pounds. 'That's my dad.' I point him out in the line-up.

The Marble Cat manages to locate his glasses and moves his face closer to the frame. Then suddenly he booms, 'Hamish O'Neill! That's your dad?'

'No, no,' I laugh. 'That's wrong. His name is Fergus Boggs. But that's him. Definitely him. Oh my God, look at him, he's so young.'

'That's Hamish O'Neill,' the Marble Cat says, prodding Dad's face with his thick finger. 'And he was a regular. Sure I know him well.'

Spud steps in now too. 'That's Hamish,' he says defensively, looking at me as though I'm a liar.

I'm stunned. My mouth opens but nothing comes

out. My head is racing, too many questions, I'm too confused. I study the photo myself to see if it's Dad at all, maybe I'm the one who's wrong. It was almost twenty years ago, maybe it's somebody that looks like him. But no, it is him. Are they messing with me? Is this a joke? I study them, and their faces are as serious as mine.

'She says her dad is Hamish,' the Marble Cat says to Spud, excited, his voice booming through the pub so that the two men in suits are listening now.

'I heard her.' Spud narrows his eyes at me.

The Marble Cat laughs, his laughter filling the whole place. 'Gerry!' he yells into the bar next door. 'Get in here, you'll never guess who is here!'

'I know who's in there and I'm not going anywhere near him. Not until he apologises!' a man yells back grumpily.

'Well, then you'll be a long time in there,' Spud yells back.

'Ah, would you ignore your feud for a few minutes. What is it, a year now?' the Marble Cat hollers. He walks to the bar, there in three long strides, and shouts through the doorway that leads from the lounge to the bar. 'Hamish O'Neill's *daughter* is here.'

I hear a string of expletives and everyone laughs. Then Gerry appears in the bar, beer in hand, faded jeans, leather jacket. A few men are behind him, they've followed him through to take a look at me.

'Hamish is your da?' one of the men asks.

'No. Fergus Boggs . . .' I say quietly.

The Marble Cat finally recognises my discomfort and tries to calm down what he has revved up. 'Okay, okay, let's take this over here.' He leads me to the nearby table. 'Dara!' he yells as if he's back on the pitch. 'Get this woman a drink! I'm sorry,' he says to me. 'What's your name?'

'Sabrina.'

'Get Sabrina a drink!' he yells and then to me, quieter: 'What will you have?'

'Water, please.'

'Ah, have something stronger, you look like you need it.'

I feel like I need it too, but I'm driving.

'Sparkling water.'

They all laugh.

'Just like your da,' Gerry says, joining us, the other men slinking back to the darkness they came from. 'Never drank when playing. Said it affected his throw.'

They laugh again.

'Gerry, call Jimmy, he'd love to see this,' the Marble Cat barks at him.

I try to interject, more people isn't necessary, I'm feeling overwhelmed and dizzy as it is, but they talk over me, like excited kids. Spud starts to explain in detail how his team, the Electric Slags, won the championship, almost throw by throw, setting up the scene, describing the tension between the Americans and the Irish, and then how Dad threw the winning throw. They're talking over each other, interrupting, fighting, debating, Gerry and Spud absolutely unable to agree on anything, even the slightest detail such as the weather, while I listen, feeling stunned, thinking this all must be a mistake, a misunderstanding. They must be talking about another man. Why was Dad calling himself Hamish O'Neill?

Then Jimmy arrives, twenty years older and with less hair than in the photograph, but I recognise him. He shakes my hand and sits down, seeming quieter and perhaps a bit stunned himself, having been dragged out of wherever he was to be here.

'Where's Charlie?' Spud says.

'On holiday with his missus,' Gerry explains to me, like I know who Charlie is, but I should, he too is in the photograph, a member of the Electric Slags.

'Peter passed away last year,' the Marble Cat says.

'Liver cancer,' Gerry says.

'Shut up, you – it was the bowel,' Spud corrects him, elbowing him in the ribs, which makes Gerry spill his drink and they go at it again.

'Lads, lads,' the Marble Cat tries to calm them.

'I preferred it when you two weren't talking,' Jimmy says.

I smile.

'So you're his daughter?' Jimmy asks. 'Well, it's a pleasure to meet you.'

'She says his name was *Fergus*,' Gerry says excitedly, as though Dad's name was the most exotic he's ever heard. 'I told ye, lads. I always knew it. Something didn't add up with our boy. Spud always said he was a spy, better not to ask him questions in case we got killed.'

They laugh, apart from Jimmy, and Spud who looks at me in all seriousness. 'I did. Was he a spy? I bet you he was.'

They try to quieten him and it turns into a debate: remember the time he did this, remember the time he said that, until they finally shush and look at me.

I shake my head. 'He did a few different things . . . mostly sales.' I try to think of everything about him, to prove that I know him. 'He started in meat, then later mobile phones, mortgages . . .' My voice sounds as though it's coming from very far away, I don't even trust my knowledge any more. Did Dad do any of those jobs or were they all lies?

'Oh yeah, travelling salesman, I heard that before,' Spud says, and they shush him like he's a child.

'His last job was as a car salesman. My husband bought a car from him,' I say pathetically, proving to myself that Dad was in fact *something* that he said he was.

Gerry laughs, hits a stunned and disappointed

Spud in the chest. 'You should see your face,' he laughs.

'I could have sworn he was a spy,' Spud continues. 'He was so cagey. His right hand wouldn't know what his left hand was doing.'

'Come on now,' Jimmy says softly, and they realise I'm here, and this is new to me, and they pipe down.

'When's the last time you saw him?' I ask.

They look at each other for the answer.

'A few months ago,' Gerry says.

'It wasn't,' Spud snaps. 'Don't be listening to him, he can't remember what he had for breakfast. It was more than that. Over a year ago. With that woman.'

My heart beats faster.

'So in love. Jaysus,' Spud shakes his head. 'He never introduced us to a soul in all the years and then all of a sudden he shows up with a woman. Blonde. What was her name?'

'German,' Gerry says.

'Yeah, but what was her name?'

'And Irish,' Gerry continues. 'Funny accent. Funny woman.' He tries to think. 'You must know her?'

'I don't.' I clear my throat.

'It was Cat,' Jimmy says.

They all agree on that.

Cat?

'But she could be using a different name too, for all we know,' Spud says. 'She could be a spy. German one.'

222

They all tell him to shut up.

'Why Hamish?' the Marble Cat asks me, leaning in intently. 'Why did he call himself Hamish O'Neill if his name was Fergus Boggs?'

I search my mind but there's nothing that links to that name. 'I have absolutely no idea.'

Silence.

'I only found out yesterday that he ever played marbles.'

'Mother of divine!' Gerry says. 'So you didn't know about us? The Electric Slags? He never talked about us?'

I shake my head.

They look at each other in surprise and I feel like apologising on his behalf. I know how they feel. Were they not important enough to him?

'Well, maybe you're right about one hand not knowing what the other hand was doing, Spud.'

'Did you say I'm right, Gerry? Jaysus! And I've witnesses and all.'

'So where is he?' Gerry asks. 'It's been a year and none of us have heard from him. Can't say we're too happy with him about that.'

'How is he?' Jimmy asks quietly.

Breathe.

'He suffered a stroke last year which affected his movement and memory. He's been in hospital under full-term care since then. We didn't realise that it had affected his memory as hugely as I think it did

223

now, but recently I've discovered some things about my dad that I never knew, like the marbles, and I'm quite sure he doesn't remember ever playing them. Obviously I don't know everything about his life to know what he remembers or not, that much is quite clear . . .' I try to control my voice. 'He had, has, a lot of secrets, I don't know what he's keeping a secret and what is a lost memory.'

Jimmy looks sad. They all do.

'I can't imagine Hami— your da, not knowing about marbles. They were his whole life,' Gerry says.

I swallow. Then what was I?

'Not his whole life,' Jimmy corrects him. 'We don't know about the rest of his life.'

'Well, we never bloody knew. But I figured the rest of his life at least knew about us,' Gerry says, annoyed.

'You would think,' I say, agreeing with him, sounding a little more snappy than I intend.

There's a silence. A respectful, understanding one, which becomes uncomfortable. I would rather they were bickering.

'Tell me what my dad was like when he was playing marbles,' I say, and then I can't shut them up.

'Sabrina,' Jimmy calls after me when I'm outside.

I have tears rolling down my cheeks and him catching me is the last thing I want. I thought I'd make it to the car at least, but I don't. I don't know if I can hear any more. Who was my dad? Who is my dad? This man that I grew up with that everybody seems to think something differently of. The words of Regina haunt me: He's a liar. Simple as that. As if that answers everything. Does it? No. Does it hurt? Yes. Why did he lie to me? His own daughter. How foolish and stupid I feel for letting him in on my life, on all aspects of my life, even the moments I had marriage troubles. He was always so caring, yet he wouldn't share a thing with me. I feel used, irritated, and even worse I can't storm into the hospital and have it out with him. The man in there simply doesn't remember. How convenient for him. I sound like Mum now, this silent rant in my head. I try to calm myself, forget about it all until I'm in private.

Jimmy takes me by the arm and leads me down the road. We stop by a door beside a tools and hardware shop and Jimmy takes out a set of keys and lets himself in. I follow him upstairs to a studio apartment above the shop. It's basic and I think he must live alone, but then I see a bucket of toys.

'For the grandkids,' he says when he sees me looking. 'I take them every Friday, when my daughter's at work.'

He fills the kettle and boils it. He watches me for a while, concerned.

'It's hard, what you're going through.'

I nod. Trying to pull myself together.

'I know a little bit about that feeling. Your dad made me feel like that too. On his wedding day.'

He has my full attention but he doesn't start talking until he's poured us both a cup of tea and as much as I want to urge him to speak, I know it would be impolite. In his own time. A plate of pink Snacks comes out. Then finally.

'I was a guest on his wedding day. A first proper date with a girl I half-liked. Michelle. She was a bridesmaid, begged me to go to the wedding. Figured there'd be free food and drink, so why not? So I went. Iona Road Parish Church. I remember it well. Big church, all decked out fancy. Her friend Gina was marrying Fergus Boggs. That's all I knew. Wore my brother's suit, showed up, sat down. Didn't know a soul. Or at least, I didn't think I would. But all of a sudden a good friend of mine arrives, and I'm chuffed that I know someone. He's looking pretty dapper too, in a light blue tuxedo suit. Flares. We all wore them then. He walks all the way to the top of the aisle. Stands there, waits. *Is that the best man?* I ask the fella next to me. *Who? Him? No, that's the groom*, the fella says. *Hamish O'Neill is the groom?* says I. Yer man starts laughing. *Are ye at the wrong wedding? That's Fergus Boggs.* I'd swear the floor went from under me. It was as if he'd punched me in the stomach. Couldn't breathe, couldn't get any air. I felt . . . well, I felt like you do now probably, but not as bad for me. He wasn't my dad. But he was my pal. For two years we'd hung around. Hamish O'Neill. Couldn't figure it out.'

'Did you confront him?'

'Never did.'

'Why?'

'I thought about it. Stayed away from him for a while. Easy enough, he was away on honeymoon, then working extra hours to save up to buy a house, that much I knew. But odd thing is, when he was gone, someone came into the pub looking to set up a marble team. Charlie, you didn't meet him, he was away. He'd heard there were two of us in the Marble Cat who played. I told him I was interested, wasn't sure about the other. Had no intention of telling him. But then Hamish . . . Fergus, came back, phoned me to meet for a game and a pint. I told him about Charlie wanting to set up the team and we arranged to meet. We met in the Marble Cat, it was up to me to introduce him to Charlie. I thought about it, it could have been my moment to catch him out, show him I knew, but instead I said, Charlie, this is Hamish, Hamish this is Charlie. And that was that.'

'I don't know how you could do that,' I say, shaking my head. 'If I'd known I couldn't have hid it.'

'Look, none of us are perfect. I certainly don't claim to be. We all have our . . . complications.

227

Thing is, the man must have had his reasons. That's what I always told myself. I thought it would be best to let him tell me, or I'd figure those reasons out. Over time, like.'

'And did you?'

He smiles. A sad smile. 'Well, I am now, aren't I?'

'You and everybody else,' I say angrily.

'He was a good man, as simple as that. Hamish O'Neill, Fergus Boggs or whoever he says he was, it doesn't matter. He was just him. He was fun, sometimes he was grumpy, I don't think he changed his personality, no way a man could do that over forty years. I don't think he was pretending to be someone else. He was just the same man with a different name. That's all. It really didn't matter to me about the name. He was a good man. He was a loyal friend. Was there when I needed him; I'd like to think I was there when he needed me. Didn't have to tell me why or what was wrong. We just played marbles. Shot the breeze and I don't think that a single conversation we had was pretend or made up, it was all real. So your dad is your dad, who he was, who he is – he's the same man you've known all along.'

I try to take that on board but right now I just can't. 'You didn't try to find him when he disappeared last year?'

'Nah, I'm no stalker, or private investigator,' he laughs. 'We'd stopped being a marble team for nearly ten years. We played together sometimes, but we didn't compete. Too difficult to get the lads together, then with Peter getting sick . . .'

'But you were his friend. Did you not wonder where he went?'

He thinks about that. 'He doesn't talk about marbles now at all?'

'Today was the first day. I showed him a few bloodies and I think something happened, they triggered something. I don't think he remembered them before.'

He nods sadly. 'People come and go. Lots of my friends have died,' he says. 'Happens when you get to this age. Cancer, heart attacks . . . it's depressing really. You ask about someone, hear that they've gone. Think of someone you haven't seen in a while and hear that they're dead. Open the paper and see an obituary for someone you once knew. It happens at my age. The way I see it is, when I stopped hearing from him, my pal Hamish O'Neill died too.'

This brings tears to my eyes again. 'Maybe he'll want to see you.'

'Maybe,' he says uncertainly. 'It would be nice to see him. We didn't share everything, but we shared a lot.'

I thank him for the tea and I make a move to go. It's six p.m., I've nowhere to be but I need to leave. I'm not finished yet.

Jimmy leads me downstairs to the door to the street and before he opens it he turns to me. 'He slipped up sometimes, you know. The lads might not remember now, but they definitely noticed it at the time. We used to talk about it: what's Hamish on about now? Who's he on about? Usually it was when he'd had a few. He'd mention names – by mistake, I think. He didn't seem to notice. I think he confused things then, what he'd told us and what he hadn't. I'm sure it got to him in the end.'

I nod and plaster a smile on my face, not feeling any sympathy for Dad right now.

'You know there was only one other time that I ever saw him as happy as when he was with that woman, Cat. Couldn't figure out what it was then, but it makes sense to me a little bit later in my life.'

'What was it?'

'He came practically dancing into the pub one day, bought everyone a drink. *Jimmy*, he says, taking my head in his hands. *Today is the happiest day of my life*. It took something happening in my life to realise what it was that made him like that. When I had my first baby. Happiest day of my life, went dancing into the pub just like your da had. And I knew then what had happened to him. I knew he'd had a baby. April time about thirty years ago. Maybe a little more.'

My birthday. 'Is that true?' I ask, unable to wipe the smile off my face.

'On my grandkids' lives,' he says, holding up his hands.

I'll take that.

21

PLAYING WITH MARBLES

Cat's Eyes

The best thing about having had to sell my car is meeting her. The bills were totting up, the income wasn't, the car had to go. Thirty grand would go a long way. It took a while to make that decision – what's a man without a car? But then when I made it, I never looked back. A financial advisor with no money, no car, and no clients. I was always going to be the first to go; subsequently the company folded, I didn't feel any joy. We're all in the shit together. More fellas like me, looking for the same kind of jobs.

I'm a salesman, have been all my life, it's what I do best, it's all I know. Today is my first day as a car salesman. I'm trying to feel positive, though I feel anything but. I'm fifty-six years old and I don't have a car to get to my job as a car salesman – not that the boss knows that, but he'll figure it out soon enough when he sees me huffing and puffing up the hill from the bus stop to work every morning. My doctor has been at me to exercise, my cholesterol, my blood pressure, everything is bad news. Every envelope I open is bad news. I'm officially a granddad and even little Fergus likes to remind me that I'm fat Granddad as he jumps on my belly. At least these short walks to and from the bus stop will give me some movement.

She's standing alone at the bus stop, trying to figure out the timetable. I know she's trying to figure it out because she's wearing her reading glasses, is chewing on her lip and looks confused with a screwed-up face. It's endearing.

She sighs and mutters to herself.

'Can I help you?'

She looks around in surprise like she thought she was alone. 'Thank you, I can't understand this thing. Where is today? Is this today?' She points with a manicured pink fingernail. 'Or is this today? I'm looking for the number 14 bus, am I even in the right place? And this, you can't read this at all, because some clever person decided to tell the world with a Sharpie that Decko is a fag. I mean, this is no big deal, I know some very happy fags. Decko might be extremely lucky, but not if he wants to get on the number 14 on a Monday morning. Then Decko will be a miserable fag.'

I laugh, it explodes right out of me. I adore her instantly. I study the timetable for some time, not because I'm concentrating, but because I want to be near her, because she smells beautiful. She finally looks at me, lowers her leopard-print reading glasses and I'm faced with the most stunning pair of eyes which illuminate her entire face, make her glow from within.

I must be making my feelings quite obvious because she smiles, in a flattered, knowing way. 'Well?'

'I have absolutely no idea,' I say, which makes her throw her head back and laugh heartily.

'I love your honesty,' she says, taking off her glasses and letting them fall down on a chain to her chest, which is incredibly large and inviting. 'You're new to the bus too?'

'Relatively. I just sold my car. All I know is that I'm to get on the seven fifty bus and stay on it for eighteen stops. My daughter. She likes to make sure I'm safe.'

She smiles. 'My car is the reason I'm here too. Yesterday morning it decided to give up. Poof! just like that.'

'I can sell you a new one.'

'You sell cars?'

'Today is my first day.'

'Then you are doing rather well so far, and not even in the office,' she laughs.

Together we try to figure out how to pay the driver, who won't take our money but insists on us dropping it into a machine. She lets me go first, which means I take a seat first and I'm left wondering will she sit or pass me by. Praise the lord she sits beside me, which makes me feel warm.

'My name is Cat,' she says. 'Caterina, but Cat.'

'I'm Fergus.' We shake hands, her skin is smooth, soft, she's not wearing a wedding ring.

'Scottish?'

'My dad was. We left when I was two, moved to Dublin. What about you? Your accent is peculiar.'

She laughs. 'Thank you very much. I'm from the Black Forest in Germany. The daughter of a good forester. I moved to Cork after university, when I was twenty-four.'

She is addictive, I'm interested in everything about her and I forget the first-day nerves and relax completely in the seat, almost missing my stop. I ask her too many personal questions but she answers and asks back. I tell her too much about me – my debts, my health, my failures – but not in a gloomy way, in an honest way, in a way that we can both laugh.

Leaving her on the bus is like a bubble bursting, I don't have the time or the courage to ask her for her phone number. I almost miss the stop. She presses the bell just in time. The bus pulls in, everybody is waiting for me to squeeze my way out of the seat to get off, all eyes on me. I can't ask her out, it's too rushed, too panicked. I get off the bus feeling enraged.

I spend the first few hours of my first day of work feeling like a spare part that can't quite find its place. The other men aren't too impressed by my hiring. They know I'm a friend of the garage owner, Larry Brennan. It was one of the only favours I had left in my life and the only way I could get a job after five months out of work. We grew up together and he couldn't say no. Probably wanted to, but he couldn't.

As an unpopular man on the floor it is difficult to get to the customers. They jump in before me, manage to somehow distract my clients and poach them. It's dog eat dog.

'No, I want him,' I hear a familiar voice in the afternoon when I feel like I want to go home and eat an entire box of Roses.

And there she is. My colourful, vivid, larger than life, foreign sparkler. On my first day, I make my first sale.

Rather unprofessionally I use her number from the paperwork to call her and ask her out. She is more than happy to hear from me and tells me she wants to cook for me. I go to her apartment on Friday night with a bouquet of flowers, a bottle of red and a clear mission. Tell her everything.

No more secrets. No more separation of my life.

I've come to hate the man I've become. No more secrets. Not with Cat. This is my chance at a fresh start.

Her apartment is a sweet set-up, two bedrooms, one for her and her remaining daughter that she's trying to get rid of. The walls are filled with her own paintings; drying on the windowsill are painted vases and paperweights, with lilac and pink flowers crawling upward, swirls and spirals on the paperweights. I study them while she prepares the food in the tiny kitchen, which smells delicious.

'Oh, I've just started a painting class. Painting on glass, to be specific.'

'It's different to paper?' I ask.

'Indeed, and it costs seventy-five euro to know about it,' she teases.

I whistle.

'Do you have any hobbies?'

It's an easy question, such an easy question for so many people. But I pause. I hesitate, despite my mission I'd firmly decided on all week while waiting for this evening.

Because of my hesitation, she stops what she's doing. She moves to the opening that joins the kitchen to the open-plan dining and living area, oven gloves still on. Those green eyes meet mine.

I feel short of breath suddenly, like I'm admitting something huge. Feel sweat break out on my brow. Do it, Fergus. Say it.

'I play marbles. Collect marbles.' It is not a full sentence, I don't even know it means anything, but I'm gripping the back of the kitchen chair and she quickly takes me in, my posture, my nerves and she smiles suddenly.

'How wonderful. When do you play next?'

'Tomorrow.' I clear my throat.

'I would love to come and see. Can I?'

Taken aback, I agree.

'You know, I was playing with marbles myself today.' She smiles, and has the cop on to talk while I try to compose myself again. 'Yes, I'm a vet. And some very clever people came up with the idea of using a glass marble to keep mares out of heat. Today I put a thirty-five-millimetre glass ball into the uterus of a mare. First time for me, and for the horse. But do you know what? I think she's been learning from these ping-pong clubs: she popped it straight back out again. Expelled it immediately. Got it right second time round, though. You know, the company I got them from call them "mare-bles"!'

I laugh, totally surprised by the ease of her taking my news, then by her own marble story.

'I'll get you one,' she says, going back to the oven. 'I bet you don't have one of them in your collection.'

'No,' I laugh, a little too hysterically. 'No I don't.'

'So tell me about your marbles, tell me about your collection.'

And so I begin at the beginning with Father

Murphy and the dark room with my bloodies, and then I can't stop. I tell her about Hamish and the hustling, I tell her about my brothers, I tell her about the world championships. We drink wine, and eat roast lamb, and I tell her about the games, about my team Electric Slags, I tell her the pubs I play in and how often. I tell her about Hamish, all about Hamish, and I tell her about my collection. I tell her about the marble swearing jar, I tell her about the cheating, I tell her that Gina and Sabrina have never known and I try, with difficulty, to explain why. We drink more wine, and we make love and I tell her more as we lie naked in the dark beside each other. It's like I can't stop. I want this woman to know who I am, no secrets, no lies.

I tell her about my brothers, how I pushed them away and will never forgive myself, and moved by my story, she says that she will cook for them, and I say no, that is too much, I couldn't, we all couldn't. But she is an only child and has always wished for a big family. So over the course of the next few months, she cooks for Angus and Caroline, then Duncan and Mary, Tommy and his date, Bobby and Laura, Joe and Finn. And it's a success, so we do it again, with her friends.

She asks me what was it that struck me about her, that had me hooked on her so quickly – because we were like that, addicted to each other. I say it was her eyes. They're like cat's eyes. Ironically. More specifically foreign cat's eyes, mostly made in Mexico and the Far East. Most cat's eyes are single colour four-vane and the glass has a light bottle-green tint to it. The outer rim of her eyes are bottle rim, the inside almost radioactive they're so bright.

'So what am I worth, in mint condition?' she teases me one morning in bed. 'Me at twenty-one, before my babies, perhaps?'

'You're in mint condition now.' I climb on top of her. 'Look at you . . .' I lift her arms above her head, hold her down. 'You're beautiful.' We kiss. 'But you have no collectable value whatsoever,' I add, and we both erupt with laughter.

She tells me that when I revealed to her my marble-playing hobby she knew from my face that just saying it was a big deal. She said I looked like it was life or death, that for whatever reason it had taken a lot for me to say it, and if she said the wrong thing I would be gone and she didn't want me to leave.

The first gift she gives me is a mare-ble, painted by her, of course.

The only regret I have, each day I spend with Cat, is that I haven't completed the perfection; I have not tied up all of my loose ends. This part will take me time, the part where I introduce Sabrina to Cat. It's not because I don't think they will get along – I know they will – but Cat knows about me, the real me, the marble persona, and Sabrina and Gina are completely unaware. To tell Sabrina about it would be to tell her that I cut her and her mother out of a part of my life for so long that I effectively lied to the two people who were closest to me, who I was supposed to trust, and allow to trust me. I can't think of the words for them. Cat tells me to hurry. She says to say things to people when you can; her ma died before she had a chance to make amends over their falling out. She says you just never know what can happen. I know that she's right. I'll do it soon. I'll tell Sabrina soon.

22

POOL RULES

No Shouting

'Dad had a secret life,' I say, hearing my voice shake as the adrenaline continues to surge through me at the discovery. In the background I hear Alfie having a meltdown over baked beans; he doesn't want beans, he only wants marshmallows, or Peppa Pig shaped pasta. Aidan tries to calm him down while listening to me. I keep talking. 'He was an entire *other person. Hamish O'Neill*,' I say angrily. 'Did you ever hear him use that name?'

'Hamish O'What? No! Alfie, stop. No way, honey. Tell me more. Fine, you can have marshmallows for dinner.'

Confused by who Aidan is addressing at any time, I just keep talking. 'I met these men in the pub, they were on his marble team, they had never even heard of me. Said Dad was secretive, one of them thought he was a spy . . .' My voice breaks and I stop talking, concentrate on the road. I've taken two wrong turns and an illegal U-turn where everyone beeped me out of it.

'Sabrina,' Aidan says, worrying, 'do you want to wait until I'm home to look into this further?'

'No,' I snap. 'I think it's rather apt. Don't you? With everything you've been saying about me.'

He's quiet. 'Sabrina, you're not him, that's not what I was saying.'

'I'll call you later. There's somebody else I need to see.'

'Okay. Just . . .'

'Don't say *if I think it will help*, Aidan.'

He's silent.

Alfie suddenly roars down the phone, 'Beans make you fart, Mammeeee,' before we're cut off.

I never called Mattie Granddad because Dad never called him Dad. I must have questioned it at some stage as a child, but I don't ever remember the answer, I don't remember ever wondering why he wasn't Granddad, I just always knew he wasn't Dad's dad. I was told that my granddad died when Dad was young and Mattie married my grandma, who quite honestly scared me. They both did.

But it strikes me as odd now, at thirty-three years

old, that despite the fact Mattie raised my dad from the age of six, I never considered him my granddad. Disrespectful.

Grandma Molly was tough, not soft like my Nana Mary, and I felt she viewed me as though I never acted grateful enough, reminding me of my pleases and thank yous a thousand times a day and leaving me jumpy and never completely comfortable.

In later years Mum told me Grandma Molly always said to her, 'You give that child too much.' She also used to have a go at Mum about not having any more children, which for some reason wasn't happening for them. Now it could be treated, but back then, Mum just kept trying. I think that had a huge part to do with how their relationship went sour, apart from the fact they were very different people who had different opinions on almost everything. Mum couldn't take the criticisms from her mother-in-law, who'd spent her entire life having and raising children, it was the entire point of her life.

'I wasn't used to someone not liking me,' Mum once told me. 'I tried really hard with her, but she still didn't like me. She didn't ever want to like me.'

The one thing they had in common was their love of Fergus.

When Dad visited Grandma Molly he did so mostly on his own. He called in on her from time to time, on the way home from work or on the way into town. Sometimes I was with him, sometimes not. We'd all meet at Christmas for an hour on Christmas morning. I'd sit quietly, overly thankful for my new set of pyjamas, while they all chatted. She died when I was fourteen and it felt like somebody I didn't know had died. Secretly I felt a bit relieved that I wouldn't have to visit her any more. Visiting her was a dreaded chore. Then at the funeral I saw my cousins, who I barely knew, all in tears and being consoled by my uncles over their loss, and I felt so guilty because I didn't care as much as they did. I didn't feel the loss like they did. And then I cried.

When I married Aidan I felt the right thing to do was invite Mattie to the ceremony and reception. Mattie didn't come.

I have rarely given Mattie much thought. My children don't know him, I never visit him. My mum abhors him, thinking him a vile old man who got even worse when Molly died. But again, I feel guilty about that. I thought Dad wanted nothing to do with his family, he certainly behaved that way, and I thought it was no big deal if we went along with that, if it was a relief to us. But now I wonder why I didn't probe, press, encourage, wonder. Why? And as his secrets come to the fore, I want to know these people. I want to know why Dad became the way he became.

Mattie is almost ninety years old and lives alone in a ground-floor one-bedroom flat in Islandbridge.

I know his address because I send him an annual Christmas card. A photo of the kids every year. He's not expecting me to call.

'Who is it?' he yells.

'Sabrina,' I say, then add just in case: 'Sabrina Boggs.'

'Who?' he yells.

I hear the door being unlocked and we stand face to face. After squinting and glaring, looking me up and down, it is clear that a further explanation is required.

'I'm Fergus's daughter.'

He takes me in again, then turns and shuffles back to his armchair in front of the TV. He's wearing a short-sleeved shirt with a stained white vest beneath and he makes an effort to button it up with his gnarled fingers. He's older but pretty much exactly as I remember him during my childhood visits. In an armchair, distracted by the TV.

'Sorry I didn't go to your wedding,' he says straight away. 'I don't go out much to social things.'

I'm embarrassed. The wedding was in Spain and I knew he wouldn't make it. 'I know Spain wasn't easy for a lot of people, but I wanted you to know you were welcome.'

'Made a change for me to be invited somewhere instead of the Boggs,' he chuckles. He's missing some teeth.

'Oh, yes,' I redden again. 'It was a numbers issue,

my family is so big that we just couldn't include everyone.'

His stare doesn't make it easier for me.

'You're not in touch with them.'

'With . . . my uncles? I wish that hadn't happened,' I say, genuinely meaning it, though I never realised it before. Sitting before me is the man who raised my dad and he's a stranger to me. 'Dad wasn't close with them, unfortunately, and I suppose that had an effect on me and them,' I explain.

'They were as thick as thieves,' he says, the thick sounding like 'tick'. 'They called him that. Tick. Did you know that?'

'They called Dad thick?'

'No. Tick. Because he was the smallest. The smallest Boggs.'

I have a feeling the house was split into Doyles and Boggs. I never asked Dad about whether it was an issue for them growing up. Why didn't I?

'But he held his own,' he says. 'He outsmarted them.'

I feel proud.

'Not that it was hard, with them pack of feckin' eejits,' he snorts.

'Does the name Hamish O'Neill mean anything to you?'

'Hamish O'Neill?' he asks, frowning, like it's a test and he's failed. 'No.'

I try not to express my disappointment.

'But there was a Hamish Boggs,' he says, trying to be helpful. 'The eldest Boggs boy.'

I nod, my mind whirring. I'd forgotten about Dad's eldest brother up until now, his name hardly mentioned. 'I've heard of Hamish. Were he and Dad close?'

'Hamish?' he says, surprised, as if he hasn't thought of him since he died. 'Him and Hamish were glued together. Your da would follow him around like a lapdog; Hamish would throw a stick and your dad would scramble to get it. Hamish was clever, you see. A dumb git, like I said, but he was clever. He'd find the smartest fella in the room and he'd keep him under his thumb. Did that to your da. It worried his ma no end.'

This is new to me. I sit up.

He thinks for a while.

'Smartest thing to do was keep Hamish away from the lot of them. I kept telling Molly that.'

'And did she?'

'Well, he died, didn't he?' he says, and laughs a cruel laugh. When I don't join in, he brings it to a slow end. 'That lad didn't get what wasn't deserved,' he says, finger wagging at me.

'How did Hamish die?'

'Drowned. London. Some fella punched him, he was worse for wear, fell into a river.'

I gasp. 'That's awful.' I'd known he'd died, but never knew the details. Never asked for them. Why hadn't I?

He looks at me, surprised that someone would think it so tragic after all these years, as though Hamish wasn't a real person. And now I can see he's wondering what my visit is about.

'Was my dad very upset when Hamish died?'

He thinks about it, shrugs a little. 'He had to view the body. Flew over on his own. Angus wanted to go, but sure I couldn't be sending all my staff away to London.' He raises his voice defensively, still fighting a forty-year-old argument over sending Dad over on his own. 'Ara' it was probably tough for him on his own over there. His ma was worried. First time away and all that, seeing his brother dead, but he had to go – the authorities thought it was him that was dead.'

'They thought my dad was dead?' I'm not sure I've heard correctly.

'Seems good ol' Hamish had been using Fergus's name in London. God knows why, but if you piss off enough people like that boy did you'd have to change your name ten times over. He'd probably have worked his way through the entire family if he hadn't died.'

My heart pounds at that discovery, a clear link to Dad's alternate name.

'Come to think of it I remember hearing about a Hamish O'Neill,' he says suddenly. 'Funny, you've reminded me now. Knew it was familiar when you said it. Here's a funny story . . .' He shifts in his chair, livens up. 'I'd been hearing things about a lad, Hamish O'Neill, playing marbles locally. Didn't mean anything, but Hamish wasn't a common name around and when you'd hear it, a fella would listen out, and O'Neill, well, that was Molly's maiden name, before she became Boggs, and then Doyle. It didn't mean anything, but I told Molly. I was drunk, shouldn't have said it maybe, we were at the wedding – Fergus's wedding – and, no offence to your ma, but it was so hoity-toity the fuckin' thing drove me to the drink and gave me a loose tongue. So after I tell her, she chats to your da, him in his fancy blue suit and frilly shirt and looking like a poofter, and I see her slap him across the face. "You're not him," she says.'

He's laughing at this, laughing so hard, at the image of my dad being slapped by his mother on his wedding day. My eyes fill with tears and I try to blink them away.

'That put him in his place,' he says, wiping his eyes. 'Now I never knew if it was your da playing or if it was another fella, a coincidence as they say, but there weren't many who played marbles at that age, not around where we lived anyway. Ever since he was a mucker he'd be out on the road all day, playing, you'd have to bait him to get in for dinner. Every birthday and Christmas present, all he wanted for was feckin' marbles. All the lads were the same, but your da was the worst because he was the best.

He even hung out in some dodgy places with Hamish, Hamish taking him under his wing, thinking he was some bigshot agent making a few quid from his baby brother. I told your da when he was a teenager: "You'll never meet a wife if ye keeps playing those feckin' things." He gave up when Hamish died. At least it did him good that way.'

I came here looking for answers, for insight into Dad's life, though I wasn't sure if I'd get them. But if Hamish used Dad's name in London, it explains why Dad used Hamish's name for marble playing. As a sign of respect? Remembrance? To honour him? To bring him back to life? And no wonder Dad played marbles in secret, when everyone around him was telling him to stop. But why continue this into his adult life?

'How did Dad feel about Hamish having used his name?'

'Couldn't understand it myself, but your da took it as a compliment. Proud as punch that Hamish had stolen his name. Like he was something special. Puffed-out chest and all at the funeral. Silly boy didn't realise that Hamish was getting him in a world of trouble using his name. If Fergus had set foot in the wrong place at the wrong time, Hamish could have got his brother killed. But Hamish was like that, I told you: a leech. Sucking up everything in a person and moving on.'

There's a long silence.

'How did you and Grandma meet?' I ask suddenly, wondering what possessed her to marry this man after the death of her husband.

'Met her in the butcher's shop. She bought her meat from me.'

That was it.

'Must have been true love to marry a woman with four children,' I say, trying to bring positivity to it.

'Those four runts?' he asks. 'She's bloody lucky I married her at all.'

I take in the surroundings. It's simple and clean, he is keeping it well.

'Laura will be here soon,' he says, following my gaze. 'Tommy's daughter.'

'Oh, right. Of course.' I try to think of the last time I met my cousin.

'She comes on Fridays, Christina on Mondays, the lads every day in between, checking up on me to make sure I haven't keeled over and have maggots coming out of my eyes. That's why they moved me over here: Laura lives across the way, they can keep a better eye on me that way, stop me getting up to mischief,' he chuckles. '"Are ye all right, Grandda? Are ye still alive, Grandda?" Ah, they're a good lot, the Doyles. Tommy and Bobby's kids. Bobby's not with the ma any more, you hear that?'

I shake my head.

'Sad to hear that, I liked her. But Bobby can't get

enough of the women, never could, and Joe can't stand them. He's a queer, you know that?'

'He's gay, yes, I know.'

'I blame his ma for that, always suffocating him – don't go here, don't go there – while the rest of them went out and about and raised themselves.'

'I'd say he was gay no matter how she was with him,' I say, having had enough of him now.

He laughs, 'That's what he says, but what do I know?'

Silence then. Uncomfortable. We've both reached the end of our chat.

'How's your da?'

'He's okay.'

'Still doesn't remember much?'

'Not everything.'

'No harm,' he says, almost sadly to himself. 'They wish he'd remember them though. Talk about it all the time.'

'Who?'

'The Boggs boys. The Doyle boys.'

'Of course Dad remembers them.'

'Not the recent years.'

'Well, I suppose they weren't close in recent years,' I say.

'But they were,' he says, riled up like I've accused him of lying. 'These past few years they'd started meeting up again. They played marbles, would you believe. Them and his new woman. They all liked her. No offence to your ma, but they said this one was good for him. Kept them all together. He doesn't remember any of that?' He looks at me like he doesn't believe my dad's memory loss.

I shake my head, completely taken aback.

'Do you know her name?'

'Whose?'

'His . . . girlfriend. This woman.'

'Ah, now,' he waves his hand dismissively. 'Never met her. But the boys know. They can tell you.'

With a weak, 'Tell your ma I was asking for her,' he closes the door and I just manage to avoid my cousin Laura, who's carrying a vacuum cleaner and a bucket and mop across from an opposite flat on the other side of the courtyard. I sit in my car feeling stunned by what I've learned.

I search through my phone for my Uncle Angus's number. He is my godfather, the one I have most contact with, which is limited to text messages on birthdays on the years that we remember.

I dial his number and hold it to my ear, my heart pounding. Hello Uncle Angus, Sabrina here, you haven't heard from me in almost a year but I've just learned that you and Dad were pals again before his stroke and I've also just learned that you knew his girlfriend. Could you please tell me, who is she? Because I don't know. I seem to be the only one, apart from Dad, who doesn't know.

No answer. I hang up the phone, feeling angry

and stupid once again. As the anger surges through me I turn the key in the ignition and pull out. As I drive towards the hospital I hear Mattie's words in my head, calling Hamish a leech.

At the time I felt Mattie was overly harsh. I could understand Dad feeling special and honoured by the fact Hamish hadn't forgotten him when he'd moved away. Dad obviously looked up to Hamish his whole life, thought the world of him, it was an honour for his brother to have taken his name. But as the anger seeps through me, I feel Mattie's words now.

Whether he planned to or not, Hamish did suck some of the life from Dad, and in doing so not only stole a part of Dad from me, but worse, Hamish stole a part of Dad from himself.

23

PLAYING WITH MARBLES

Aggravation

Cat leaves me after a dinner of salmon, garlic fondant potatoes and peas and green beans made by Mel, who's a marvel in the kitchen and often cooks with produce from the small allotment here on the yard, helped by a few of the inmates, but not grumpy Max. He has nothing to do with anything and complains about everything. Cat kisses me gently on the forehead and I like it, it is so long since I've felt that kind of intimacy. I now realise that visits from Gina are cordial in comparison, not affectionate. Sabrina's boys shower me with cuddles and hugs and thumps and clambering, and I love that; Sabrina's hugs are maternal-like, always worried about me; but Cat, I feel a connection with her, an intimacy. I look up to her for more, but perhaps that is asking for too much on what we jokingly call our first date. My great fear, as Lea wheels me to my bedroom for the evening, is that I won't remember Cat tomorrow. How many times did this very event occur in the last year for me to forget it again the next day or a few days later, maybe even a year?

'Penny for your thoughts, Fergus,' Lea says, picking up on my concerns as usual.

'I don't know.'

'You don't know?'

She helps me up out of my chair and I sit on the toilet. She leaves to give me privacy and returns to help when I'm finished.

Do I want Cat to have to do this for me? Is there a future for us? Am I going to improve? I was happy here, bumbling along, existing, living, being cared for, no pressures. But with her out there, knowing there is a life that I had but didn't know it until today, it makes me uneasy. I need to be there, I should be there. I need to get better, I need to wipe my own bloody arse.

'But,' Lea says, cutting into my thoughts, 'the other way of looking at it is that there's someone there for you, waiting for you, helping you. Someone who loves you. That should motivate you, Fergus.'

I'm confused. Have I said those thoughts aloud?

'And the other thing is, you've remembered quite

a lot more today than usual. That's major progress. Remember when you couldn't move your right arm? And then all of a sudden you did? Knocked that glass of water right over on top of me, but I didn't care, I was jumping up and down like a happy lunatic, had to hold my boobs and everything, remember?'

I laugh along with her, remembering the moment.

'Glad that smile is back now, Fergus. I know it's scary, changes can be scary. But remember it's all good, you're getting better every single day.'

I nod, thankful.

'Have you had enough for the day?' she asks, standing at the end of my bed, holding my feet like she doesn't even realise it.

'Why?'

'Because you've a few visitors to see you. I thought I'd wait and see how you're doing before telling them if they can come in or not. Just maybe you've had enough today. I don't want to tire you out.'

'No, no, I'm not tired at all,' I lie. I do feel exhausted from the day, the places my mind has brought me, the day with Cat, but I'm curious. I look at the clock. It's eight p.m. 'Who's here?'

'Your brothers.'

'All of them?' I say, surprised. I've seen them of course over the past few years, but never all of us together.

'Well, there's five of them, I don't know if that's all of them.'

Five. Is that all of them? No Hamish. There hasn't been a Hamish for forty years, but I've always felt that he's missing. No. Five is not all of them.

'Will I tell them to come in? It's okay if you don't want to,' she says, concerned.

'It's okay. Tell them I want to see them.'

'Okay. And Dr Loftus will probably call in to see you as well.'

Dr Loftus, the resident psychologist I have weekly sit-downs with, has obviously heard the news of my memory today.

'I'm off to the office to do some paperwork, but Grainne is here if you need her.'

Grainne. Who grunts when she lifts me from my chair to anywhere like I'm a sack of potatoes she wants to get rid of. 'Thanks, Lea.'

'You're welcome.' She winks, then she's gone.

I hear them before I see them and they have me smiling before they even arrive in the door, a bunch of teenagers pushing, shoving and bouncing off each other as they make their way in, though they don't look that way any more.

Angus, the oldest, is sixty-three and has practically lost all his hair, Duncan is sixty-one, I'm fifty-nine, Tommy is fifty-five, Bobby the charmer is fifty and Joe the baby is forty-six.

'Surprise!' they announce, ducking their heads in the door.

'Shh,' someone says outside, probably Grainne,

and they all grumble and give her abuse as they close the door on her.

'We heard you had a good day,' Angus says. 'So we thought we'd celebrate.' He takes out a bottle of whiskey from his coat. 'I know you can't drink it, but we fucking can so not a word out of you.'

They laugh and try to find enough places in the small room to perch, settle and sit.

'Who told you I had a good day?'

'Cat,' Duncan says easily, to a few disgruntled stares from the others.

'You know Cat?'

'Who doesn't fucking know Cat? Oh, that's right, you didn't until today,' Tommy says, and that's the ice-breaker everyone needed. Tommy slides the chair over to Bobby for him to have. Bobby sits down despite his brother being older, but some things never change.

'She said you told her about the swear jar,' Bobby says.

'I did.'

'When did you remember that?'

'I'm surprised you even remember that,' Duncan says. 'You were always off stuffing worms up your hole.'

They explode with laughter while Bobby protests with, 'That was one time, all right!'

Dr Loftus enters. 'Do I hear a party in here?' he asks jovially, then fixes me with that intense look.

There's barely room for all of us in here; it gets hot quickly, particularly under his gaze.

'So tell us, Fergus,' Angus says, pouring Dr Loftus some whiskey. 'How did you remember the swear jar?'

I look out of the window, the moon high in the indigo sky, full and perfect, and I think of Sabrina. Lea's dimples, Sabrina's nose. That got it started.

'The moon,' I say.

'You don't believe in that voodoo stuff?' Angus says.

'I do,' Tommy says. 'I could tell you a thing or two.'

'I do too,' Duncan agrees.

'There could be something in it, all right,' Dr Loftus says, rubbing the stubble on his face. 'It's been an interesting day so far.'

'Sabrina could never sleep during a full moon,' I say, and they keep a respectful silence. They're a rowdy bunch but they know their place.

Joe hasn't said anything at all since he entered, the baby in the corner, observant and concerned. Self-contained. I'm surprised he's here at all, but appreciative.

'Which one of you stole the fucking marble swear jar?' I say suddenly, which sends them into a spin, laughing. Angus literally nearly pisses himself and launches into a spiel about his prostate, Tommy who smokes too much almost coughs to death. They argue and blame one another, voices raised over each other, fingers pointed, the banter flying.

I remember the moment. There were about fifty marbles in the jar, we'd had a busy swearing month that time. I'd made a new friend in secondary school, Larry 'Lampy' Brennan, who was big into swearing. He'd get himself into trouble and I'd get him out of it. My favourite rainbow cub scout had landed itself in the jar after I'd told Bobby he was a fat fuck and I desperately wanted it back. I'd been to the chemist every week, not caring what was in the brown paper bag, I'd helped peel potatoes, carrots, cleaned the toilet outside, I was the best boy that month.

'It was probably you and you can't remember,' Angus says as soon as he's gathered himself. 'You're not getting away with that.'

We all laugh.

'I don't think it was me,' I say, really believing it, feeling the wrench of finding it gone.

'To be honest, I always thought it was you,' Tommy says. 'You were always going on about the . . . what was it called, lads?'

'Rainbow cub scout,' they all say in unison, apart from Joe.

Dr Loftus laughs at them.

'You kept on at Ma about swapping it with another one, but she wouldn't let you,' Tommy recalls.

'She was a hard one,' Angus shakes his head, 'bless her soul. I thought it was you too, to be fair.'

'It was me,' Joe finally speaks up and everyone turns to stare at him in surprise. He laughs, guiltily, not sure whether he's about to be beaten up.

'It can't have been you,' I say. 'What were you – two? Three?'

'Three, one of my first memories. I remember pulling the kitchen chair over to the shelf, pulling it down. I put it in my cart – remember the wooden one with the blocks?'

Bobby nods.

'Just you two lads had that, we never had anything so fancy,' Angus teases, but there's truth in it. Bobby and Joe always had more than we ever did, the last two babies while we were all out of the house working and giving Ma money that she poured into those babies, mostly Joe.

'I pulled it down the alley, behind the house, then threw it over the wall at the end. It smashed.'

'Where was Ma?' I ask, stunned. I never suspected Joe, not for a second, the rest of us fought for weeks about that.

'Chatting to Mrs Lynch about something, something important, heads together, smoking, you remember.'

We chuckle at the image.

'She noticed I was gone at one point. I remember

her grabbing me in the alley and dragging me and the cart home. So it was me. Sorry, lads.'

'Jesus, good one, Joe. You got us.'

He's earned some respect in the room and we think about that revelation in a surprised silence.

'You could've caught a cold, I suppose,' I say, thinking of Ma's fear of losing Joe, and they all look at me in surprise and laugh their arses off again.

'We brought you something,' Angus says as the laughter dies down. 'One game and we're gone, if that's okay with Dr Loftus?'

'Perfectly fine with me.'

'Tada!' Duncan lifts up a game of Aggravation.

When a member of the family leaves or dies, it changes the dynamics of a family. People move and shift, take up places they either wanted to have or are forced into roles they never wanted. It happens without anybody noticing, but it's shifting all the time.

The week that we hear Hamish left Ireland for London, and the week I'm in trouble with the gardai for being with Hamish when he beat up those boys in school, Ma is like a banshee. She won't let any of us leave the house, go anywhere, do anything. Angus has a school dance she won't let him go to, which is a big deal, so he's in a foul mood especially as Siobhan was going to let him pop her cherry. It's pissing rain outside and we're killing each other, testosterone levels high as we're all on top of each other in the two-bed house. Mattie is close to beating the living daylights out of all of us and he goes to the pub for the umpteenth time that day.

I come up with an idea. I spend an hour in a corner of our bedroom, the only space and peace that I can find, and I work on it. Duncan accuses me of wanking and gets a clatter over the head from Angus, which is surprising, the first protective action from him. He's probably surprised himself but he stands by it and for the first time Ma doesn't punish him because he only did her job by telling Duncan off, which makes Angus and Ma allies, and Angus and me allies. The dynamics are shifting and it's confusing.

I come into the living room with a handmade game of Aggravation, a game I'd seen in my marble book. It's a board game for up to six players and the object of the game is to have all players' pieces reach the home section of the board. The playing pieces are glass marbles, and we can choose our own as long as we can tell them apart. The game's name comes from the action of capturing an opponent's piece by landing on its space, which is known as aggravating – something we'd been doing to each other all week since Hamish left for good.

We play the game. We sit around the dining table, and Ma and Mattie can't believe it as for one whole hour we battle it out on the cardboard game. Bobby wins the first game. I am the best marble player, but this game has nothing to do with skill and everything to do with the roll of the dice. Bobby the charmer has always been the luckiest bastard of all of us.

We play that game all day, every day for a week until Ma is sick of us under her feet and says we can go out. In a way it teaches us about finding our place, our base, in the family and not just through the game, but from the sitting down and spending so much time together, quarantined together and learning to live without Hamish.

We play it again in my room forty years later; not the homemade version but a real game that Duncan has bought. Bobby wins again.

'You lucky bastard!' Angus says disbelievingly. 'Every single time.'

I roll the marbles in my left hand, my right side was the paralysed side, the side that now has limited movement, so I couldn't knuckle down like I used to, even if I wanted to. But I like the feel of them in my hand, rolling them around, and I like the familiar clink as they tap against each other. It's rhythmic and it's relaxing. 'I'm sorry,' I say suddenly.

They stop bickering and look at me.

'For all those years. What I did. I'm sorry.'

'Ah, would you stop it, you've nothing to be sorry

for,' Angus says. 'We were all . . . we all had our own thing going on.'

I start to cry and I can't stop.

Dr Loftus politely tells them to leave, and I feel their supportive hands on my head and shoulders, patting me as they say their goodbyes. Angus stays with me, my protective big brother that stepped up to the plate when his nemesis had disappeared. He hugs me, holds me, rocks me, cries with me, until my tears finally subside and I fall asleep, utterly exhausted.

24

POOL RULES

No Littering

I'm driving and I can't breathe. My chest feels tight and my muscles are tense and I'm about to shout at anybody who so much as looks at me the wrong way, and whoever makes the slightest mistake on the road will get it. I'm racing to confront Dad and I know this is a bad idea. He remembers nothing, I know we are to be gentle with him, no aggressive pushing on matters he simply can't remember as it will upset him, but I am raging. It seems everybody knew about this woman and these marbles apart from me and Mum. His own family. It took the arrival of a box of marbles to learn this? What else is there about Dad, about everything in my life, that I don't know?

I park in the car park and clamber out. The car park is quiet, it's after nine p.m., not many visitors now that they've returned home for their Friday night out, or their Friday night in.

I race through the front doors, and as I wind my way through the corridors I slow down, my chest heaving with the effort of holding back an emotion I don't want to release. What am I doing? I can't go into Dad like this, it will worry him, upset him, set him back, stress him. I'm not even sure I can talk. I slow down to a stop. I smell chlorine. It's comforting. I have lived in the water since I was a child. I liked that it was my own world, I could float and drift and not have to speak to anybody, explain anything, just swim beneath the surface. It was always my escape. It still is now.

I've slowed down but my mind is still racing. It's getting darker and the moon is visible, perfectly round and full, keeping an eye on me as I've gone about my day, on this most peculiar day. And the biggest thought of all which occurs to me now is this: am I this closed, inside person that Aidan tells me I am because my dad was somehow shadowy and secretive? Did I get this trait from him? Though I never picked up on it when I was younger, never thought of Dad as shadowy and never considered myself as closed, until Aidan started mentioning it. Perhaps it's true that you never know yourself until someone else truly knows you. Today's mission stopped being about looking for missing marbles early on, it grew to become a quest to look for the man who owned them. I didn't know that it would mean eventually looking at myself. And I don't like what I've found. I don't like any of these discoveries. I can't breathe.

I stop walking altogether and instead turn and make my way towards the swimming pool. Through the viewing pane of glass I can see that it's empty; of course, nobody swimming at this time, and physio all finished for the day. It's 8.5 metres long, the tiles beneath are blue, the tiles on the wall are blue, with a wave effect in shades of blue mosaics. I pull the door open and the chlorine hits me.

I hear somebody call out. I'm not supposed to be in here. I can hear footsteps behind me. I speed up. They speed up. More footsteps. Then someone calls my name. I can't breathe, I can't breathe. My chest is tight. I think of Dad, I think of Hamish, I think of the marbles and the secret woman. I think of Aidan and me. I kick off my shoes. I rip off my cardigan. I dive in. I escape. And I breathe.

I don't want to ever come back up. I stay close to the floor of the pool, feeling weightless and free, the tension gone. I don't have to think, my body relaxes, my heart rate reduces. I see the legs and feet of others by the edge of the pool, shimmering like mirages, like I'm the only real thing here. I hear the water in my ears, smell the chlorine, love how my hair tickles my skin, feeling like velvet as it moves with me. I tumble and twirl around the pool floor, perhaps looking like a beached whale, but feeling like a ballerina, graceful as can be. I don't know how long I've been under. Over a minute, maybe two, but I'm feeling the need to go to the surface to get some air, just a quick gulp and then under again. This is what I love about being in a pool, this is my territory, I'm safe here.

I hear the sound of clapping or slapping and look around to see a hand slapping the water like they're calling a dolphin.

I whoosh to the surface.

Gerry, the kind porter, is looking at me with worry, concern, confusion, like I've completely freaked out and lost the plot. Mathew from security is halfway between amused and angry, but Nurse Lea is smiling.

I've attracted quite the crowd at the viewing pane. No sign of my dad, thankfully. I float on my back.

'Come on, Sabrina,' Lea says, reaching out her hand.

I'm tempted to pull her in with me.

The moon made me do it.

But I don't. Instead I climb out, a sopping mess.

'Feel better?' she asks, wrapping a towel around me.

'Much.'

25

PLAYING WITH MARBLES

Bottle Washers

The last time I saw Hamish before he was a corpse in London was when we parted ways in the alley after he beat up those two schoolboys. I was fifteen, he was twenty-one years old.

It was the last time I saw him.

But it wasn't the last time I heard from him.

I'm seventeen, I've finished school, the only one out of Hamish, Angus and Duncan who made it to the end. They're working with Mattie and I know that will be what I'll have to do too, there's nothing else I can think of that I want, but before that begins, I'm going to have an entire summer ahead of me to do whatever I want. Mattie can't give me a job until September because he has another young lad as an apprentice. Doesn't mean I get to sit on my arse though. I got a job working on the school grounds with the groundskeeper, Rusty Balls. Not his real name but we nicknamed him that because he's so old he practically squeaks when he walks. I'm making my own money but I pay Ma every penny I earn. She gives me back an allowance as she sees fit. It's always been that way with everyone. All the bills are in Mattie's name and Ma takes care of paying them all. It's unusual for me to get anything from the postman is what I'm saying.

I go home at lunchtime covered in muck, thorns and pine needles stuck in my skin, calluses on my hands, scratches on my face from clearing the bushes of beer bottles and rubbish. Bobby and Joe are playing outside on the road, down on all fours, dirty legs and hands as they concentrate on racing snails against each other. There hasn't been a marble played on the road since we all went to work. I always want to play but the lads are too lazy. They want to go out with their girlfriends or go to the pub with Mattie. No one ever wants to play marbles with me. Tommy's twelve and he's still as useless as a chocolate teapot. Neither Bobby nor Joe ever caught the marble bug, it seems to have been a solely Boggs trait. I know a few lads that still play but they're hard to find; seems as though everyone is outgrowing marbles except for me.

Bobby and Joe warn me about Ma's mood, so I

kick off my dirty boots and leave them outside and intend on doing everything right from the get-go. I can't think of anything I've done wrong today.

'What's this?' she snaps at me when I walk in.

She's standing beside the table, knuckles resting on the plastic cover like she's an ape.

'What's what?'

'This.' She jerks her head at it like it can hear her.

I look at the table and see a parcel. 'I don't know.'

'Don't tell me you don't know, you do know,' she snaps at me.

I step closer and look at it. My name is written in capital letters in black pen on the only piece of brown paper that hasn't been covered in brown sticky tape.

'I don't know, Ma, honest.'

She can tell I'm genuinely surprised. The ape knuckle goes from the table to the hip.

'Is it from Marian?' I ask. Ma's brother Paddy lives in Boston and his wife Marian is the only person who ever sends me anything. She's my godmother, I've only met her once and I don't really remember her but every birthday and Christmas card has some sort of miraculous medal inside. I don't believe in them but I stuff them in the bottom of my underwear drawer, because it would be bad luck to throw them out completely.

Ma shakes her head. She looks worried. The only

reason she didn't open it is because she's afraid. Ma doesn't believe in privacy, what is in her house is hers, but she's looking at it like it's a bomb about to explode in her face. She's like that with new things, or if anything out of the ordinary happens. The same with new people in the house: she's quiet, looks at them like they're about to attack her, and she gets all defensive and snappy because she doesn't know how else to react.

I don't want her to watch me open it but I can't figure out how to say that to her.

'I'll get you a knife,' she says, going to the kitchen. At first I think it's so I can defend myself from whatever jumps out and then I realise it's to open it.

While she's in there we hear a blood-curdling scream coming from outside and Ma goes rushing outside to her baby Joe. While Bobby tells Ma about the bee that stung Joe, I grab the knife and slip upstairs to my room. The parcel has been badly wrapped, a lot of brown tape all over the place makes it a tough job to open, but I manage it finally and toss the paper aside. All I can see is a load of scrunched-up newspapers. Inside is a blue glass bottle. I'm confused. It takes me a while to see what I'm looking at but after some inspection I see that it's empty and on the top there's a rubber washer in the neck. Inside, there's a marble. My heart starts pounding and I know who it's from. Well, I don't know for sure, but I'm guessing it's from Hamish.

It's been a year and a half since he left and I haven't heard a thing, but this feels like a message from him. I root through the crumpled-up newspaper pages on the ground, searching for a note, but there's nothing. My eyes finally fall upon a pair of tits. And then another pair of tits. I quickly uncrumple every single piece of paper to find it has been protected by two weeks' worth of the *Sun*'s page three. Loads and loads of tits. I laugh and hope Ma doesn't hear me. I quickly fold them up and stuff them under the carpet that comes away from the floorboards. I rush back to work, taking the bottle with me, before Ma finds me and demands answers that I don't have.

'Do you know what this is?' I ask Rusty.

Rusty, who always has a cigarette in his mouth, looks at it and smiles. He flicks his cigarette into the trees that I just spent the morning cleaning out.

'You find that in there?'

'No. It's mine.'

'It's mine if you found it here.'

'I didn't. It's from my brother. In England.'

'You don't even know what it is.' He gestures, 'Give it to me.'

I move away.

He grabs it from me, strong for an old man, and he studies it. 'Codd Neck bottle or marble-in-the-neck bottle. Haven't seen one of these for some years. My mother used to have them, all stored in the shed before the Black and Tans destroyed them all. She had poteen in the shed. Not what these bottles were supposed to be for, but that's why she put the poteen in them. It was designed for carbonated drinks, fizzy drinks,' he adds when I'm confused. 'Problem with glass bottles is that the pressure of the gas would force the cork stopper out, especially if the cork dried out. So a man named Codd came up with these marbles in the neck. The bottles were filled upside down, the pressure of the gas in the bottle forced the marble against the rubber washer, sealing it in.'

'How do you get the marble out?' It's all I want to know.

'You try to do that and I won't give you this back. You don't get the marble out. Some kids smashed them to get them out, but don't you go doing that. Some things are better left the way they are.'

The marble is plain and simple, just clear glass, no signs or markings that I can see that tells me it's a certain brand or make. There's nothing special about the marble at all, just that it is in the bottle.

'These bottles are rare. Blue was a colour for poisons so any smart mineral company wouldn't have used blue. I doubt there are many of these around.'

He looks at it closely, checking it for marks as I would a marble, and my heart starts pounding, feeling possessive. I reach for it and he pulls it away.

He chuckles. 'What will you give me for it?' he asks, gripping it tight.

I could tell him what I think of him, put up a fight, but that won't get me the bottle back. Besides I've to spend every day for the rest of the summer with him. Reluctantly I reach into my pocket and give him a folded-up page three. I was planning on having a go in the bushes when I got time to myself; Beverly, nineteen, hot tits. Rusty looks at her and hands the bottle back instantly, and disappears into his woodshed with the page for twenty minutes.

I sit on the grass outside and stare at the blue bottle, wondering what it means. Does it mean anything? I know instinctively that it's from Hamish, it could only be from him. The fact that it's a marble and the page three girls make it obvious, his kind of humour. He was probably hoping Ma would open it, or that I'd open it in front of her. I can hear his chesty chuckle as he wraps it all up, probably wishing he could be there to see our reactions. Homebird Hamish, stuck away from us all. I search the bottle for answers; does it mean Hamish is working in a bottle factory? Does he want me to find him? Is he a bottle washer? I remember we called larger taws 'bottle washers' but never knew why; now I know it's because of the marble in the neck. Is the large taw a link to my big brother? Is he trying to tell me something? I look for hidden messages but then I realise that it's clear as day: there is a message in the bottle. Hamish didn't write it on a note and stuff it inside, but instead he found a bottle with a marble in it.

A message in the bottle.

It speaks loudly and clearly to me.

It says to me, *I'm still here, Fergus. I haven't forgotten you, I haven't forgotten the marbles like everyone else has, I know how important they are to you. Saw this, thought of you. Still thinking of you. Sorry for all that stuff that happened. Let's be pals.*

It says, *Truce.*

26

POOL RULES

No Glass

I sit in the cafeteria with Lea, who has the ability to make you feel that the oddest thing you've ever done in your life is the most normal, like she sees it all the time, does it all the time, and maybe that's true. She emanates warmth and care and I can understand why she's Dad's favourite, and why he grumbles so much about the others.

It's evening now. The cafeteria is all closed up apart from the tea/coffee facilities, which we help ourselves to. Dad is asleep, he was asleep from the moment I parked and ran inside like I was hunting him down. I'm glad. Even though the swim calmed me down, it stops me from barging in there and asking him about everything that has come out today.

I don't have to say anything and Lea just knows, Dad has always said that about her. A skill we all wish we had, and wish the nearest and dearest to us had. Like Aidan, for example. I would just like him to know how I feel without him having to ask, because he asks me all the time, convinced something is so wrong with me, with us, that he needs to fix it. Two months we've been going to a marriage counsellor yet there's nothing wrong with our marriage. It's me. I'm closed. I'm all inside. This is what he tells me. But I've always been like that, I don't know why it's bothering him now.

Yes, I do know; he said so at the last session: he feels like I'm not happy with him. But I am. There's nothing wrong with him.

Are you happy?

Yes, I'm happy with you.

Are you happy with yourself?

Jesus, Aidan, you're starting to talk like one of those counsellors.

Yeah, I know, but are you happy with yourself?

Yeah. I am. I like my job, I love my kids, I love you.

Yeah, but that's not yourself.

What is it if my job, my kids and my husband aren't myself? I shout.

I don't know. Relax, I'm just asking, you're stressed.

I'm only bloody stressed because you keep asking.

Okay, fine, you want to do this, let's do this. Am I happy with myself? Yes, I am mostly, but I'm tired, exhausted, up at seven, breakfast, school lunches, school drops, work, collection, lunch, activities, dinner, bath, bed, sleep. Do it again. Butter, ham, cheese, bread, slice. Raisins. Next.

But we can't really change that, can we? The kids have to get to school. You have to work.

Exactly, so stop asking.

But would you like to change your job?

No! I like my job.

Do you?

Do I? Yes, I do. But lately, no.

And another thing: I'd like to lose the weight I put on after Alfie. Seven pounds. My tits are full of fat, I want that gone. I want to be able to do the splits in a bikini on the beach while we're at it, while everyone's looking.

So work out.

I don't have time.

Yes you do, in the evening, I'll stay home, you go out. Go walking with the ladies around the block.

I don't want to fucking walk with the fucking ladies around the fucking block – all they do is gossip and ramble, I don't want a gossipy ramble. Stop laughing at me, Aidan.

Sorry. So join a gym. Go swimming for yourself, you never get to do that any more.

In the evenings, Aidan? When I'm so tired all I

*want to do is lie down or watch TV on the couch.
Or be with you, because if I went out in the evening,
when would I be with you?*

Stay up an hour later.

But I'm already fucking wrecked.

Okay, okay, stop swearing so much.

*Sorry. I just don't want to have to ask you a
favour to mind the kids while I go to the gym of
all places. I'd rather do something else, like go out.
Feels like a wasted favour.*

*Is that it? You want to go out more? You always
say you're too tired, that you don't want to go out.*

I am too tired. And I'm tired of this conversation.

I just want to help you, Sabrina, I love you.

*And I love you too. Really, it's not you, it's not
anything, you're just making it something.*

You're sure? It's not because of . . .

*No. It's not because of that. I'm over that. I don't
even want to talk about that. It's not that.*

Okay. Okay – you're sure?

Am I sure?

Yeah. Yeah I am.

*Do you want me to do more around the house?
Help out more?*

*No, you're great, you do enough, remember we
filled out that list of duties at the last session, you're
great, you do way more than I thought, you're great,
Aidan, it's not you.*

But it's something?

Aidan, stop it. No, it's nothing. There's nothing.

If there is, tell me, because it's hard to tell with you, Sabrina. I can't read you. You're quiet, you know. You keep it all inside.

Because I don't want to make a big deal of things, because there's nothing wrong, because you're making this all dramatic and really everything's fine. I'm just tired that's all, some day the kids will be older and I won't be tired.

Okay. And I'll take them camping on Friday and you can have a day to yourself, rest after work, don't lift a finger, don't do anything, okay?

Okay.

'Tell me, what did you discover?' Dr Loftus asks.

Dr Hotness, in Lea's words, was about to leave work when I dived into the pool, but word spread and he came to see me. And while I appreciate it, I hope I don't have to pay for this session. I tell Dr Loftus about everything I've learned today about Dad, about his double life, and I wonder how much of this Dr Loftus already knows, if he has been speaking with Cat and Dad's brothers for the past year, if everyone has known everything all along, apart from me. I now know how it feels to be Dad, for everyone around you to know things that you don't know, and it's upsetting. It has knocked me off my axis. And I think what hurts me the most is that in some version of his life, I didn't exist, that

285

he chose for that to happen. I swallow the lump in my throat before continuing.

Dr Loftus is quiet.

'Did you know about this?' I ask.

He ponders this slowly. 'They came to me at various points during Fergus's rehabilition to try and help, offer information that they felt I should know about him that he no longer knows, and so yes, I do know about some of what you say, but not its entirety, and certainly not that he had been using his brother's name. This is new.' He thinks. 'With a stroke there is often memory loss. You know this, we've discussed it before. Confusion or problems with short-term memory, wandering or getting lost in familiar places, difficulty following instructions – we've seen some of these with Fergus. The memory can improve over time, either spontaneously or through rehabilitation, and we've seen signs of both of these working using the brain retraining techniques. However . . .' He shifts in his seat and moves forward, elbows on the rickety table, shirtsleeves rolled up, the tired eyes of a man who's had a long day. 'Repression, or dissociative amnesia as it's sometimes referred to, is a different matter altogether. Repressed memories are hypothesised memories having been unconsciously blocked, due to the memory being associated with a high level of stress or trauma. Repressed memories are a controversial issue; some psychologists think it occurs in victims of trauma, some dispute that. Some think it can be recovered through therapy, again others dispute that.'

'You think my dad has deliberately repressed the marble memories?'

He takes his time. There are no yes/no answers with him, there never have been with Dad's condition, which is stressful and confusing. Why does he remember some things and not other things, why does he remember some things on certain days and not others? The stroke affected the memory, that's the only response that ever made sense to me.

'He remembers you and your mother and the life you've had together, he remembers his childhood and his relationship with his family, he doesn't recall his recent reunion with his brothers which preceded his stroke, this woman that he was in love with, and he doesn't remember the marbles at all.'

'But you said that people block out things that have been stressful and traumatic. Marbles made him happy. This woman and his brothers made him happy, by the sounds of it.'

'But by your telling, marbles forced him to separate his life into two. They forced him to become two different men, living two different lives. He was clearly under a lot of stress in his life before his stroke, his financial strains and losing his job, but this stress would have been heightened by the fact he was trying to live two separate lives. Now this is just a theory, Sabrina,' he says more casually, and

I realise we're off the record here, this is not an official diagnosis. 'And it's late, and I'm tired and I'm just offering theories, but if he blames the marbles for bringing that stress on him, then it would offer some explanation as to why he has repressed the marble memories, despite the obvious joy they brought him before. They began as a kind of freedom to him, a place he could get lost in and then, as the years went by, they trapped him. He may not have seen a way out of it.'

'So forgetting them is a way out?' I have been so angry with him, so selfishly hurt about it all, that I didn't think of the pressure he must have been under, albeit self-imposed pressure.

'Again, repression is an unconscious thing. He wouldn't have consciously made the decision to block it out, but to survive . . .' He leaves it hanging in the air.

I think of Dad's expression when I showed him the bloodies. Recognition. Joy. Turmoil. Confusion. 'If I showed him the marbles, would it have a negative effect on him? Send him into . . . a stroke again?'

He's shaking his head before I've even finished. 'It wouldn't give him a stroke, Sabrina. It could upset him. But it could also bring him joy,' he says, with a shrug of the shoulders. No yes and no no.

I think of Dad's face when he saw the bloodies this morning, of how it changed from innocence to confusion, the other part of him caught between who he is now and who he has blocked out, both battling against each other. I don't want to cause him more stress.

'He had both reactions when his brothers showed him the marble game tonight. Delight at seeing them, followed by tears, but he seems to be working out something today, dealing with it all on an unconscious level.'

He's healing, I think to myself.

Lea had told me that my uncles had visited, I'd just missed them when I arrived and dived into the pool. Meanwhile Dad had fallen asleep, exhausted by his day.

'I discovered the marbles in the boxes that were delivered this morning,' I explain. 'Some are missing and I started out trying to find them. They're worth a lot of money. But then I found all of this out.'

He nods along encouragingly.

I cover my face in my hands. 'Or maybe it's me that's losing it.'

'You're not,' he laughs. 'Go on.'

'I thought if I could find all the marbles, and then show them to him, then they would magically unlock whatever is blocking his memories. I know you can't just fix a person like that, but . . . at least I'd be doing something to help.' My head pounds at the revelations the day has brought me, not just over

Dad's secrets but, as the night draws in, my own intentions slowly surface, perhaps feeling safer under the cover of dark.

'Sabrina, just being here for him is helping. Talking to him. No one knows the triggers for the reoccurrence of memories; it can be sense, sound, or aided triggers like guided visualisation, trance writing, dream work, body work, hypnosis. And in my field, the existence of repressed memory recovery has not been accepted by mainstream psychology, nor proven to exist. Some of my fellow memory and cognitive experts tend to be sceptical.'

'And you?'

'I have a roomful of books on all of this stuff, what to say to Fergus, what to do with Fergus, but really,' he opens his arms, looking utterly exhausted and I feel so guilty for keeping him so long, 'really what matters is, whatever works.'

I'm thinking fast as I know he's about to leave any moment, return home to his real life with his own concerns. I've now decided that I don't want to upset Dad by showing him his marble collection; each will have a memory attached, it could be too much for him. But I want him to remember the joy of marbles. 'What if I buy him new ones, make new memories, make new joy?'

He smiles. 'I don't see what harm that could do.'

'What time is it?' I look at my watch. 'It's almost ten. Who sells marbles at ten at night?'

He laughs, 'Why does this have to be solved all in one day?'

Because it does. Because I can't tell him why, but I have a deadline. Fix things today or else. Or else what? Everything remains unfixed forever? Tomorrow I'm back on the hamster wheel.

As Dr Loftus bids me farewell, I take stock of myself. My jeans are still wet from the pool no matter how much I've tried to dry myself under the heater in the changing rooms, and I'm braless and T-shirtless beneath my hooded top, with the wet T-shirt and underwear in a plastic bag. Reality is setting in. I'm contemplating the fact that my mission to save my dad in one day is just not going to happen. Tomorrow I will wake up, Aidan and the children will come home and I will be all consumed by them, and this dream will have vanished, like so many other daily aims that never happen. I should go home, get some sleep, get the rest and recuperation I should have been getting while Aidan has the boys. That was the whole idea. But then Nurse Lea clears her throat from the doorway.

'Dr Hotness gone?'

I laugh.

'I wasn't eavesdropping . . . okay, I was, but don't ask any questions.' She hands me a folded piece of paper. 'I met a fella on Facebook, we were supposed to go out tonight to a party, meet in person for the first time – okay, it wasn't on Facebook, it was a dating site, but if by some divine miracle he looks anything like his profile then I'll marry him tomorrow.' Nervous laugh. 'Anyway. He's an artist. Does stuff with wood. And he has lots of artist friends. Here.'

She hands me a piece of paper with an address.

'What is this?'

'I'm mad about your dad, I've never seen anyone come on so much in one day. I want to help.'

27

PLAYING WITH MARBLES

Reproductions, Fakes and Fantasies

Cat is sitting at a table dressed in a white dress, white flowers pinned in her hair. She sips on a glass of white wine and throws her head back and laughs, a naughty, dirty laugh which instantly makes the others laugh. That's the way with Cat, it's not always what she says that's funny, it's her reaction to it that is the hilarious part. It would be naïve to say she is always in flying form, she certainly is not, especially with her eldest daughter who gives her so much grief, a troubled young woman who is constantly problematic, not happy unless she is making her mam unhappy. Aside from that and almost in spite of that, Cat has the ability to put those things aside and enjoy life for what it is, or at least enjoy the other part of it. She never allows things to overlap, she separates her worries. Despite the way I have separated my life, I have never been able to do that. A problem in Hamish O'Neill's life is a problem in Fergus Boggs's life and vice versa. For example, today, this beautiful day, she says, 'To hell with all of life's problems, let's just enjoy now, this moment, what we are doing now.'

I both admire it and am driven crazy by it. How can she ignore problems? But she doesn't, she puts them aside, chooses her moments to dwell on them. I have never been able to do that. I constantly dwell until they're gone away. And where are we ignoring our problems today? Five thousand miles away on the central coast of California's wine region at the wedding of Cat's dearest friend. At fifty years of age and the groom at sixty they're no spring chickens and it's not the first time for either of them, though they appear like two love-struck teenagers, as in love as I feel with Cat when I'm in her company. It seems to be the year of second marriages, this is my third wedding this year, and I remember the first on all three occasions, especially as one of them was mine. I wasn't invited to Gina's wedding but it was the one which affected me greatly. I wasn't expecting to be invited, Gina and I haven't had a pleasant word to say to each other since our separation over fifteen years ago but still, despite boyfriends after me, I considered her my wife. Now she's someone else's and I think of all the things that I did wrong. How good it was at the beginning, how I looked up to her, worshipped her, and only ever wanted to please her. It was that thinking that ruined our relationship, that ruined me. Why couldn't I just have seen her for what she is, known that she loved me for who I was? No matter how hard I tried to change myself, the roots of me were the same and she loved that. For a time at least. That sweet young woman with the freckle face is gone, now just a scornful woman who snaps at the slightest chance. Did I make her that way? Is it all my fault?

We are in Santa Barbara county, in July, in the sweltering heat. Cat, who is in her element, is bronzing herself in the full blaze of the sun, shoes off, manicured toes wiggling, cleavage big and tanned, jiggling when she laughs. She is the sunshine in my life and yet the greater she shines upon me the greater I feel the shadow cast behind me. Time is creeping up on me. I'm away from the sun, unable to take the heat. I have completely soaked my white shirt and because of that can't take off my jacket, which makes me all the warmer. I'm in the shade as much as I can be, drinking gallons of water, but at the heaviest weight I have been. Four stone above my usual weight, I'm feeling the heat, the discomfort, the heat of my balls, my thighs sticking together, my shirt too tight around my neck. The man who has plonked himself next to me in a white casual suit and a white hat tells me he's an art dealer, he talks of nothing but golf courses that he's played all around the world in such detail I want to tell him to shut the fuck up, shut the fuck up. But I hold back, for Cat's sake. I made the mistake of mentioning I played golf, which I once did, though it feels like many moons ago. I played mainly for work purposes, when I was a financial advisor and was keeping up with what was going on. I've had to sell my golf clubs, lose my membership as I couldn't keep up with paying the fees and I don't have the time for leisure any more. Anybody I played with has done the same and instead invested in Lycra and a bike and goes cycling on Sundays. Hearing about a game I had to give up does nothing to help my mood.

I didn't want to come away. As soon as Cat told me of the invitation I didn't want to come. I said as much, but she put her foot down. She insisted on paying. Whatever I felt when I was younger on honeymoon, I don't feel it now. I don't want anyone else paying my way. I want to pay my own way, but I couldn't afford the flight and now that I'm here I can't afford anything. Cat is covering it all. Every gesture, every kindness just makes me feel even worse, like my balls have been chopped off. And the company I've been in has been horrendous. I'm sure she's wishing she left me behind after all.

She looks over at me and I see the concern in her

eyes. I put on a fake cheery grin, fan myself comically to let her know why I'm over here in the shade. She smiles and rejoins the conversation, and I even keep up an extremely animated conversation with the art dealer beside me so she can see I'm enjoying myself in the moments that she sneaks a peek at me, thinking I don't notice.

Midway through talking about the par something on the eighth hole in Pebble Beach, my phone vibrates in my pocket. I'm happy to excuse myself and disappear inside to the air-conditioned reception of the vineyard. I take off my jacket, away from anyone's view, and sit down. It's the text I was waiting for. Sonya Schiffer, a woman I contacted a few months ago as soon as I heard I was coming to Santa Barbara. Communicating with her behind Cat's back has stirred those old feelings inside me that I used to get when arranging nights out or nights away from Gina, but when I feel the feeling it is accompanied by guilt. My conscience has grown since meeting her, but it doesn't remove the need I have to get away and meet this other woman. I think hard about how to get away from here, I had a plan in action but now that I'm here I need to rethink it. Our hotel is further from the venue than I thought, it isn't easy for me to slip away, I must arrange a shuttle bus or get a lift from somebody, and if I feign sickness I'm sure Cat will want to come too. The music will start shortly and Cat loves to dance. She'll be up all night dancing non-stop with anyone and everyone, like she always does. She's a beautiful dancer and usually I watch her, but perhaps that's my time to escape. Wild horses couldn't drag her away from a dance floor. I can say I'm jetlagged or that I've a dodgy stomach. I had oysters for my starter.

Our inn is twenty minutes away from here, the hotel I've arranged to meet Sonya in Santa Barbara is forty minutes away. I need to get to our hotel to get the car and drive to the city. Can I make it? Meet Sonya, and be back in time before the wedding is over, before Cat finds me gone? I don't know, but the sooner I go the better the chances. When she sees me coming towards her she looks concerned. I rub my belly and explain to her, in a rush, that I must get back to our bedroom toilet. She knows I don't like to use the toilet when I'm out and about. I tell her I won't be long, I need to change my shirt too, I'm embarrassed; enjoy yourself, I'll be fine, I'll come back for the dancing. She wants to take care of me, of course. Cat is a nurturer but she also likes her space having lived alone for twenty years and is good at giving it to others and so I leave the party. I have a quick shower, change into a clean shirt and pants, take my overnight bag and drive to Santa Barbara.

The meeting place is a motel and I park in the car park and climb the stairs to the second floor.

At the end of the corridor all the doors of the bedrooms have been left open as I was informed they would for the room trading. I know Sonya straight away, I recognise her from her photograph and also because she's the only woman. At seventy-four years old she has published two books about marbles, playing and collecting, and is one of the leading experts in the marble world. I have asked her here to value my marbles, or rather Hamish O'Neill has, and after sharing photographs with her of my collection she was sufficiently intrigued to agree to come. At over three hundred pounds, and with arthritis in both knees, she is surrounded by fanatics eager to get a moment of her time. But as soon as I enter, it's just me and her. She, like me, wants to get straight down to business. The four rooms on this floor are all involved in the room trading, where people can discuss, swap, value their marbles. I've been to marble conventions before as Hamish O'Neill and have always thrived on the pure buzz of being surrounded by people as committed to marbles as I am. Seeing their eyes light up at the sight of a mint-condition Guinea cobra or a striped transparent or an exotic swirl or even at a sample box they haven't seen before, or haven't seen in the flesh, reminds me that I'm not alone in being mesmerised by this world. Of course some of the people are even nuttier than me, spending their entire lives and savings on collecting without ever playing, but I always feel among friends at these meets, like I can truly be myself, though it's under my brother's name.

I owned both of Sonya's books before I contacted her. I had bought one in particular with the intention of trying to value my own collection but quickly realised I could be easily misled and tricked. I contacted her on the Internet, one of the most knowledgeable collectors there is. I haven't brought my entire collection, I couldn't have afforded the airline's weight charges nor could I have fitted any more in my bag without Cat suspecting. I've brought what I think are the most valuable. I haven't brought them to sell them – that I made abundantly clear to Sonya Schiffer. I don't know if I'll ever sell them or not; I always thought I never would, but the time is coming close. The banks are after me for an apartment I own in Roscommon, a stupid investment in an apartment block in the middle of nowhere that cost too much at the time and now is worth nothing. Because the school, shopping centre and anything else that was in the plans didn't go ahead, I can't let the apartment, never mind sell it, which leaves me in a difficult position of trying to pay the mortgage as well as my own.

I need to start gathering my pieces and seeing what I have in play.

Despite the fact that I have driven and need to drive back, Sonya insists that we drink whiskey together. I have a feeling that my response has a great bearing on whether she values the pieces or not. She has come for a night out, not to be rushed. I can worry about the car tomorrow, give an excuse to Cat, I don't know what yet. I'll come up with something.

'My, my, you have quite the collection,' Sonya says as we sit down at a table in a bedroom. People swirl around us, talk, swap, play, even watch her at work, but they're not registering in my mind. I keep my eye on her. She's huge, so big her arse sticks out on both sides of the chair. She thinks I'm Hamish O'Neill, winner of the World Championship of 1994, individual best player in the same year. She wants to talk about that for a while and I don't mind reliving my glory days when there are very few people I can tell the story to. I tell her all about it in detail, how we beat the Germans' ten-in-a-row run and the bar fight that broke out afterwards between Spud on my team and one of the German teammates, and USA having to act as peacemakers. We laugh about it and I can tell that she's impressed and we return to the marbles.

'I bought your book to value them myself but I quickly learned there's an art to it, one that I couldn't master,' I say. 'I learned there are more reproductions out there than I thought.'

She looks at me intently. 'I wouldn't worry about reproductions as much as people want you to worry, Hamish. When it comes to the collectable world, reproductions are not a new thing. Sparklers and sunbursts were an attempt to mimic onion-skins, cat's eyes an attempt to mimic swirls. Bricks, slags, Akro and carnelian agates and 'ades were an attempt to mimic hand-cut stones, but despite this, all these marbles – except of course cat's eyes – are highly collectable today.'

I smile, thinking of my joke with Cat about her not being collectable at all, though she is the most valuable thing in my life, and Sonya looks at me over her glasses which are low on her nose. She watches me, as if evaluating me and not the marbles, twirls them around with the 10x loupe in her thick fat fingers, gold rings squished down on most fingers, with fat gathering around them. Those suckers are never coming off. 'But usually everyone and everything is mimicking something or other.'

I swallow, thinking it's a direct evaluation of me. As if she knows I'm not Hamish O'Neill, but she couldn't possibly.

After a time studying, during which I've downed too much whiskey, she speaks, 'You've got some reproductions here and this, this has been repaired to fix a fracture, see the tiny creases and the cloud-iness in the marble?'

I nod.

'That's from re-heating the glass. And you've a few fantasies,' she says, moving everything around.

'Items that never existed in original form. Polyvinyl bags with old labels.' She looks disgusted. 'But no, you're generally looking good here. You obviously have a good eye.'

'I hope so. We'll see, won't we?'

'Yes, we will.' She looks at the collection and laughs wheezily. 'Hope you've got time, because this will take all night.'

It is four a.m. when somebody called Bear drops me back at the inn in a pickup truck and speeds off. I can barely see straight after downing a bottle of whiskey with Sonya. I try to concentrate on the path ahead of me and fall with my bag of marbles into the vines. Laughing, I pull myself out and stumble to the room.

As the pickup truck passed the vineyard I saw to my surprise that the wedding had wrapped up and there wasn't a guest in sight, not even my Cat. Unusual for an Irish wedding, though I suppose we aren't in Ireland and I should have known that it would be over early, with such a conservative bunch. I stumble into the inn, receiving angry glares from the owner who had to let me in at such an hour, and I bang into everything, door frames, furniture, on the way to the stairs. When I reach the bedroom, as if by magic Cat pulls the door open, hurt written all over her face.

'Where the hell have you been?'

I know I've done it again. No matter what I think

about myself, how I think I can change, I always slip back into hurting people. The Hamish in me comes out, but I can't blame him any more, I never really could. It's me. It's always been me.

28

POOL RULES

No Alcohol

I wait in my car for Lea as she gets ready for the party. I blare the heating, trying to dry my jeans, which stick to my legs. I take the inventory out of my bag again and flick through it. Scanning his lifetime of memories, all catalogued in a neat script. I look through the photographs I took of the newspaper article on the Marble Cat wall. It's grainy and Dad is hiding in the back row, but it's him all right. For the first time I notice the date on the newspaper.

I call Mum, who answers quickly for so late at night.

'Mum, hi, I hope I didn't wake you.'

'Not at all, we're still up drinking wine – Robert

is drunk-tweeting NASA,' she giggles as I hear Robert in the background shouting about aliens waving at him from the moon. 'We're out on the balcony watching the moon, isn't it marvellous? I should have known you'd be awake, you know you could never sleep as a little girl when there was a full moon? You used to sneak into our bed. I remember Fergus brought you downstairs for a hot chocolate one night, I found you both sitting in the dark at the kitchen table, him asleep, you looking outside.'

The moon made us do it.

I smile at the image. 'I haven't changed much.'

'Did the boys have a great day?' she asks.

'The best.'

She laughs. 'And I'm sure you have too. Nice to have the day to yourself. You don't get that much.'

Silence.

'Everything okay?'

'Do you remember my thirteenth birthday party? We had a marquee in the back garden, didn't we?'

'Yes, about forty people, catering, the works.'

'Was Dad there? I can't really remember.'

'Yes, he was.'

'So he wasn't away that day?' The newspaper report is dated the day of my birthday, though it refers to the championships being held the day before.

She sighs. 'It was a long time ago, Sabrina.'

'I know, but can you remember?'

'Of course he was there, he was there in all the photographs, remember?'

I remember now. Me in my short skirt and high heels, looking like a tart. I can't believe Mum let me dress like that, though I know I didn't give her much choice.

'And what about the day before?'

'What did you find out, Sabrina? Just spit it out,' she snaps.

I'm taken aback by her coldness.

'I suspected,' she fills my silence, 'which is probably what you're about to tell me, that he was having an affair, away with somebody. He said he was in London for a conference, but when I called the hotel they had no record of him. I suspected something, he'd been doing his usual secretive thing leading up to that, heading off to places I knew he wasn't going to. He did that a lot. He came home the day of your birthday. I confronted him, I can't remember now, but he managed to weasel his way out of it as usual. Made me feel like I was going crazy, as usual. Why? What did you find out? Who was she? Was it that Regina woman? God knows there were many others, but he never admitted to her. I always thought they were together before we split.'

'I don't think he was with another woman, Mum. He was having a love affair all right, but not the one you think.' I take a deep breath. 'He was at the World Marble Championships in England. His team of six men, the Electric Slags, won. A newspaper published a photograph and an article about it on the day of my birthday. He's hiding in the back, but I know that it's him.'

'What? Marble championships? What on earth are you talking about?' She slurs as she talks and I don't think this is the best time to discuss it with her. I was wrong, I should have waited, but I couldn't.

'I told you about them, Mum, he's been playing marbles all his life, competitively. Secretly. He's been collecting them too.'

She's silent. So much to take in, I'm sure.

'It's him in the photograph, but he used a different name. Hamish O'Neill.'

I can hear her intake of breath. 'Sweet Jesus! Hamish was his brother, his older brother who died when Fergus was young. He wouldn't talk much about him, but I learned a few things about him over the years. Fergus thought the world of him. O'Neill was his mother's maiden name.'

So Mattie was right. This was all about Hamish. Hamish died using Dad's name, Dad in turn took Hamish's name. I don't know if I'll ever truly know why. I don't know if I need to.

'There was a best individual player trophy for a Hamish O'Neill. I met with his team, they say that Dad is Hamish.'

Mum is quiet. Food for thought. I can't even imagine the memories she is accessing as she tries to understand it and piece it all together.

'Mum?'

'And he won this the day before your thirteenth birthday?'

'Yes.'

'But why didn't he tell me?'

'He didn't tell anyone,' I say. 'Not his family, not his friends.'

'But why?'

'I think he was trying to breathe life back into his brother. Honour him in some way. I think he didn't think anybody else would understand. That they'd think it was weird.'

'It is weird,' she snaps, then sighs and goes quiet. Then, as if she's feeling guilty, she adds, 'Nice though. To honour him.' Silence. 'Who on earth was I married to?' she asks quietly.

I don't know how to answer that, but I do know that I no longer want my husband asking the same thing of me.

Lea slowly lowers herself into the front seat wearing a neutral-coloured bandage dress, black leather jacket, smelling of perfume, caked in make-up and almost unrecognisable as the girl-next-door nurse I see most days.

'Too much?' she says anxiously.

The colour of the dress makes her look naked. 'No,' I say, starting up the engine. 'So tell me about where we're going.'

'You know just about as much as I do.'

I throw her a warning look. 'Lea.'

'What?' she giggles. 'I met him online. His name is Dara. He's delicious. We haven't met in person, but you know . . .' She shrugs.

'No, I don't know, tell me.'

'Well, we met on an online dating site. We've Skyped a few times. You know,' she repeats, like I should know something.

'No, I don't know. What?'

She keeps on staring at me, jerking her head at me as if it will spark the answer, which it in fact does.

'Oh!' I say suddenly.

'Yes, now you've got it.' She faces front again. 'So we're pretty much well acquainted, but we haven't actually met yet.'

'You've had Skype sex and you're nervous about meeting him?' I laugh.

'My camera had a filter,' she explains. 'I don't.'

'And what does this mysterious Dara do that he knows where we can find marbles at eleven o'clock at night?'

'He does wood carvings. For chairs, tables, furniture. The party is at his office. I remember him saying there is a glass artist.'

I'm dubious.

We find the address of the full moon party that Dara gave her. We stare at it from across the river in silence, both deep in thought, probably thinking the same thing. We've been duped.

The address is a multistorey car park. It is on the graveyard site of a ripped-down old shopping centre which was to make way for a new €70 million state-of-the-art shopping centre and cinema which never was and so the multistorey car park stands alone in the wilderness far from any businesses which can utilise its parking. The moon sits above it, big and full, guiding us to it like the North Star, keeping a watchful maternal eye over our progress. But I can't help but think she's laughing at us now.

It's an enormous concrete monstrosity, but it's old school, ugly and red brick, tight and low ceilings, unlike the spacious light-filled car parks of today. It climbs eight levels high, not a car in sight on any floor. Halfway up, on the fourth floor, a glow appears from the mesh-gridded openings.

'Looks like he's home,' Lea says, trying to make light of it.

'Do you smell smoke?' I ask.

She sniffs and nods.

'Do you hear music?'

It is faint but it drifts from the fourth floor, a calm rhythmic bass.

Neither of us make a move.

'So maybe this is a party,' I say. 'Do you think this is dangerous?' We're in a neglected part of town that should have been developed but wasn't and then was left for dead, invited by a man who's good with tools, who Lea met on the Internet. I wonder if goodwill has run out for the day.

The site is completely surrounded by fencing, the wooden construction kind, and it is too high to climb with no gaps to pass through. We circle the entire thing and find that it has been opened at one section, inviting us in. We slowly walk through the fence, pass the barrier where ghost cars collect their parking tickets, and into the darkness of the multistorey. The ground level has been completely covered by graffiti, every single inch of the concrete walls and supporting pillars have been sprayed. I don't concentrate too much on the darkened corners, I don't want to linger, I need to keep moving. We follow the signs for the stairs, choose to ignore the lifts, which I guess aren't working anyway, and even if they are, I'm not interested.

Every scary movie I've ever seen has told me to be wary of car parks on my own late at night or even during the day, and yet here I am, going against every single instinct in my body. The sound of music and laughter gets increasingly loud as we tread lightly up the steps, not wanting to make a sound to alert them. There is a hum of conversation and that relaxing bass keeps us going; there is some kind of civilisation up there, one which doesn't sound like murderous screaming, gunshots and violent gang dance-offs. I expect to happen upon a homeless community, with laptops on Skype; I have prepared myself to run, to give them my money, my phone, whatever, just in case they get angry at my intrusion.

Lea readies herself, checks her reflection in her pocket mirror and reapplies her thick lipstick that makes her look like she's had collagen injections, then with a flick of her hair, she pushes open the door. I am stunned when we peek around at the inside. Everywhere I look I see trees, beautiful large greenery covering the grey concrete. They sit in stunning pots, Spanish and Mexican in style with beautiful mosaic tiles. Fairy lights run from tree to tree and candles light the meandering pathway through the trees. It feels like we're in this wonderland in the middle of a concrete car park. Grey and green, dark and light, man-made and natural.

'Hi, guys,' a young man says beside us and we turn to him in surprise. 'Can I see your invitation, please?'

Our mouths open and shut, we are visibly shocked.

'She's a guest of Dara's,' I finally say, when Lea doesn't say a word.

'Oh, cool!' He stands up. 'Follow me. Sorry about

the invitation thing, it's Evelyn, she's pretty insistent after last year. Apparently the party got crashed and it all got a little crazy.'

We follow him through the winding path, through the trees, and I feel like I'm in a dream.

'You guys did all this?' I ask.

'Yeah. Cool isn't it? Evelyn just got back from Thailand where she had full moon parties all the time. Doesn't exactly feel like Thailand, but concrete jungle was the theme.'

The path ends as it opens up to what looks like a living room. An enormous chandelier of beautiful twisted glass hangs low from the concrete ceiling, large pillar candles sit in the chandelier, the wax dripping down over the sides. Below it is a vast Oriental rug and copious brown battered leather couches where a dozen or more guests gather and chat like they're at a house party. Music plays, not too loud chill-out music that we could hear from across the river, and a nymph-like girl in a sequined catsuit dances on her own with her eyes closed, fingers running through invisible harp strings in the air. Some look up to see us, most don't, they're a friendly bunch just checking us out and smiling their welcomes. A bunch of all ages, the artsy kind, very cool, very edgy, not at all like me and Lea, the mother of three and Nurse Kardashian.

'There he is,' she says, pointing quickly. Lea skitters

over to Dara and they embrace. A moment later, out of their scrum, she shouts, 'Marlow,' to me.

I nod. Marlow. I'm here to see Marlow.

'Marlow,' Dara calls, then whistles and nods at me. A stunning man looks up from the group on the sofas. He's dressed in tight black jeans, a charcoal T-shirt, workman's boots, perfect physique, toned arms, long black hair, one side behind one ear, the other falling down over his face. Johnny Depp twenty years ago. He has one eye squinted as he inhales on a cigarette, and he holds a bottle of beer in the other hand. He looks at me, his eyes running over me. I shiver under his intense stare, don't know where to look. Lea laughs.

'Good luck!' She throws me a thumbs up and heads towards the barrel of beer in ice.

I swallow hard. Marlow smiles and leaves the company of a cool butterfly girl with body jewellery wrapped around her toned abs. He stops right in front of me, standing quite close for an absolute stranger.

'Hi.'

'Hi.' He smiles and sits down on the back of the couch so we're at the same eye level. He looks like I amuse him, but not in a teasing way.

'My name is Sabrina.'

I look around and see Lea settling down on a couch with a group of people, beer in hand, relaxed as anything. I try to relax too.

'I've lost my marbles,' I say with a smile.

'Well, you've come to the right place,' he grins. 'Why don't we go into my studio.' He stands.

I laugh at that and he seems confused by my reaction, but walks away anyway. I look at Lea, who motions at me to follow Marlow. I follow him through the trees on the other side of the gathering and discover he hasn't been lying. Hugging the walls of the car park are offices and art studios.

'What is this place?'

'The art council let us work here. They came up with a great idea to utilise the space. The plan was to put something new on each floor, exhibitions on the third level, theatrical performances on the fifth floor . . . We've been here a year.'

He unlocks the door and steps inside.

There is glass everywhere, it glistens as the moonlight hits it.

'Wow, this is beautiful!' I look around, unable to stop as everywhere I turn is a glass masterpiece, either a jug, glasses, vases, panes, chandeliers – a myriad of gorgeous colours, some smashed and put back together again to make stunning creations.

He's sitting up on a counter, legs hanging, watching me.

'You make marbles,' I say, spotting a cabinet in the corner, little globes winking in the light, my heart suddenly pounding.

I remove my bag from my shoulder and take

the inventory out, feeling on fire. I walk towards him, offering the folder. 'My dad was a marble collector. I found this inventory in his things, including the marbles, but there were two collections missing.' I try to rush to the exact pages that list the missing marbles but he stops me, a hand on my hand, which he keeps a hold of while reading at his own pace.

'This is incredible,' he says, after a while.

'I know,' I say proudly, and uncertainly, looking at his hand wrapped around mine like he doesn't notice it's happening, as though it's the most natural, normal thing in the world. He turns page after page, fingers running over my knuckles, which makes me nervous and thrilled at the same time. I'm a married woman, I shouldn't be standing here close to midnight holding hands with a handsome cool dude, but I am and I don't want to let go. He takes his time reading through the inventory, his fingers still slowly moving over mine.

The moon made me do it.

'This is quite the collection,' he says, finally looking up. 'So he was only a fan of glass.'

'What do you mean?'

'Marbles were also made from clay, steel, plastic. But he only collects glass.'

'Oh, yes. I didn't realise.'

'Apart from steelies – he's got a few of them. But the most beautiful ones are handmade glass,' he says with a smile, 'then again, I'm biased. Which ones are missing?'

Tragically, I must let go of his hand to leaf through the pages and point them out. 'This. And this.'

He whistles when he sees the price. 'I can try to replicate them, but it's impossible for me to make them look exactly the same, and he'll notice the difference,' he says. 'A collector like him will know straight away.'

'He won't,' I swallow. 'He hasn't been well recently. Actually, I was hoping to find something new. I want him to make some new memories.' *Don't go back, Sabrina, move forward. Make new.*

'With pleasure.' He smiles, eyes playful, and I have to look away. 'So, Sabrina, I see here that the thing your dad was beginning to collect was contemporary marbles. He only has one, which is damaged – a heart, which is rather ironic, isn't it? This is where I feel I can come in. I can make you a contemporary art marble. See over there.'

He points to the display cabinet and I'm entranced by the variety he has. It's like a treasure trove of precious gems. So many intricate swirls and designs, colours and reflections bounce from the glass.

'You can touch them,' he says.

Opening the case, I'm drawn to a chocolate brown marble, like a snooker ball, and I'm surprised by the weight. They're larger than Dad's collection, not your usual playing marbles, but their colours and design are far more intense and intricate. Swirls and bubbles, they are hypnotising to look at and when I hold them up to the moonlight it seems they have even more depth, glowing from the inside.

'Interesting you picked that one,' he says. 'Is that your favourite?'

I nod, wrapping my fingers around it. It's almost as if I can feel the heat of the fire inside. 'But it's not for me.' I examine the collection again. 'He'd love any of these, I'm sure.'

It's not what I began the day searching for, but it feels right, like a better solution to driving myself insane looking for lost marbles that I probably will never find.

'No, no.' He takes the brown marble from me gently, and he places a hand on my waist as he examines it from behind me. 'I'll make you a new one now.'

'Now?'

'Sure. Have you somewhere else to be?'

I look out at Lea; she's lost in Dara's eyes, Dara running his fingers through her hair. It's almost midnight, I'm going home to an empty house anyway. I need to end my night with some kind of conclusion. Learning about Dad was satisfying, exhausting, draining, but I need to find a solution. I've opened a wound and I need to find something to help heal it. If I can't complete Dad's collection, then I must complete my own personal mission.

'How long will it take to make?'

He shrugs coolly. 'Let's see.'

He doesn't walk around, he kind of glides, drags his feet but not noisily, like he's too relaxed to lift them. He turns on a gas canister, leaves me momentarily, disappearing behind the trees in the car park, and returns with a six-pack of beer, a joint and a mischievous look in his eye.

I hear Aidan's voice in my head. *I just don't know if you're happy, Sabrina. You're distant. I love you. Do you hear me? Do you love me?*

Maybe I should leave, but if I haven't learned anything else from today, I've learned that I'm my father's daughter. I stay.

29

PLAYING WITH MARBLES

Increase Pound

I'm sitting before Larry Brennan, aka Lampy, known as such due to his teenage pastime of lamping animals late at night, usually rabbits, when we were teenagers. He had an uncle in Meath that he used to be sent to on weekends; his dad was an alcoholic and his ma had a nervous breakdown and couldn't cope with much, so he was sent to his uncle, his sister sent to their aunt. His sister got the better deal. They were thinking he'd be in a better place than at home but they were wrong. His uncle wasn't much better than his da, he just seemed more responsible because he didn't have his own family to care for. He was functioning okay by himself. He was fond of the drink, too fond of Larry too, though I don't think I realised that until I was older and looked back on it. Larry always wanted me to go with him, I think his uncle didn't bother with him if he had a friend there, but I didn't like his uncle one bit. Tom was his name. I went once for the weekend and, despite the adventure, the misadventure, the freedom to do and eat and drink whatever we wished at whatever time of the day or night, I wouldn't go back whenever he asked. His uncle wasn't right. I should have known what was going on but I didn't.

The lamping was fun. Larry would take his uncle's air rifle and we'd go out to the fields in the pitch-black of night. It was my job to hold the light, one-million-candle strength, and stun the rabbits, then he'd shoot them. Half the time he didn't even get their bodies. I always remember thinking Ma would make a great stew with it, but I had no way of keeping it fresh and bringing it back, or I didn't ever ask anyone how. It wasn't about the food for Larry, it was about the kill, and I'm sure every rabbit he shot was really his uncle or his dad, or his ma or whoever else was letting him down in the world. Maybe even me for being right there and not doing anything about it.

Lamping was best done at the darkest hour; cloudy nights were good, but the best conditions were when the moon was new. I remember Larry checking the weather as it got close to the weekend, almost going mental and causing all kinds of hell in school when the weather wasn't good for lamping. I suppose he knew that he'd have to stay in the house all night and he knew what that meant. Hamish wasn't around then. I was sixteen and he'd headed off to Liverpool, but he would have loved it there, he would have come with me. And he would have sorted Larry's uncle out too.

I look at Larry 'Lampy' Brennan now, the same age as me, fifty-seven, but slim, trim, respectable. I'm sitting across from him at his desk, and I think of all of the things that I know about him. He's wearing a smart suit, employs a few dozen people, he's doing well for himself, dragged himself out of the shit and washed himself off. My heart pounds as he smooths down his tie with manicured fingernails as he waits for my response, and I feel the tension in my chest that just never goes away and I'm so heavy these days I'm constantly wheezing, trying to catch my breath.

'I bet there's no one in your life now that knows where we came from,' I say.

He pauses, unsure of what I mean.

'You know what I mean, Lampy.'

He freezes then and I know that I've brought him back to being someone he's tried so hard to run away from in an instant. He's sixteen again. He's Lampy Brennan and it's mayhem in his head, the world is against him and he's fighting for himself against everybody and everything.

'What are you saying, Fergus?' he asks quietly.

I feel the sweat trickle down my right temple and I want to catch it but to do so would be to bring attention to it. 'I'm just saying that I'm sure a few people would be surprised by the things I know about you. That's all.'

He leans forward slowly. 'Are you threatening me, Fergus?'

I fix him with a stare, a long hard look. I don't need to answer, let him take from it what he may. I need this to work, I'm fifty-seven years old, I've cashed in every single favour everyone ever owed me and more, now I owe more favours than I'll ever have time to repay. I've hit a wall, this is the last trick up my sleeve, reduced to threats like the desperate lowlife I've become.

'Fergus,' he says quietly, looking down at his desk. 'This decision isn't personal. These are difficult times. I took you on because I wanted to help you out, out of loyalty.' He seems shaken. 'We said we'd look at it after six months. After six months I told you you had to up your game, you were selling the least – and yes, I know it was early days. But it's been nine months now, it's not good here, I have to start losing people. You were the last person in, which means you're the first person out. And frankly,' the anger seems to explode from nowhere as if he realises he should forget about being polite to me, 'threatening me isn't going to endear you to me, and it doesn't take away the fact that you are the worst salesman on the floor and you have earned the company the least amount of money.'

'You need to give me more time,' I say, feeling the panic rise, trying to sound cool, assured, like I'm someone he can trust. 'I'm still finding my feet. The first year is hard, but I'm getting there now. I have a real understanding of how things work around here.'

'I can't afford to give you more time,' he says. 'I just can't.'

I fight it out some more with him, but the more I push, the further he backs away, the tougher he becomes.

'When?' I ask quietly, feeling my entire world cave in on me.

'I was giving you one month's notice,' he says, and I think about one more month until it all falls apart. 'But in light of your threat, I am suggesting immediate termination.'

I have one more trick up my sleeve, the worst one of all, the one I have never wanted to resort to in all of my life.

'Please,' I say and he looks at me in surprise, the anger evaporated. 'Larry please. I beg you.'

Favours, threats and, last but not least, begging.

'What on earth is going on here?' Cat yelps as she finds me on the floor of my apartment.

I've pushed all the furniture to one wall. The armchairs are piled up on the couch, the coffee table is filling the tiny cubby kitchen and the rug is rolled up and out on the balcony. A perfectly large space has been cleared before me on the floor and I have a Sharpie in hand and am about to deface the wooden floors.

I've drawn a small circle eight inches wide and am in the middle of drawing a larger circle around it eleven foot in diameter. I can't talk to her because I'm concentrating.

'Fergus!' She looks around, eyes wide, mouth open. 'We were supposed to have lunch with Joe and Finn, remember? We were all waiting for you at the restaurant. I called and called you. I ate with them alone. Fergus? Can you hear me? I went to your work, they said you'd gone home.'

I ignore her, working on the circle.

'Did you forget, Fergus?' her voice softer. 'Did you forget again? This has happened a few times now, are you well, my love? Something is not right.'

She is down on her knees beside me on the floor, but I can't look at her. I'm busy.

'Are you okay? Are you feeling well? You don't look . . . Fergus, you are dripping wet.'

'Right,' I say, putting the marker down and sitting back on my haunches as I feel another drip of sweat fall from my nose. 'This game is called Increase Pound, and that is exactly what it's going to help us do. The small circle is the pound, the large circle is the bar. You shoot the taw from—'

'Me?'

'Yes, you.' I hand her some marbles, which she takes as though they're hand grenades.

'Fergus, it's three p.m., shouldn't you be at work and not playing marbles? This is ridiculous, I have to get back to work myself. I don't understand, what's going on?'

'I was fired!' I shout suddenly, which silences her and makes her jump in fright. 'You're the bank,' I say, more aggressively than I intend. 'You throw the marble and anything you hit in the pound becomes your property. If you don't hit anything your taw stays where it is and you go again. You have ten tries.'

I place my watch collection in the pound, the smaller inner circle. 'Throw the marble. Hit it.'

She looks at the watch collection and then at the items lining the circles which will follow and her eyes fill.

'Oh, Fergus, you don't have to do this. Joe can help you. You know that he's offered already.'

'I'm not taking handouts,' I say, feeling dizzy at the thought of baby Joe paying my way. Joe who was never really part of my family until Cat welcomed him in with open arms. It wouldn't be fair to him. 'I got myself into this mess, I'm going to get myself out of it.'

It was the marbles that got me into this situation in the first place. Getting rid of them will get me out of it. The lies, the deceit, the betrayal, me messing around, not focusing on the life I was living, splitting myself from myself and from my family. It's Alfie's birthday party and I can't bring Cat to visit, because Sabrina doesn't know Cat, she doesn't even know my great love, and I don't know where to start. To tell Sabrina about Cat would be to tell her about the marbles, and how can I do that? After a whole life of lying. Cat says she won't say a word until I find a way to tell Sabrina, but it will slip out, it's bound to, and then not to say it would be lying. Both of us lying to my daughter. Getting my marbles secretly valued in California was the real marker of how bad my financial situation had gotten. I was embarrassed, and that lie almost ended us, me showing up blind drunk back at the hotel. But she's sticking with me. She says she understands, but it's all a mess, it's all a mess. It's the marbles' fault.

Cat throws the marble. It's a crap throw, a deliberately bad one, and it misses. Cat and I have played marbles together on many occasions. As soon as I opened her up to my world I welcomed her into it; she has been to marble games with me, to marble conventions, she's not a great marble player, but she's not this bad.

'Do it properly!' I yell, and she starts to cry. 'Do

it, do it!' I pick the marble up and force it into her hand. 'Throw it!'

She throws it and it hits the watch collection in the pound.

'Right, it's yours. It's the bank's.' I pick it up and toss it aside. 'Next!' I place down my ma's engagement ring.

She misses. I yell at her to try harder.

'Fergus, I can't. I can't, I can't, I won't, please stop.' Tears are streaming from her eyes and she collapses in a heap on the floor. I grab the marbles from her and I throw. I hit a ring box, that's it, Mammy's wedding ring: property of the bank. I throw it again and hit the Akro Agate Sample Box from 1930 valued between seven thousand and thirteen thousand. Of course I hit it, it is almost bigger than the pound.

Next are the World's Best Moons, in the original box, valued between four thousand and seven thousand. I hit it. My two most valuable collections. Them first, then everything else, everything must go.

'I've found a buyer for these,' I tell Cat a few days later, as I put the marble collections down in order for me to put on my coat. 'I'm meeting him in town later. At O'Donoghue's. He's flown in from London to buy them. Twenty thousand dollars' worth, we agreed fifteen thousand euro cash.'

'You don't look well, Fergus.' She runs her hand

over my face, and I kiss her palm. 'You should lie down.'

'Didn't you hear me? I will, after I meet him.'

'You don't want to sell these. These are precious. All of your memories . . .'

'Memories last forever. These . . .' I can barely look at them as I say it. 'These will pay the mortgages for a few months, give me time to sort something out.' What though? No job, no one hiring. Not at my age. Think, think, what, what. Sell the marbles.

'You're pale, you should lie down. Let me go for you.'

It's the best idea and we both know it. If I go I won't be able to part with them and I need to, or the bank will take my home from me.

She leaves with the marbles and I go to bed. She returns some time later, it's dark, I don't know what time it is and I feel like I haven't slept but I must have. She comes to my bedside and I smell wine on her breath.

'Did you sell them?' I ask.

'I got the money,' she replies, placing an envelope by the bedside.

'The marbles are gone?'

She hesitates. 'Yes, they're gone.'

She rubs my hair, my face, kisses me. At least I have her. I want to make a joke about her value but I can't figure it out.

'I'm going to take a shower,' she says, sliding away.

As soon as I hear the water start I do something I haven't done for a very long time, I cry. Deep and painful, like I'm a child again. I fall asleep before Cat is out of the shower. When I wake up I'm in hospital and the next time I see Cat is the first time I meet her, in a rehabilitation centre that I call home, where she is visiting a friend.

30

POOL RULES

No Lifeguard on Duty

Marlow hands me a pair of glasses, tinted pink so that the world is immediately rosy and helps my beer buzz. The glasses are to help my eyes when I'm looking directly at the flame.

'Cute!' He pinches my nose lightly and fires up the kiln. 'I love to work with glass because it's so easy to manipulate and shape,' he explains, moving around the studio with ease and comfort, knowing where absolutely everything is without looking; reaching, placing, like a dance. 'Do you bake?' he asks.

'Bake? Yes, sometimes.' With the kids, and thinking of them snaps me into gear. I have kids. I have a husband. A beautiful husband. A kind husband who wants me to be happy. Who tells me he loves me, who actually loves me. I take a step back.

'It's okay.' He pulls me closer again, hot hand on my waist. 'Glass reacts similarly to sugar when melted. You'll see. But first, here's one part I prepared earlier.'

I move closer and take a look at an image he lays out on the table.

'I've wanted to do this for a while but I was waiting for the right project to come along . . .' He looks at me through those long lashes again, marble blue eyes as though he's crafted them to perfection himself.

'You designed this?' I try not to look at his face. He's doing hypnotic things with his face. In fact with his entire body. Can't look, won't look, concentrate on the flame.

'Sure. It's made of finely ground glass powders. So there are two ways I could make your marble: here at the lamp, which creates the swirl effect you've already seen, but your dad has a lot of German swirls, not all handmade, so I think we should give him something different.'

He gathers a nucleus of opal glass on the end of a long stainless steel rod. He stands at the kiln, perfect posture, and slowly starts twirling the glass in the fire. The glass becomes illuminated, shiny and dripping like honey. He continues turning it to shape it into a sphere. Then he pulls it out of the kiln and I duck as the burning, dripping glass is carried across to an armchair on the other side of the studio. He sits on the wooden chair with high arms and he places the rod across the arms, and rolls it back and forth so that the glass at the end of the rod takes shape. The arms of the chair already have the indentations of the number of times he has done this. He's deep in concentration, no conversation now. In fact there's none for quite some time. He does this routine a few more times, moving back and forth from the kiln to the chair, beads of sweat on his forehead. He grabs hold of a newspaper in his palm and directly starts rolling the hot glass around in his hand to shape it.

At one stage during the process I remove my eyes from him, feeling giddy and light-headed from the bottle of beer and an unusually emotional day, taken away by the chill-out music and the atmosphere, and I see Lea through the trees, dancing with Dara. There is a celebration in the air, things are great, life is great. Life is full of adventure. I can't remember the last time I felt like this. While I watch this all happen my body relaxes, I even sway a little to the music. I can't take my eyes off Marlow, and the beautiful honey-like syrupy glass.

I stand back as he pulls the rod from the kiln and instead of sitting in the chair, he carefully rolls it over the powdered glass drawing he has prepared earlier. Once the drawing is on the glass, he continues to shape it into a sphere, careful not to distort the intricate image inside. He plunges the glass into a pot of crystal glass for the final layer.

Marlow dips the shaped boiling-hot glass into a tin bucket of water, steam hissing and rising as it sizzles and hardens. He knocks it and it falls off the end of the rod, landing in the water and bobbing to the top.

'We'll leave it there to cool,' he says, mopping the sweat from his brow.

He must be able to see the way I've been looking at him because he finally looks up at me and smiles, that sweet amused look he's had since he saw me. He reaches for his bottle and slugs the entire thing down. It's after two a.m. and my head is spinning.

I remember the marble he's just created and make an effort to look in the bucket.

'No peeking until it has cooled,' he says, coming close to me. He pushes me up against the work surface, his hips against my ribs and he takes off my pink glasses. I try to adjust to the fact nothing is rosy any more, it's real, unfiltered, not just in my head. It sobers me quickly. He traces a line all around my face, over each of my features, taking all of them in, slowly and softly. My heart is pounding and I'm sure he can feel it through his thin T-shirt.

He kisses me, which begins slowly but very quickly becomes urgent. For someone who moved

336

so rhythmically and slowly at work, there is something panicked and urgent about how he moves now.

'I'm married,' I murmur in his ear.

'Congratulations,' he continues, kissing my neck.

I laugh nervously.

Five years ago, when I was pregnant with Fergus, a friend came to me and told me that Aidan had had an affair. I confronted him, we dealt with it. I made a decision. Stay or go, go or stay. He stayed. I stayed. We remained, but we didn't remain as we were. We got worse, and then we got better. We've had Alfie since. In my angry moments, which come far less regularly than they did, I always felt that I would grab the closest opportunity I could get to getting him back, by having an affair too, to make sure he truly understood how I felt. I know it's childish but it was real. You hurt me, I'll hurt you. But years on and there has been no opportunity, not at the school run, not at the empty pool, not at the supermarket with the kids, or at karate, or at football, or at art class. No chance for an affair during the mum-related activities that fill my day. Butter, cheese, ham, bread, slice. Raisins. Next. And that made me even more depressed about it, because even if I wanted to get him back, I couldn't.

I know that Aidan loves me. He's not a perfect husband and not a perfect dad, but he's more than enough. I am not a perfect anything, though I try to be. Sometimes I wonder if love is enough, or if there are levels of love. And sometimes I wonder if he can see me, even when he's looking right at me. Last Sunday I went an entire day with green paint on my upper lip, from a morning of painting with the kids, and he never told me it was there. We went to the supermarket, we went to the playground, we walked around the park and not once did he say, 'Sabrina, you have green paint on your face.'

When I went home and looked in the mirror and saw it there, a big green gloop on my upper lip, I cried with frustration. Did nobody see me? Not even the boys? Am I this thing that is expected to be covered in dirt or food or green paint? Sabrina, the woman with paint on her face, the woman with the sticky stain on her trousers, the woman with the finger marks and food splashes on her T-shirt. Don't tell her it's there because it's always there, it's supposed to be there, it's part of who she is.

I asked Aidan about it, some high-pitched unhinged accusation about gloop on my face. He said that he just didn't see it there, which made me wonder, did he look at me and not see it or did he not look at me at all for the entire day. Which is worse? We spent an entire session at counselling talking about it, about this green gloop that he didn't see. Turns out I'm the green gloop.

The green gloop started it, the near-drowning

tipped me over the edge. And then I went looking for lost marbles in an attempt to fix things, save things, complete things for Dad, when perhaps it is myself that I'm trying to figure out.

Aidan is afraid that I'll leave him. He has told me this, he has been afraid of this since his affair. But I have no intention of leaving him. It's nothing to do with him or what he did so long ago that I don't even feel the pain any more, just an echo of it. It's all to do with me. Lately I've been trapped, not myself, or being my real self and not liking it, whatever. Butter, cheese, ham, bread, slice. Raisins. Next. Watching an empty pool. Saving a man that doesn't want to be saved. Not being immersed in the thing I am most passionate about, but on the edges, on the outside looking in. Window-shopping with a full wallet. Shopping with an empty wallet. Whatever. Feeling outside, pacing the edges, feeling redundant.

I lived with a dad who I've just today learned was incredibly secretive, and despite never knowing this, I too became a secretive person, maybe unconsciously mimicking or shadowing him, not opening up to Aidan. It might have happened after his affair, maybe it was before. I don't know the psychological reasons for it and I don't even care. I'm not going to dwell, I'm just going to move on. The important thing is, now I have no secrets.

The past year I was feeling something. I was bored.

But I'm not bored any more.

I smile at the realisation.

Marlow is looking at me with a lazy grin. 'Don't you want to get him back?' he guesses. 'Tit for tat, tat for . . .' his hand travels up my top, '. . . tit.' We both laugh at that, and he removes his hand good-naturedly. 'I'm sensing no.'

'No,' I agree, finally.

He backs off then, respectfully, easily. 'It's cooled off now, if you want to take a look.' He scoops out the marble, polishes it and studies it before handing it to me.

'It's beautiful,' I say, transfixed. 'How much do I owe you?'

He gives me a final kiss. 'You're so sweet. This is for you –' He hands me a second marble. 'I have a theory that the marble is a reflection of its owner. Like with dogs,' he smiles. Then he picks up his beer and drags himself lazily back to the party that is still in full swing.

The marble he has given me is the brown one I was immediately drawn to when I first arrived. It looks like a plain brown marble when you see it first, but when I hold it up to the moonlight, it glows with orange and amber like it has a fire burning brightly inside. Just like its owner.

It is four a.m. when I finally drag myself and Lea from level four of the multistorey. The sun is rising over the city, my watchful moon no longer in sight; she has left me to my own devices now that my mission is complete. Lea collapses into the seat beside me, exhausted. For all her free love and serenity earlier, she now looks green in the face. She insists on coming to the home with me. She has an early shift, she'll sleep it off in the staff room. Besides, I know she cares enough about my dad to want to be with him first thing in the morning.

I don't intend on staying long. I just want to leave the marble by Dad's bed so that he sees it when he wakes. So that it's hopefully the first thing he sees when he wakes.

Of course the home is closed. I ring the doorbell and security recognises Lea and lets us inside.

'Jesus,' Grainne whispers, looking at her colleague. 'Look at the state of you.'

Lea giggles.

'Did you meet him?'

She nods.

'Well?'

'I'll tell you in the morning.'

'It is the morning,' Grainne laughs.

I tiptoe down the corridor, into Dad's room. He's lying on his back, looking old, but happy, snoring lightly. I balance the marble on his bedside locker, alongside a note, and kiss him on the forehead.

31

PLAYING WITH MARBLES

Heirloom

I wake up feeling like I've lived a thousand lives in my dreams. Fragmented memories linger in the moment I first open my eyes then delicately disintegrate like a morning frost in the sunrise. The ghosts of the past and present and their voices begin to diminish as I take in my surroundings. It's not Scotland where I have images of green and grass, lakes and rabbits, my da's hunched shoulders, sad eyes and the smell of pipe smoke; it's not St Benedict's Gardens where I woke up every morning as a child with another brother's feet pushed up against my face as we sleep top to toe in bunk beds. Not Aunty Sheila's bungalow on Synnott Row where we woke up on the floor of her house for the first year after arriving in Ireland, not Gina's ma's home in Iona where we slept for the first year of our marriage while we saved up enough money to buy our own, and not the home we lived in during our marriage. It is not the apartment that I lived in alone for so many years that for the first time in a long time is now so vivid to me and I can hear the calls and shouts from the football field beside me as I lie in on a Saturday and Sunday morning. Nor is it the bedroom I slept in with Cat, the one that feels orange and warm, sweet and glowing when I close my eyes. I'm here in the hospital, my home for the past year, the place where up until some time yesterday I was content to be, to stay and call home. But I have a feeling now, no not a feeling, an urge, to leave. This is an empty place and outside is full, whereas before I felt the opposite. There has been a shift in my mind, something has moved ever so slightly, but that slight movement has had seismic implications. I feel hungry to know, where before I felt full. I want to hear now, where before I was deafened. In fact I had deafened myself. Self-imposed, for protection, I assume. Dr Loftus will tell me. We have a session this morning.

This change does two things to me. It makes me feel hope and it makes me feel hopeless. Hope that I'll get there, hopeless that I can't get there now.

My mouth is dry and I need water. I look around

for my glass of water which is usually on my bedside locker, on the right side so that they make me practise moving my right arm. Where there is usually just my glass, I see a marble. A large, beautiful royal blue marble. It is lit up by the morning light coming through the window and it takes my breath away. It is a sight to behold, its beauty, its elegance, its perfection, such a rarity.

It is a sphere of the world. Within its royal blue ocean there lies a map of the earth, created to perfect proportions. The land, mountains, in browns, sandy and honey colours, every continent, country accounted for, every island. There are even wispy white clouds in the northern hemisphere. The entire world has been captured inside this marble. I reach over with my left hand to pick it up, I will not risk using my weakened right side, not at such a moment, for such a task. I turn it around, inspecting every inch. The islands are intact, the ocean seems to glow from the inside. There is not a scratch, not a scuff. It is perfect. What a marvel, what a marble. Larger than usual, it is 3.5 inches in diameter; I let it sit in the palm of my hand, big and bold. I sit up, pull myself up, heart pounding at the discovery, I must get my glasses to see. They are on the bedside locker to my left, easier to reach for. I see, once they are on, that there is a note. I place the marble on my lap carefully and reach for the note with my left hand, a strain to reach so far and I must be careful not to knock the marble to the floor, which would be catastrophic.

I reach for it and settle back to read.

Dad,

You have the world in the palm of your hand.

Lots of love,
Sabrina
X

As the tears roll down my cheeks and I stare at it for what feels like an endless time, I believe her. I can do this. I can take my life back again. Sleep starts to call me again. Tired eyes, I take off my glasses and make sure the marble is safe. It reminds me of a marble I saw while on honeymoon, one I really wished to buy but couldn't afford. I suddenly have an image of Gina on honeymoon, of her face, young and innocent in a hotel room in Venice, freckles across her nose and cheeks, not a stitch of make-up, moments before we made love for the first time. That image of her is in my mind forever, a look of love, of innocence. I have an overwhelming urge along with that memory to give her this marble, to give her the world. I should have done it then, but I will do it now, I will give her the part of me I held back for so long.

Sabrina will understand, as will Cat, as will Gina's husband Robert. In time Gina can pass it on to Sabrina or to the boys when they're older. It can be like an heirloom, passing the world on to the next generation.

And to Cat, I will give my full heart.

32

POOL RULES

Do Not Swim Alone

I arrive home at five a.m. It's been a long day and night. I yearn to fall into bed for at least a few hours before Aidan and the kids return.

I'm not sure about Amy's moon theories, but there's a comforting one that I heard while in the waiting room at Mickey's yesterday. A new moon is a symbolic portal for new beginnings, believed by some to be the time to set up intentions for things you'd like to create, develop and cultivate. In other words, make new. Make new memories.

I think of myself as a little girl during the night of a full moon, wide awake, alert, head constantly thinking and planning, unable to rest, as though a beacon was sending messages. Was it the moon that made me do this? I don't know. I should probably not cancel my therapy sessions though. The real conversation has just begun.

It's bright as I walk up the path to my door, I see Mrs O'Grady, my neighbour, peeking out at me through lace curtains as I do the walk of shame. As I slide the key in the lock I don't feel like a different woman, but the same woman, slightly changed. For the better.

I dream of kicking off my shoes, stripping off my clothes and falling into bed, having a few hours until the kids come home, but the door opens before I have the chance to turn the key, and it is then I notice Aidan's car parked outside.

Aidan greets me, an exhausted, handsome mess of a man whose expression makes me laugh instantly.

'Mummy!' the boys run to me, throwing themselves at me and grabbing a limb each. They squeeze me tight, as though they haven't seen me for a week instead of less than twenty-four hours.

I hug them tightly while Aidan looks at me, exhausted, but concerned.

'Where have you been?' he asks, when they give up on their cuddles and instead drag me down the hall to show me something so incredibly exciting that they have found. They bring me to the containers of marbles all laid out on the floor; I'd left them there before rushing out the door to Mickey's office yesterday morning.

'I was teaching them how to play,' Aidan says, guiding me away from them. 'I hope that's okay, they know to be careful with them. Although all I wanted to do is ram them down their throats – they've been a nightmare,' he groans, wrapping his arms around me and pretending to cry. 'Alfie has not slept. At. All. Charlie pissed on the sleeping bags and Fergus wanted to eat a frog he caught for breakfast at four. We had to come home. Mind me,' he whimpers.

I laugh, hugging him tight. 'Aidan . . .' I say, a warning tone for what's about to come.

'Yes,' he replies, still in place, but his body stiffens.

'You know the way you said not to let *another* man kiss me . . . ?'

'What?' he pulls back, his face contorted.

'Dad! Mum! Alfie swallowed a marble!'

We both run.

An hour later I kick off my shoes, peel off my clothes and fall into bed. I feel Aidan's lips on my neck, and I've barely closed my eyes when the doorbell rings.

'That's probably your lover,' he says grumpily, turning over and leaving me to answer it.

I groan, pull on my dressing gown and drag myself to the door. A blonde woman smiles nervously at me. I recognise her and try to place her. I recognise her from the hospital. I speak to her in the canteen, in the halls, in the garden, when we're waiting for our loved ones. And then it all falls into place. Our loved one was the same person all along. I smile, feeling a major weight lift from my shoulders. I hadn't been completely in the dark. *I know her.*

'I'm so sorry,' she says, apologetic. 'I know it's a Saturday morning and I didn't want to disturb you and the children. I've been awake most of the night waiting for day to come, this was as long as I could wait. I just have to give you this.'

I turn my attention to the large bag she's holding out with two hands. She hands it to me and I take it. It's heavy.

'It's part of your dad's marble collection,' she says, and I stop breathing. 'I took them from him before he had his stroke, before he sold the apartment, for safekeeping. He sent me out to sell them. I pretended to him that I did. The money I gave him was a loan from his brother Joe.' She looks haunted by that admission. 'I felt it was important to keep them safe, they are so precious to him.' She looks at them as though she's unsure of letting them go. 'But you should have them. The collection should be complete, just in case he asks for them again.'

I look at the bag in total surprise that they're here, in my arms.

'I haven't even told you who I am,' she says shakily.

'Are you Cat?' I ask, and her face freezes in shock.

'Please, come in,' I say, grinning and opening the door wide.

We sit up at the breakfast counter as I carefully open the bag. I want to cry with happiness. An Akro Agate Company original salesman's sample case from 1930 and the World's Best Moons original box of twenty-five marbles. I run my hands over them, unable to believe that they are here, that after a day of searching for them, they eventually found their own way home.

33

PLAYING WITH MARBLES

Bloodies

I'm lying on the floor of Aunty Sheila's living room. Around me, Hamish, Angus and Duncan are in sleeping bags, fast asleep. My hand throbs from where Father Murphy walloped me today and I can't help it, I start to cry. I miss Daddy, I miss the farm in Scotland, I miss my friend Freddy, I miss the way Mammy used to be, I don't like these new smells, I don't like sleeping on the floor, I don't like Aunty Sheila's food, I don't like school, and I particularly don't like Father Fuckface. My right hand is so swollen I can barely close it and every time I close my eyes I see the cold, dark room he locked me in today and I feel panic, like I can't breathe.

'Hey!' I hear someone whisper and I freeze and

stop crying immediately, afraid that one of my brothers has heard and will tease me.

'Psst!'

I look around and see Hamish sitting up.

'Are you crying?' he whispers.

'No,' I sniffle, but it's obvious.

He shuffles over on his bum, moving his sleeping bag closer to mine so that we are side by side. He gives Angus's head a kick and Angus groans and rolls over to make room for his feet. At eleven years old Hamish always gets what he wants from us and he always does it so easily. He's my hero and when I grow up I want to be just like him.

He puts his finger on my cheek and wipes my skin. Then he tastes his finger. 'You are fuckin' crying.'

'Sorry,' I whimper.

'You miss Da?' he asks, lying down beside me.

I nod. That's not all of the reason, but it's part of it.

'Me too.'

He's quiet for a while and I don't know if he's fallen back asleep.

'Remember the way he used to do the longest burp?' he whispers suddenly.

I smile. 'Yeah.'

'And he belched the entire happy birthday song on Duncan's birthday?'

I laugh this time.

'See? That's better. We can't forget things like that, Fergus, okay?' he says, full of intensity like he really means it, and I nod, very serious indeed. 'We have to remember Da the way he was, when he was happy, the good things he did, and not . . . not anything else.'

Hamish was the one who found Da hanging from a beam in our barn. He wouldn't tell us exactly what he saw, none of the gory details, and when Angus tried to make him, he punched him in the face and almost broke his nose, so none of us asked again.

'Me and you, we'll remind each other of stuff like that. I don't sleep either most nights, so you and me can talk.'

I like the sound of that, just me and Hamish, having him all to myself.

'It's a deal,' he says. 'Shake on it.' He grabs my hand, my sore one, and I whine and cry out like Aunty Sheila's dog when you step on its paw. 'What the fuck happened?'

I tell him about Father Murphy and the dark room and I cry again. He's angry about it and puts his arm around my shoulders. I know I won't tell the others this, he would flush my head down the bog if I did that and I like him holding me this way. I don't tell him about me pissing myself though. When I came home, I didn't tell anyone about what Father Murphy had done to me. I would have, but

Aunty Sheila noticed it and helped clean my hand and bandage it up, and she said not to bother Mammy with it because she's upset enough. Everyone's upset, so I didn't tell anyone else.

'What have you got there?' he asks, as my marbles clink in my other hand.

'They're bloodies,' I say proudly, showing him. I sleep with them that night because I like the feel of them in my hand. 'A nice priest gave them to me when I was in the dark room.'

'For keeps?' Hamish asks, studying them.

'I think so.'

'Bloodies?' he asks.

'Yeah, they're red, like blood,' I explain. I don't know much more about them, but I want to.

'Like you and me,' he says, clinking them around in his hand. 'Blood brothers, bloodies.'

'Yeah.' I grin in the dark.

'You bring them into school with you tomorrow,' he says, giving them back to me and settling down in his sleeping bag again.

Angus tells us to shut the fuck up and Hamish kicks him in the head, but we're silent until his breathing tells us he's fallen asleep again.

Hamish whispers in my ear: 'Put them bloodies in your pocket tomorrow. Keep them there, don't tell anyone else, none of the lads, or the Brothers will hear and they'll take them from you. And if he locks you in that room again, you'll have them.

While everyone's working and getting their heads slapped off them, you'll be in there, playing. Do you hear?'

I nod.

'That thought will help me tomorrow, thinking you're in there having a blast, pulling the wool over their eyes. You can't cross a Boggs,' he says.

I smile.

'And the more they put you in there, the greater you'll be. Fergus Boggs, the best marble player in Ireland, maybe even the whole world. And I'll be your agent. The Boggs Brothers, partners in marble crime.'

I giggle. He does too.

'Sounds good, doesn't it?'

I can tell even he's excited by it.

'Yeah.'

'It'll just be our secret, okay?'

'Okay.'

'Every night you can tell me what you learned.'

'Okay.'

'Promise?'

'I promise, Hamish.'

'Good lad.' He ruffles my hair. 'We'll be okay here,' he says to me. 'Won't we?'

'Yeah, Hamish,' I reply.

He holds my sore hand, gentler this time, and we fall asleep together.

Partners in marble crime. Bloodies forever.

EPILOGUE

On Monday morning I return to work.

'Good weekend?' Eric asks, studying me, and I know he's assessing my mental stability after the mug-throwing incident.

'Great, thanks.' I smile. 'Everything is fine.'

'Good,' he says, still watching me, blue eyes luminous from his orange fake tan. 'You know I checked that phrase for you. The one about feeling antsy.'

'Oh yeah?'

'It can also mean sexually aroused.'

I laugh and shake my head as he chuckles his way back into the office.

'Eric,' I call. 'I'm going to start teaching my dad how to swim next week. And I was thinking of trying something different here. Aqua aerobics classes. Once a week. What do you think?'

He grins. 'I think that's a great idea, Sabrina. Can't wait to see Mary Kelly and Mr Daly do the samba in the water.' He gives a sexy little hip roll, which makes me laugh.

Grinning happily, I sit on the stool and watch the empty pool, the pool rules sign glaring down on us all like a crucifix in a church. A reminder. A warning. A symbol. Don't do this, don't do that. No this, no that. So negative on the surface, and yet, a guide. Take heed and you'll be grand. Everything will be fine.

Mary Kelly is in hospital recovering from her heart attack, in a stable condition thankfully. I'm feeling anything but empty though, I feel rejuvenated, with fire inside, like I could look at nothing all day and still be okay, which is what will happen.

Mr Daly arrives in his tight green swim shorts, like an extra layer of skin, tucking tiny wisps of hair he has left into his too tight rubber hat.

'Good morning, Mr Daly,' I say.

He shuffles by me grumpily, ignoring me. He grips the rail and slowly descends into the water. He steals a glimpse at me to see if I'm looking. I look away, wanting this to happen straight away. He lowers his goggles over his eyes, grips the metal bars of the ladder and goes under.

I walk over to the ladder, reach into the water and pull him up.

'You're okay,' I say to him, lifting him out of the water, helping him up the ladder and sitting him on the edge of the pool. 'Here.' I hand him a cup of water which he downs, with trembling hands, his eyes red, his body shaking. He sits for a while, staring into space, in silence, me beside him, arm around him rubbing his back, while he calms. He's not used to me sitting with him after. I gave up on that some time last year when I could tell it wasn't going to stop him. All I had to do was save him and take my seat again. He gives me a sidelong look, checking me out suspiciously. I continue rubbing his back, comfortingly, feeling skin and bone, and a beating heart.

'You left early on Friday,' he says suddenly.

'Yes,' I say gently, touched that he noticed. 'I did.'

'Thought you mightn't be coming back.'

'What? And miss all this?'

He bites the inside of his mouth to stop himself from smiling. He hands the cup back to me, gets back into the pool and he swims a length.

ACKNOWLEDGEMENTS

I'd like to thank all the people who shared their marble memories with me; in all of my twelve novels, I don't think I've ever received quite the reaction when I've shared the topic I'm writing about. Personal stories just tumbled out of people, and whether those stories were big or small, each of them reinforced my belief that marble memories go hand in hand with key moments in adolescence. All of these shared memories encouraged me along the way.

Thank you Killian Schurman, glass artist and sculptor, who spent many hours showing me the process of marble making. Anything incorrect in the marble making scene is entirely my doing.

Thanks Orla de Brí for connecting us and for inspiring me through your own work. Thank you to Lundberg Studios for sharing your expertise, and inspiring 'Marlow's' universe marble. Two books in particular were constantly in use: *Marbles Identification and Price Guide* by Robert Block, and *Collecting Marbles: A Beginners Guide* by Richard Maxwell. Thanks to Dylan Bradshaw for answering my odd questions about the silent hairdryer that I'm sorry never made it to the final edit!

As ever, all my love to David, Robin and Sonny. Mimmie, Dad, Georgina, Nicky and the gang. Fairy godmother Sarah Kelly, Marianne Gunn O'Connor, Vicki Satlow and Pat Lynch.

Thank you Lynne Drew and Martha Ashby for the epic edit. The ever joyful Louise Swannell, Kate Elton, Charlie Redmayne and all of the HarperCollins team, and Kate Bowe and Sarah Dee from Kate Bowe PR in Ireland. Thanks to the booksellers, big and small, independent and chain, physical and electronic. And most important of all, thank you readers.

THE
MARBLE COLLECTOR

READING GROUP QUESTIONS

1. How believable did you feel it was to hide a part of yourself from your family for so long?

2. Why do you think Fergus didn't feel able to talk to his wife about his passion once they were married?

3. Is it possible to pinpoint one moment that changed Fergus's life, or do you think it was a gradual process?

4. Why do you think Fergus strived so hard towards a better life?

5. Do you think Sabrina is like her father or completely different? Why?

6. Do you think Sabrina was justified in her kiss at the end? And why did she tell Aidan about it?

7. Why do Sabrina's chapters start with pool rules? Discuss the significance of the pool and water to Sabrina.

8. Did you feel the book showed Sabrina changing even though it all happened in one day, or did you feel it was predominantly Fergus's story?

9. Have you ever hidden something about yourself, however small? And do you think it has changed how your life unfolded?

Q&A WITH
CECELIA

Can you tell us about your inspiration for this novel?

The inspiration for this novel came from the simple phrase 'I've lost my marbles,' which is something that I say a lot. For the past few years I've been writing a collection of short stories called 'The Woman Who...'. Each story begins with that title and so I came up with the idea of 'The Woman Who Lost Her Marbles,' which was about a woman who literally loses her glass marbles and goes on a quest to find them. While searching, her journey helps her resolve her personal dilemmas. I hadn't started writing the story yet but as it was developing in my head, I quickly realised that this wasn't a short story, this would be better suited to a novel. As I asked the questions – whose marbles has she lost, why are they so important, what do the marbles represent, why does she desperately need to find them? – so Fergus came alive and his story gave the story so much more gravitas. Researching the marble world was a really interesting and inspiring experience for me and so the marbles themselves inspired each chapter and helped shape the overall story.

The research for this novel must have been fascinating: the collecting and making of marbles and some presumably emotionally fraught research on the effects of having a stroke. Can you tell us about your process?

I did a huge amount of research into marbles. There were two books in particular that lived on my desk; *Collecting Marbles: A Beginner's Guide* by Robert Block and *Marbles Identification and Price Guide* by Richard Maxwell. The marbles that Fergus owned, lost, collected were all real, and their valuations were real too. Glass artist and sculptor Killian Schurman was incredibly kind and gracious to welcome me into his studio and showed me how to make marbles in two ways, one method by Bunsen burner and the second using the kiln. I even attempted it myself. It was very inspiring being able to see it happen in reality, feel the atmosphere and soak it all up. Part of what drew me to writing about marbles is their beauty. There is a huge amount of artistic skill that goes into creating them and I wanted to capture that magic in the novel. Lundberg Studios were also very helpful in explaining the process of how their universe marble was created. The story is driven by Fergus's passion for marbles so I needed to immerse myself in it.

Since writing this book, what does the phrase 'losing your marbles' mean to you now?

Oddly I feel quite a bit of ownership over that expression now! I took a phrase that I used to say a lot but never thought of its true meaning, and gave it meaning in my life. I always knew that it is an inappropriate phrase for mental illness, so it was never a phrase designed for Fergus. It always alluded to Sabrina's journey. She feels like she has lost her marbles, it is the everyday, muddled, exhausted and busy mind of a young mother who feels like *she* has lost her marbles and not, of course, Fergus. She goes on the journey to find them and while doing so, discovers secrets about her father, and in turn solves some of her own personal issues.

Sabrina carries out her treasure hunt all in one day: was the idea of a woman with many demands on her time something that you felt strongly about?

With each of my novels I always set myself new challenges. With *The Year I Met You* I set myself the challenge of telling the story over one full year. It's become a natural process for me to immediately move in the other direction from my previous novel, when I begin a new novel. I wanted to set myself the challenge of writing a novel based on one day. I'd never done it before, I like reading novels set in one day, and wondered if I could do it. While the novel spans over Fergus's lifetime in the chapters dedicated to his story, all of Sabrina's story occurs in one day. What makes this a believable journey is because she is given one day where she is allowed to change her routine. She's been given the day off work, her husband has taken the children off camping, and for the first time, she actually has time to herself. I also set it on the day of a total solar eclipse, where the sun, moon and earth line up differently, and this is mirrored in Sabrina's personal adventure. Everything is lining up in a way it has never done before. If she doesn't find the answers to her questions by the end of the day, she knows that she will never find the answers, because tomorrow her life returns to normal, resuming her hectic schedule that revolves around her family.

If you had just one day free from any other demands, how would you spend it?

I tend to not know what to do with myself when I'm not working or with the children. Life is one insane routine of jumping from one to the other, trying to make sure that nobody is missing me. The correct answer should probably be to try to help the world in some way, but I think it would be more important to first take care of myself. Read a book, get a massage, get my hair done, then save the world.

Who inspires you as a writer?

I'm inspired by bravery, inner strength and people who aren't afraid to be different. Anybody who has a unique voice and has the ability to express how they see the world from a different angle are the kinds of people who inspire me as a writer. Whether it's through art, fashion, or in business. Originality and individuality is very inspiring. But they need to be kind. Kindness is key. They make me want to tell stories in ways that feel true and honest to me.

Can you tell us something about your next book?

My new novel is called *Lyrebird*. It's about a young man who falls in love with a mysterious woman. A lyrebird is an Australian ground-dwelling bird known for its ability to mimic every sound in its environment. In *Lyrebird* a documentary crew discover a young woman living in the Cork mountains with similar qualities to the lyrebird. She becomes the subject of their documentary which is embraced by the world.

Lyrebird leaves the peace and serenity of her world behind for a new beginning, with much to learn and even more to teach others. But as the world embraces her, and in a way wants to change her, she has to learn to stay true to herself. For the young man who discovered her, he has a dilemma: when you find someone rare and precious, should you expose them, or should you protect them?

Look out for the captivating new novel from

cecelia
ahern

LYREBIRD

A Lyrebird is a ground-dwelling Australian bird known for its striking beauty and extraordinary mimicking skill. When a documentary crew discover a young woman living alone in the mountains of West Cork who possesses similar abilities, she becomes the subject of their story, a story that the entire world embraces.

As the Lyrebird leaves her peaceful life behind to learn about a new world, it is quickly evident that, as she learns, she has much to teach others. But as she assimilates into the world she sees, and mimics so accurately, is she losing a part of herself?

And for Solomon, who stumbled upon her first, the relationship carries a great responsibility. One that changes his life. Because when you discover something rare, should you expose it? Or protect it?

Coming in autumn 2016